"Jack?"

Sophie's voice drew him like a siren's song. He could no more let her fend for herself than fly to Mars in a Venetian vaporetto. But what would he find in the bathroom? Sophie wrapped in a wet towel? Or in nothing? *Hell!*

When he opened the door, he entered a cloud of fragrant steam. Sophie had wound the bath towel around her upper torso. Her hair hung in glistening ropes over her shoulders. She wore yellow cotton-pajama boxers that bared her long, tanned legs. Jack realized she was mostly covered. Desire and dismay dueled in his struggling system.

His hungry gaze climbed her legs' slender length until it reached a massive yellowing bruise on her left thigh.

Reality slapped him back to Earth. He could do this. His brain knew his duty, even if his body didn't. Add to that, she was still a suspect and under official protection. All kinds of tangles to trip him if he didn't keep tight control. She needed care, not sex.

"Your *agent* reporting for duty, ma'am."

Dear Reader,

Benvenuto al Italia! Welcome to Italy in another of my books about the men and women of the ATSA, the Anti-Terrorism Security Agency. The hunt for stolen uranium and their personal searches take my hero and heroine to that ancient land of extravagant food, wine and people.

My memories of a trip to Italy and my research allowed me to indulge myself with Italian culture and lore. I steeped myself in the language and history, architecture and scenery as I created villas and villages. Of course, I had to sample the wine and recipes that accompanied my characters' journey from Venice to Tuscany. You can find one of those recipes on my Web site.

My characters' memories are not so pleasant. Jack Thorne's deadly memories focus him on vengeance. Sophie Rinaldi's memory of a villain's deadly intent could get her killed—before she can recall his secrets. As they drive mountain roads and hide in remote villages to escape the villain, they find beauty and warmth as well as passion and danger.

In *Deadly Memories,* I hope you enjoy immersion in the romance of Italy along with the adventure. I love to hear from readers. You can write to me at Saint George, ME 04860 or e-mail me by visiting www.susanvaughan.com or www.intimatemomentsauthors.com. At my Web site, you can find other books and an excerpt and enter my contest.

Andiamo! Let's go!

Susan Vaughan

DEADLY MEMORIES
SUSAN VAUGHAN

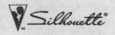

INTIMATE MOMENTS™
Published by Silhouette Books
America's Publisher of Contemporary Romance

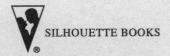 SILHOUETTE BOOKS

ISBN-13: 978-0-373-27500-7
ISBN-10: 0-373-27500-5

DEADLY MEMORIES

Copyright © 2006 by Susan Hofstetter Vaughan

Visit Silhouette Books at www.eHarlequin.com

Printed in U.S.A.

Books by Susan Vaughan

Silhouette Intimate Moments

Dangerous Attraction #1086
Guarding Laura #1314
Code Name: Fiancée #1342
Breaking All the Rules #1406
Deadly Memories #1430

SUSAN VAUGHAN

Susan Vaughan is a West Virginia native who lives on the coast of Maine. Battles with insomnia over the years fired her imagination with stories. Living in many places in the U.S. while studying and teaching gave her characters and ideas. She once lived with a French family and attended the Sorbonne. With her husband, she has kissed the Blarney Stone, canoed the Maine wilderness, kayaked the Colorado River, sailed the Caribbean and won ballroom dance competitions. Susan's books have won the NJRW Golden Leaf and finaled in the Booksellers' Best Contest.

To my sisters in spirit—
Virginia Kelly, Ann Voss Peterson,
Sheila Seabrook and Linda Style.

And to my research assistant—
thanks for always being my rock.

ACKNOWLEDGMENTS

Grazie mille, many thanks for your help and expertise—
Sheila Franklin, Elizabeth Jennings, Mary LaRochelle,
Dennis Lombardi and Helen Vaughan.
Any errors or fabrications are mine.

Prologue

"I bring you a fortune in diamonds." The gaunt man shifted from foot to foot on the villa's flagstone terrace. Sweat misted his forehead.

Sebastian Vadim leaned back in his chaise longue and savored the last sip of grappa. The fiery liqueur, Italy's best-kept secret, would level his nerves. His grueling buying trip had ended in frustration, and upon his homecoming, this unwelcome visitor had descended on him.

The grappa also allowed him to temporize while he decided how best to deal with Dobrich, his second cousin from a part of the family best forgotten. Police from Paris to the capital of his native Cleatia had hosted Dobrich for offenses ranging from smuggling to picking pockets.

Vadim crossed his ankles and straightened the seam in his tailored silk slacks. He angled his face to the late-afternoon sun's warming rays as he regarded his nervous relative.

In the Cleatian of his homeland—a language he'd not

spoken for years—he said, "Cousin, did anyone observe your arrival here?" Vadim preferred to remain below the radar of the Veneto *polizia.* He'd chosen this country villa near Venice for privacy.

"No one local. The bus driver will not remember me." Dobrich's shapeless trousers, threadbare jacket and the battered metal toolbox at his feet created the cover of a laborer. A man no one would notice. "May I sit down, cousin? I am not feeling well."

"Of course." He waved a hand at the chairs surrounding the glass-topped patio table. "Not too close. My sympathies, but I do not wish to contract your illness."

Dobrich collapsed onto the cushioned seat as if he had walked all the way from Cleatia. He tucked his toolbox beneath it. "Thank you, cousin. Maybe the flu, but I think food poisoning. The inn where I stayed before crossing the Adriatic had sanitation from the Middle Ages."

"Tell me, then, about the diamonds. Where did they come from?" Vadim continued in his silky negotiating voice. "Are they in that disreputable box?"

Dobrich bent into his handkerchief with a phlegmy cough that churned up from the soles of his feet. Before he tucked away the dingy linen, Vadim saw blood on it. A nasty form of food poisoning or flu. Whatever it was, he wanted the man gone. And quickly.

"My employer is Viktor Roszca. You know of him?"

Vadim couldn't help his startled reaction. Viktor Roszca was a high-profile international arms broker. He didn't usually deal in black-market diamonds, but it was credible he might hire a fellow Cleatian, one who was expendable and not overly bright. Given Roszca's recent circumstances, Dobrich's involvement became more interesting.

Vadim wanted details. "Who has not heard of Viktor Roszca? Go on."

"Four days ago I took possession of the package. The

previous courier passed it to me. I headed to Antwerp, where my papers say I have employment. There I was to receive more instructions. I saw on the television in a bar that the Americans have Roszca in custody. If I went to Antwerp, I, too, could be picked up. I thought of my wise and generous cousin, who appreciates diamonds." Dobrich's weak smile displayed bleeding gums.

Vadim suppressed a shudder. Two meters away wasn't far enough. He pushed to his feet and strolled to the flower garden at the terrace edge, where he plucked a rosebud. "Why would Viktor Roszca take *you* into his confidence?"

Dobrich appeared to take no offense at the slur on his character and status. The man knew his worth—or lack of it. "He did not. No one told me what was in the hidden compartment of my toolbox." He tapped the side of his nose with an air of pride. "A little brainpower is all it took."

Diamonds. A niggling suspicion made the hairs on Vadim's neck itch. Apparently Dobrich hadn't seen the entire news story on Roszca. What the idiot carried were *not* diamonds. "Tell me."

Another spasm racked Dobrich's frame. Then he continued. After the news headline of Roszca's capture, he'd left the bar for his room. With Roszca gone, the package belonged to him, he reasoned. His first move was to pry open the lead lining in the bottom of the toolbox. In it he found rough, pea-sized gravel, unremarkable looking but heavy.

He guessed that the first courier had come by freighter from Africa to the Adriatic port. Dobrich was to take it to a major diamond-cutting center. Therefore, what he had must be uncut diamonds. "What else so small could be so valuable? I bit into one to test its hardness. Nearly broke a molar."

Vadim considered the freighter-sized holes in Dobrich's logic. The other courier could've come overland instead of from diamond-rich countries in West Africa. Uncut diamonds did not resemble pea-sized gravel, but he wouldn't disabuse the fool of his notions.

Dobrich should've stayed in the bar for the rest of the news broadcast. If he had, he never would've opened the lead-lined case. Or perhaps he would. He might not have the imagination to understand the danger.

What Dobrich had in his lead-lined case had poisoned him. Vadim eyed the toolbox as if it were a dragon ready to breathe fire on him. As indeed it might. "Did you then secure the lead compartment once more?"

Nodding, Dobrich mopped his forehead with his blood-spattered handkerchief. "I sealed it up immediately so no one would suspect. Are you interested, cousin?"

"I am intrigued. But I am being a bad host. You are ill and need rest and refreshment. I will have you shown to a room. We can talk more later."

"Thank you, cousin. I am quite fatigued."

As if Vadim had pressed a button, his bodyguard and assistant stepped through the doorway and bowed.

Dobrich struggled to his feet and bent to pick up the toolbox. He followed the bodyguard into the villa.

Vadim returned to his chaise, leaned back against the soft padding and poured another glass of grappa.

A miracle had fallen into his lap. His pulse raced.

Dobrich's toolbox held the key to wealth and power. With it, he, Sebastian Vadim, could achieve control of the diamond market. He might even achieve legitimacy in some eyes.

He already knew the perfect buyer. An eager buyer, a fanatic. With some clever negotiating, the deal would net him a fortune and a bonus—the destruction of his competition.

And perhaps more. Viktor Roszca's capture left a void in the international arms market. A void *he* could fill. He had the contacts. And soon he would have the means. Smiling, Vadim raised his glass in a toast to himself, then downed the rest of the grappa.

There was also the matter of his unfortunate cousin.

Dobrich presented a minor problem. Regardless, he was a dead man. Two days, perhaps less.

Definitely less, Vadim decided. An autopsy would identify the illness—another complication he could not permit.

When his man returned, Vadim said in Italian, "My dear cousin is to take a *permanent* rest. Bring me his toolbox. Then dispose of the body where it will not be found. Ever."

The toolbox had served well, but by now the Americans and Interpol probably knew about it. For such a small package, a lead-lined compartment could be built into almost anything.

He would need a new courier, one both unsuspecting and unsuspected.

Chapter 1

Six days later

Jackson Thorne strained for a bead on his enemy.

The savage hatred always coiled in his belly stretched and sharpened its claws in anticipation. Only sheer will and concentration on his goal kept his hand steady and his expression impassive.

He adjusted the lens focus and swung the view beyond the rows of grapevines and ancient lime trees, across the flower beds, until he acquired the mellowed redbrick villa.

There. The damned murderer lived in there.

If only he had Sebastian Vadim in the crosshairs of a rifle scope instead of Leica seven-by-forty-two binoculars. *Patience, patience,* he mouthed. Duty for ATSA first. The Anti-Terrorism Security Agency needed Vadim's contraband and information.

As the new addition to this Nuclear Interdiction Task Force,

Jack had to do his part. Intelligence from Interpol had prompted the American and Italian anti-terrorism agencies to cooperate on this mission—to find and confiscate a stash of weapons-grade uranium. First they had to nail Sebastian Vadim for possession.

Afterward, Jack's chance would come.

He'd waited five years to exact vengeance. Five years of investigating alias after alias, lead after lead. A few days more would make no difference.

"Nobody there but the cook and one bodyguard," drawled Jack's companion beneath the grapevine's sheltering leaves. "The other security mug—the Italian—drove him and the woman somewhere before you got here. De Carlo and a couple ATSA operatives tailed them."

Disappointment deflated Jack's tension. He lowered the binoculars and sank prone onto the rich Italian soil. He drew a deep breath of air spiced with ripening grapes and sun-heated loam.

Leaning on one elbow, he eyed the other ATSA officer, who reclined with his frayed cloth cap shading his face. Jack also wore a work shirt and trousers—cover as farm labor if anyone at the villa spotted the task-force surveillance team in the vineyard. "Any idea where Vadim went?"

Leoni affected a shrug and popped two sticks of chewing gum in his mouth to join the wad distorting his cheek.

Three others—Italian cops—were strung out along the same vine row but close enough for conversation without electronics.

When no one else replied, Leoni said, "Sometimes he takes the babe sightseeing in Venice. Sometimes they go to Treviso or the beach at Jesolo for a long lunch. Don't expect them back until three or four. De Carlo'll alert us."

De Carlo, a *commissario,* an investigative officer, Jack recalled, was the task-force leader. "And Vadim hasn't done anything suspicious? Contacted anyone?"

"Nothing that would give us an excuse to move on him." The man unscrewed the cap on his bottled water and drank.

"Wiretap?"

Leoni roused himself enough to shake his head. Jack suspected he was part of the task force mainly because he spoke fluent Italian. "Local *polizia* put up a roadblock of red tape. Vadim's been a good citizen so far, spending liberally and living peacefully."

"Hereabouts, he's a wealthy business consultant," another officer added. "They have no idea he's a major player in the diamond-smuggling trade. We're not ready to share intelligence with them."

Leoni chuckled. "Just for grins, I tried to wire in anyway, but Vadim has a scrambler. With his black-market connections, he can get anything."

The video officer spat into the dirt. "He will not get away this time. If the uranium charge does not stick, Interpol now has given us enough evidence on the smuggling."

"For now, we wait." Jack had read all that and more in the Interpol report, but impatience had goaded him to ask anyway. He laid the binoculars beside him on the ground.

At one o'clock the sun floated high among three puffy clouds. Temperatures climbed to a soporific sauna, incubating the cultivated vines and the watchers camped among their shady rows. "Unusual for early June," said one of the Italians on a yawn. Everyone nodded in a doze.

Except Jack.

Downtime or not, his mind dwelled on his quarry. He didn't need the CO's report to know the relevant events.

The uranium courier's trail had disappeared after Venice, but his kinship with Vadim was no coincidence. When De Carlo had interviewed Vadim, he'd denied any contact with his cousin and invited the officers to search the villa. They'd found nothing suspicious.

Other than Vadim and his bodyguards, a young American woman resided there. An overly courteous Vadim had introduced her as his houseguest.

Jack emitted a cynical snort. *Guest* was a euphemism. De Carlo's report stated that her bedroom—beside Vadim's—had been awash in Italian designer boutique clothes and silk lingerie with the price tags still attached. A check of Vadim's credit card history showed he'd purchased them all. A man didn't buy expensive clothing for a mere guest.

He raised the binoculars and used the rest of the time to study the villa. The house, part of it dating to the 1600s, was a sprawl of soft-red brick, native-stone chimneys and flag-stone terraces. It stood at the end of a long avenue lined with ancient lime trees. On one side was the vineyard, tended by the adjacent farmer cooperating with the task force. On the other side, opposite the watchers, Jack saw gardens, a swimming pool and guesthouses.

"They come," one of the Italians said. "De Carlo says five minutes ETA."

Jack's adrenaline surged and his temples throbbed. Deep breaths calmed him. Photographs had put a face to Vadim, but now he was finally going to see his enemy in the flesh.

When Jack heard tires crunch on the gravel driveway and the purr of a powerful engine, he raised the binoculars.

A silver-gray S-Class Mercedes sedan rolled up to the portico, and the driver climbed out, a swarthy man in a lumpy sport coat. The Italian bodyguard, Jack recalled, one Guido Mazza. He made a small bow as he opened the rear door.

The diamond dealer eased smoothly from the backseat. He gleamed like his wares, in a tailored suit the same silver-gray as his luxury automobile. At a distance he looked fit, trim and much younger than the fifty Jack knew him to be.

Fifty is all you'll have. Jack's eyes narrowed as he memorized the man's features.

Even teeth showing in a crocodile smile, bright and bogus, Vadim extended a hand for the woman.

Jack had seen photographs of her, too, snapshots taken with telephoto lenses. Hot as the Italian sun but with a freshness that surprised him. Sophie Rinaldi, aged twenty-seven, from Pelham, New York. An American tourist who after two weeks of touring Italy moved in with Vadim. She—

What he saw next short-circuited his thought processes. A slim foot in a red sandal extending from the Mercedes. Then a long, shapely, tanned leg. And the other.

"The guy is pond scum, but *mamma mia,* he sure can pick 'em." Beside Jack, Leoni had awakened.

The Rinaldi woman accepted Vadim's proffered hand as she slid from the leather interior. After smoothing her skirt— a gauzy red thing that floated to her knees—she tossed back her hair and smiled.

That soft curve of lips sent a shock wave of heat into Jack's veins. Need slammed into his groin. Never had the mere sight of a woman affected him with such power.

Why now? Why her?

Classic oval face, full lips, a mass of softly curling dark hair, toned feminine curves—the sensual Italian look. Hot but nothing special.

Except she wasn't what he'd expected, even from the telephoto shots. Softer, like her name, Sophie. With a breathless, otherworldly quality that kept his gaze riveted to her instead of to his target.

A fluke—effects of the sun and anticipation. He exhaled slowly, then again until the sensual vise began to loosen. He dragged his gaze from the woman to Vadim.

As the driver pulled the car around to the garage, Vadim and Sophie strolled toward the house. The diamond dealer leaned back his head and laughed at something she said. He brought her delicate hand to his lips and kissed her fingers.

The older man didn't have his hands all over her, but why would he when she was in his bed every night? An assumption on ATSA's part, but a logical one.

"Lucky bastard," Leoni muttered. "He's old enough to be her father."

That wasn't how Jack would've put it. But close enough. At the sight of his enemy's meticulously manicured hand on her slim one, hatred seared white-hot pain in Jack's chest and in his temples.

He should shoot right now. But he wanted the son of a bitch to know who executed him and why.

The two continued their casual conversation as the woman tucked a soft wave of thick, dark hair behind one ear.

"Why the devil can't we hear them?" Jack whispered. "No bugs or wiretaps, but what about mikes or EARS41?" The Electronic Acquiring Reconnaissance System was a high-tech listening system.

"We tried. He's got blockers we haven't cracked. So we hang out in the vineyard and tail them. Old-fashioned police work." Leoni yawned as if ready for another nap.

When the couple reached the doorway—wide double doors with a massive knocker—Vadim gestured to indicate that he was staying outside. He pointed toward the swimming pool, where his other thug waited for him. Petar, with an unpronounceable last name, came from Cleatia, like his employer.

Sophie smiled. Rising on tiptoes, she placed a hand on his shoulder. She brushed a quick kiss on his mouth.

Vadim barely reacted. Jack's face heated as though she'd kissed him. More heat dived south of his belt. He swore under his breath.

With a little wave, she pivoted, her flirty skirt allowing a glimpse of creamy thigh before she vanished inside the villa.

"Woman likes to tease. Like all of 'em," Leoni said as he angled his binoculars to follow Vadim. "A velvet trap."

Tease? Maybe. More like torture.

But Jack couldn't let himself be distracted by a woman. For damn sure not a murderer's woman like Sophie.

Sophie. Shaken, he sat back on his heels. He nearly dropped the binoculars. How did she go from being the Rinaldi woman to *Sophie?*

* * *

The day after Jack's arrival, he and De Carlo tailed Sophie and Vadim through Venice's canals and winding streets.

Tailing them afforded Jack a quick tour of Venice, but not one he could appreciate. He felt only frustration grinding like rocks on a storm-tossed shore at being so close to his quarry yet helpless to do anything.

When the couple lunched in the fashionable Harry's Bar, Jack and De Carlo washed down *risotto di mare* with a house wine in the cheaper trattoria down the street, where they could observe when the couple left. Jack didn't need the other man's reminder to limit the alcohol. He could afford no blurred senses or dulled reflexes. No amount of wine could smooth the edges of his hatred.

After lunch they strolled from shop to shop on the Merceria, a narrow street running between the Piazza San Marco and the Rialto. While Sophie bargained with shopkeepers, Vadim held her packages.

Jack and De Carlo followed, ducking behind displays and peering at merchandise. Jack's ire grew as he observed Sophie laugh at her lover's jokes. She hung on his every damned word. Excitement at a bargain and pleasure in the beauty of the day brushed her cheeks with color.

Every movement—the sway of hips, the flash of dark eyes, the tilt of chin—appeared natural, unaffected. Even if Vadim bought the artless act, Jack didn't. He knew firsthand about feminine manipulation.

Still, he couldn't help checking out her high breasts when she reached up to sweep her mass of hair from her shoulders and fasten it at her nape. And he wasn't alone.

Seeing Vadim touching and leering at this woman fanned Jack's hatred and stoked the flames to volcanic heat. His chest felt so tight with rage that he thought he'd explode.

Jack had made a solemn vow to mete out justice. He'd

waited long enough. He wanted this operation done so he could take care of the slime.

If something didn't break soon, he would act.

"And that should wrap up our plans, Ahmed," Vadim said into the telephone. "Do you foresee any loose ends?"

"What about the woman?"

"She is upstairs packing at this very moment. The goods are well hidden. Having her transport them to London will arouse no suspicions."

"And she does not suspect?"

Ahmed Saqr was a fanatic but a careful buyer. His continual worry irritated Vadim. He wanted the deal over, the danger out of his house. "She trusts me implicitly. She believes what I want her to believe."

There was a rapid intake of breath—a gasp—on the line.

"What was that?"

Click.

Vadim froze, his heart racing. *Where was Sophie?* But he feared that he knew. "Old friend, do you have someone listening on an extension?"

"Not I. What is going on?"

"I must go find out. I will call you back."

Five days after Jack had joined the task force, surveillance continued to yield no developments, only frustration.

Camped beneath the vines, Jack sat cross-legged and inhaled the warm fragrance of the ripening grapes. He let the sun slanting through the broad grape leaves soothe his aching shoulders, rigid with tension.

"Something's going on at last," Leoni whispered to him as he closed his cellular phone. "Roszca's former buyers are sending out feelers about the uranium. On the quiet, like."

Jack considered. "So that means they don't know where the package went. Vadim has it. He's got to."

"So what's he waiting for?" Leoni shook his head.

"Maybe he isn't. Maybe he's arranging a sale. They've been busy today. The Mercedes has gone out twice."

"Yeah. Returned both times with nothing more suspicious than melons. No rich-terrorist-buyer types." The officer snorted a laugh and unwrapped a stick of gum. "Lighten up, Thorne. You'd think this was personal."

Personal as you could get, but Jack didn't enlighten the man. Nobody knew. He'd kept his search secret.

"Usually the housekeeper does the marketing," he said. "Something's up." He tried to put the puzzle together but got no picture. They didn't have all the pieces, damn it.

The solid slam of the heavy front doors jarred him to alertness. He raised his binoculars as Petar exited carrying a small duffel bag. He jogged out of sight around the house. A few minutes later he drove away in the Mercedes.

"Hot damn," said another of the surveillance team. "Get De Carlo on the horn to follow that sucker."

"Roger that." Heartbeat racing, Jack hit the speed dial. Now maybe they were getting somewhere.

Moments later gravel crunched as the second bodyguard, Guido, pulled around to the front in a black Maserati. The sports car was compact and low, built to take winding Italian roads like runways. He cut to an idle and relaxed in the driver's seat. Static and then a heavy beat filled the air as the man found a station playing American rock music.

One of the double front doors swung open with a bang. Sophie appeared.

She wore a sleeveless knit top, tan slacks and low-heeled sandals. Travel clothes? Her eyes were wild, her soft mouth open. Her breasts rose and fell with rapid breaths. She trotted down the steps and jogged past the idling Maserati.

"What the hell?" Jack tensed, ready to move. He adjusted the focus on his binoculars.

After a quick glance at the bodyguard in the Maserati, she

sprinted down the gravel drive as if the devil himself snapped at her heels.

Guido stared at her in amazement but stayed in the car. Jack heard Vadim shout to his man. The diamond dealer pounded after the fleeing woman, and the car began to roll.

The hard look on Vadim's face cued Jack that this was serious. "Let's move!" He dropped the binoculars and flipped open the snap on his shoulder holster.

"No, wait!" Leoni scrambled to his feet. "It's a lovers' quarrel. Not our business."

"He's going to kill her." Jack broke cover and raced between the trees and across the open expanse toward Vadim.

"Damn it to hell! We're made anyway. Hit it, guys. *Andiamo!*" The other officers followed Jack.

Pelting down the drive, Jack heard Leoni yell to Vadim in Italian. Abruptly the man halted and looked around at the five strangers with pistols. The Maserati braked to a stop beside him.

Jack saw him assess the situation in a split second. Barking orders, Vadim jumped into the Maserati at the moment Jack reached the rear bumper.

As the powerful sports car accelerated, gravel spit like bullets from beneath the rear tires.

Ignoring the flying stones, Jack stopped, panting. Maybe he should add sprints to his running regimen. He flipped open his cell. He was about to dial De Carlo when he noticed where the car was heading.

Straight for Sophie.

She appeared in good shape, but her stride faltered with every step. She was flagging.

The Maserati would overtake her in seconds.

Jack's pulse hurtled in his veins. He took off again down the drive. *"No!"*

Sophie must've heard Jack's yell or the car's engine, because she swerved to the right. But not far enough.

The front right bumper struck her side. The momentum

threw her into the air. It tossed her onto the grass verge. She landed in a heap. She lay there, still as death.

The car stopped and backed up.

Jack saw the black muzzle of an automatic pistol protrude from the open passenger window. A tree blocked the shooter's view, and the car started to turn.

"Stop, you bastard! Throw down your gun!" Jack pulled out his 9mm and fired at the car as he ran. His first shots missed, but two bullets slammed into the trunk.

The pistol withdrew. The Maserati roared off, leaving him coughing in its dusty wake. The car swung a hard left onto the paved road. It disappeared from sight.

Awareness chewed into Sophie's brain with burning bites. Her eyelids fluttered open to a swarm of black spots like bees before her eyes. When she tried to sit up, every bone and muscle in her body protested, and she collapsed again, panting. Spears radiated into her left hip and shoulder. Her stomach lurched and her heart thumped wildly.

After taking a few minutes to recover, she forced her eyes open again. The black spots smeared into a blur, and she could make out light green walls. White sheets. White blanket. Acrid smells of antiseptic and medicine.

An IV. With a tube into her right forearm. Straps immobilized her left arm and shoulder.

She was in a hospital bed.

What happened?

Fear and panic clamped her chest, and tears burned her eyes. *Stop it right now, Sophia Constanza Elena Rinaldi. You are alive. You are safe.*

The confusion gave her something to focus on other than pain. It radiated from her shoulder and bounced around in her head like a spiked ball. Had there been an accident? The plane? Something in the airport? A mugging?

Trying to remember what happened made her head throb

more. She closed her eyes against the driving pain. Frightened anew, she fought the tears gathering in her throat.

A nurse bustled in with a pitcher of water. "Ah, *signora, come sta?*" she began, but then switched to halting English. "How are you? Is good you...wake."

"What happened to me?" Sophie said in Italian. She managed only a croaking whisper from her parched throat. "How was I hurt?"

Uttering soothing sounds, the nurse gave her some water. "You rest. I will tell the *medico*."

A few minutes later a blond woman in a white lab coat entered her room. She carried a clipboard crammed with papers beneath her arm.

The doctor. At last she'd get some answers.

"*Dottoressa*, please tell me what happened. How badly am I hurt? Where am I?"

She pushed half glasses lower on her nose and smiled gently. "Ah, *signora,* all will be answered. But first allow me to examine you. I shall try not to hurt you."

Sighing, she subsided into the soft pillows. The haze before her eyes was thinning, and the nausea, as well.

When the doctor finished checking her vital signs, she asked, "Tell me, *signora,* what is your name?"

She stared at her in surprise. Then she realized that they must check anyone who's been unconscious. "My name is Sophie Rinaldi. I'm an American. I live in New York. I came to Italy on vacation."

The doctor didn't need to know she was searching for family. That aspect of her trip would be delayed now anyway.

"*Bene.*" Very good. The doctor complimented her on her fluent Italian as she made a note on her clipboard.

"How badly am I hurt?"

"You are very lucky, Signora Rinaldi. A concussion. Bruises and abrasions and a partially dislocated shoulder, but nothing is broken. *Dieci giorni.* You will be well."

Ten days. Probably longer. Two weeks or more. Italian time was fluid. Sophie managed a weak smile.

"And what is the last thing you remember before waking up in our beautiful hospital?" She smiled expectantly. A sunbeam through the tall window reflected on the lenses of her reading glasses and made Sophie blink.

When her brows drew together in thought, she felt each muscle movement as a separate stab of pain. Marshaling her faltering reserves, she forced her aching brain to focus. "The last thing I recall is the pilot's voice announcing the descent to Rome, to Leonardo da Vinci Airport. Did we crash?"

Chapter 2

Jack paced in the corridor outside Sophie's hospital room. He knew her injuries and that she was awake but nothing else. Since his Italian extended only to basic courtesies like *grazie* and *per favore,* he could only wait until a doctor who spoke English informed him of her condition.

In yesterday's excitement, Vadim's Maserati had vanished into the Veneto countryside. Task-force vehicles didn't scramble fast enough to know even which direction he'd gone. He could be hunkered down in a cabin in the Dolomites or he could be halfway to Morocco.

The attack on Sophie Rinaldi had convinced the local authorities to give the task force free rein. Jack and ten other officers spent the rest of the day and most of the night combing through Vadim's villa. A more thorough search would take days.

Traces of radiation in several rooms, but no uranium. No courier named Dobrich. No Vadim.

Niente. Nada. Zip.

The debriefing was every bit as harsh as Jack had expected. Every one of the five officers on surveillance was interrogated and ripped from stem to stern by the task-force leader. Not surprising, as the one to blow their cover and lose the suspect, Jack received the harshest reprimand.

The only reason De Carlo didn't send Jack back to the States was the surveillance video.

The footage made Vadim's murderous intent all too clear. It showed that Jack had saved Sophie Rinaldi's life. For the moment he was still on the task force, but De Carlo and the others viewed him as a loose cannon. This snafu ratcheted up a notch the normal tension between cooperating agencies.

As long as he got to stay, he didn't give a damn.

De Carlo had given Jack an assignment guaranteed to keep him out of the loop—protecting Sophie. The *commissario* didn't consider her important, but Jack's gut said the opposite. He speculated that she'd fled in fear of her life because she'd learned dangerous information.

About the uranium or Vadim's illicit diamond trade.

More important to Jack was finding Vadim.

Sticking close to Sophie was fine with him. She might know her lover's habits and maybe his hangouts and hiding places. She was beautiful, no denying it, but he could resist temptation. A woman like that, the lover of the man he hated with all his being? No problem.

"*Permesso,* excuse me, *signore.*" The tall blond woman held out her hand. "I am Cara Manetti, the staff neurologist. I am one of the doctors treating Signora Rinaldi." She used the formal title applied to all adult women, married or single.

Neurologist? The possibility of brain damage to Sophie tightened Jack's jaw. "*Piacere,* Doctor," he replied. *Glad to meet you.* He shook her hand. "What can you tell me about Ms., um, Signora Rinaldi's condition?"

She began to smile but didn't. Jack supposed his demeanor intimidated her. Whether he meant to look harsh or not, he had that effect on people. In his work it was an advantage. But not at the moment.

Donning a professional mask, she jammed her hands in the pockets of her lab coat. "Signora Rinaldi will recover fully. In time. The pain and dizziness from the concussion will ease in a day or two, and she can leave the hospital. A sling will protect her shoulder."

Jack expelled the breath he didn't know he was holding. "So she's okay."

The doctor's lips compressed. As if unable to talk without gesturing, she withdrew her hands from her pockets and held them out, palms open. "She *will* be fine. I am certain. There is the small issue of amnesia."

"My God, doesn't she know who she is?"

"*Sì, sì.* Indeed she does. That type of amnesia is extremely rare. Signora Rinaldi's global memory is intact. Hers is what we call retrograde amnesia." She hesitated, expressive hands hovering. "Often with head injuries from an accident or attack, patients do not remember the seconds immediately leading up to the trauma."

Jack had seen it before, when fellow officers had been shot. They didn't always recover the memory later. But he needed Sophie to remember what had terrified her. "And retrograde amnesia is what she has? She's missing only the seconds up to her…accident?"

Dr. Manetti's brows drew together. She raised and lowered one shoulder. "Hers is an interesting case. *Molto insolito.* Very unusual. She has lost more memory than patients with her injuries normally do."

Sophie studied the leather bifold's contents longer than necessary. Examining the gold badge and picture ID of the U.S. Anti-Terrorism Security Agency was easier than facing the stern-faced government agent standing beside her hospital bed. Jackson Thorne was a rugged-looking man, tall and leanly muscled, with dark gold hair. His accusing blue stare and un-compromising jaw jittered her pulse. He was an intimidating man, so the flutter of sexual awareness she felt made no sense.

When he cleared his throat, she finally closed the wallet and handed it back.

When her fingers brushed his knuckles, he recoiled as if she'd contaminated him. How odd. As though a concussion was contagious.

Sophie started to smile, to reassure the agent, but even that slight movement sent shards of pain rocketing around in her skull.

She wanted to ask what ATSA had to do with her, but courtesy first, as her *nonna* would've said. "I must have you to thank for arranging such good care for me in the hospital. Did you hand out the *bustarelle?*"

Thorne, his expression already forbidding, frowned. "What do you mean?"

"In Italian hospitals, patients might not get fed or bathed unless the nurses and orderlies receive envelopes of cash, *bustarelle.*"

"My superior must've taken care of that when you were ad-mitted." Stone-faced, he conveyed an air of impatience, of intense purpose.

He withdrew a spiral notebook from his jacket pocket. He didn't open it, just held it in long, muscular, tanned fingers. White scars lacing his knuckles told of a dangerous job. No wonder he had that hard-eyed look.

"Please thank him for me," she said. "Agent Thorne, I'd like to know why ATSA wants to talk to me."

"It's Officer Thorne," he bit out. "Not *Agent.*"

"I see," she said, although she didn't, not really. "Okay, *Officer* Thorne, are you here because I was injured in some sort of terrorist attack? The doctors have told me nothing about my accident."

Doubt and suspicion chased across Thorne's austere

features. He shifted his feet. "We'll get to that. Tell me what you *do* remember."

His eyes, calm and cold, told her she'd get nowhere until she answered his questions. She subsided into the pillow. "I came to see the land of my ancestors and to find any living relatives. My trip includes Rome, Tuscany and Venice. The plane's descent in Rome on May ninth is the last thing I remember. *Dottoressa* Manetti said that today is June sixth. So that was four weeks ago."

Anguish rose up as hot tears tightened her throat. "How could I not remember four whole weeks of touring Italy? *What happened to me?*"

Other than a tightening of his already steely jaw, the ATSA officer's face betrayed no reaction to her impassioned plea. He pulled a sheaf of pictures from a manila envelope and held one in front of her. "Tell me how you met this man."

Sophie stared at the trim older man in the photo. Silver at the temples, patrician bearing. Handsome, if you liked the slick, arrogant type. But a stranger to her. "I don't know him. Who is he?"

"Sebastian Vadim." Thorne consulted the notebook. "A wealthy consultant. Owns a villa in the Veneto countryside. He says you stole from him."

Sophie did something she'd only read in books: her jaw dropped open in shock. A memory clicked. She recognized the name. "The name is familiar, but I've never met Mr. Vadim."

If Thorne's lips compressed any thinner, they'd disappear, Sophie observed. The sadness lurking in his eyes hinted that something more than his job had him strung tighter than the strings on a guitar.

"Vadim says different." Thorne glared at her, daring her to deny his accusation. "He says you stole a valuable object from his house."

"I've never been to the man's house." Sophie inhaled,

trying to remain calm. Tears burned, but she blinked them away. "Look, in New York I worked as a nanny for an Italian family, the Donatis. Mr. Donati's company moved them to London. This trip was a severance bonus."

"We have that information. Go on."

"Mrs. Donati gave me Sebastian Vadim's name as someone I could contact near Venice. He's a distant relative of hers. She wrote him that I might call on him. That's all I know."

"Then how do you explain this picture?"

She stared in disbelief at a snapshot of her with Vadim in front of a set of large double doors. She stood on tiptoes to kiss the man on the mouth. "I… That can't be me. The picture…it must be altered or something. How—" A lump in her throat choked off more speech.

Nothing made sense. If he asked one more baffling question, tears would overwhelm her. She felt like folding her arms in a gesture of finality, but her bound shoulder wouldn't allow it. So she closed her eyes.

Jack couldn't take his eyes from Sophie. Gone was the exuberant, vibrant woman he'd watched the past several days. Her shiny dark hair lay lank and dull against the pillow. Cuts and bruises marred her chin and jaw on one side, her vivid complexion pale as ivory.

Dressed in a shapeless hospital gown and with her arm held against her body like a broken wing, she looked small and vulnerable, more ethereal and delicate than before. Sympathy and other emotions he wouldn't name tugged at his chest, but he shoved them away.

She had information he needed. Concentrating on Vadim was his goal. Emotion would only get in the way. Emotion could get him killed.

He needed a new tack. Accusing her of a fabricated theft hadn't tricked her into denying it.

Amnesia for real? Or acting?

If the tears and memory loss were false, why protect the

man who'd tried to kill her? Was Vadim that great a lover? The mere thought turned Jack's stomach.

Or was she protecting herself because she was guilty? Had the sightseeing excursions been cover for passing smuggled diamonds or arranging the uranium sale?

Jack doubted that. She'd been out of task-force sight only when she'd been inside the villa.

If she was faking, returning her to the villa might give him an opportunity to trip her up. If the amnesia was real, a return might jog her brain. Either way fit his plans.

For now, he'd keep testing how good an actress she was.

Regarding her lying there weak and racked with pain, he tamped down a stab of guilt. And an urge to tuck a stray wisp of hair behind her ear.

Jack waited as she seemed to regroup and revive. Her breathing evened out and her forehead smoothed. Finally she reopened her eyes, lush brown lashes fluttering.

Distress again pleated her forehead. She gazed at him with resignation in her espresso-dark eyes. She'd probably expected him to leave.

"Ms. Rinaldi," he began.

A sigh escaped her lips. "Sophie, please. Ms. Rinaldi makes me think of my mother." She started to reach for the carafe beside her but grimaced at the effort to turn.

He waved her off and poured the water. He dropped a flexible straw into the plastic cup.

"Sophie." He'd thought the name for days but hadn't said it. A soft name, a whisper of silk on the lips. He shook off the foolish thought as he handed her the cup. Their fingers brushed, and awareness sparked into his flesh. "ATSA has pieced together the last four weeks from your travel itinerary and the American consulate. But I warn you. You may not like what you hear."

She brightened visibly, a rosy hue suffusing her high cheekbones. "Oh, yes, please tell me. I want to know everything. I *need* to know." She handed him back the cup.

Jack took the cup, careful not to touch her again. He dragged his gaze from her parted lips, moistened by the cool water. He needed to study her reactions, but, damn it, looking at the woman had unwanted physical consequences.

He flipped a page in his notebook and skimmed his notes. "You did land in Rome as planned. No plane crash. You spent a week there, stayed at the Hotel Magenta near the Pantheon. From Rome—"

"Wait," Sophie said, worry in her eyes. "What did I do in Rome? Did I find any Pinellis?"

"Pinellis?"

"My mother's people. One reason for my trip was to find family. I had letters and names—oh, my God, what hap-pened to them?" She clutched at his sleeve. "My luggage, my things…"

"Your effects are safe, including the letters." He'd gone through them himself last night. Her passport and the letters confirmed her identity if not her innocence. The rest had been bought for her by Vadim, but he'd save that for later.

Seeming to accept his word, she let go of his sleeve. She accepted the cup again and swallowed another sip of water. "Go on, please."

Returning the cup to the side table, he continued his recital of her itinerary. "From Rome you flew to Florence, where you stayed until the next Sunday. Then you rented a car and toured Tuscany. You returned to Florence and took a plane to Venice, the last leg of your journey."

Sophie reacted to his story with small frowns and a tight-ening of her mouth. She asked only one question. "Do you know whether I found my relatives?"

He shook his head. "None of your papers indicated that one way or the other. Were you searching for relatives in Venice, too?"

"No. I just wanted to see the city. What about Venice?" Her words were almost a whisper. Her agitation was palpable. "Whatever…happened to me must've happened here."

Jack stuffed his notebook away and kept his hand in the pocket to keep from gathering Sophie in his arms. If she was acting, she ought to win an Oscar. He gave himself a mental kick for letting his professional skepticism slip.

"This last part is sketchy," he said. "We obtained information from the airline and from what you told the U.S. Consulate. When you landed, your luggage didn't. That left you with only a few euros and a credit card. When you tried to use the credit card at the hotel, the card check indicated the card was stolen. The clerk cut it up."

When she said nothing, only stared at him in disbelief, he continued, "That's apparently when you contacted Sebastian Vadim. He moved you into his villa and bought you new clothes and new luggage."

"What about my own luggage?"

"We found your purse with some new traveler's checks—but no credit card—at the villa. Apparently the airline hasn't recovered your luggage." Leoni had checked with Baggage Claim. He said the clerk had merely smiled and shrugged.

As Jack studied her bewildered expression, he paused for full effect before the clincher. An assumption but a good bet. Jack wouldn't flinch from pushing her to deny or remember. "As I said, Vadim moved you into his villa—and into his bed. You are his lover."

Her mouth rounded in horror. "You must be mistaken," she whispered. "I couldn't—"

"Or *were*. Until he tried to kill you yesterday."

"Impossible. Yesterday was the return date on my plane tickets. Why wasn't I at the airport?"

"You ran from the villa in fear, but Vadim came after you in his Maserati. His right front fender did *this* to you."

His words seemed to strike her like a physical blow. She sank backward, her free hand covering her eyes. Then, tears streaming, she wrapped her fingers around his wrist. *"No, no, it can't be!* I am not this man's anything. I don't know him. Why would he try to kill me?"

Jack forced himself to peel her fingers from his arm. He leaned forward, his arms braced on the bed, close enough to feel her warm breath, see the rise and fall of her breasts and breathe her female scent. Damn it, he would not let Vadim's woman get to him.

Angry at his ambivalence, he nearly growled at her. "That's exactly what ATSA wants to know. Your lover is no business consultant. He's a murderer and a black-market dealer in blood diamonds. ATSA can protect you from him if you co-operate with us. Where is he? *Where is Sebastian Vadim?*"

"I don't know. I don't know *anything*," Sophie choked out. "What you say is impossible. *Leave me alone!*" She turned away, her tears welling to shuddering sobs.

Jack froze. Damn, he'd pushed her too hard. Questions clamped his chest. Was he wrong about her? What should he do?

He pulled his hands away from the bed. Indecision was not his style. He hated uncertainty, second-guessing, but there was something about Sophie… "Look, I didn't mean—"

The door burst open. *"Cosa sta succedendo qui?"* What's happening here?

Two nurses shoved him out of the way. One made cooing noises over Sophie and straightened her covers.

The other glared at Jack. *"Vada via!"* she ordered as she hustled him out the door.

Even in a historic building like the Venice *Questura,* the conference room looked like every other police conference room in which Jack had attended a meeting. Long polished-wood table, creaky chairs and drab walls with framed commendations, portraits and official seals. *Commissario* De Carlo was outlining strategy to Jack and other members of the Nuclear Interdiction Task Force not chasing down leads.

At the far end of the rectangular table, De Carlo was

flanked by three *polizia* colleagues who took furious notes as he talked. Jack eyed his notes—the basics, not more than ten words. What could *those* guys be writing? Two other ATSA officers sat midway down. Across from Jack, Leoni looked half-asleep, as usual.

At the other end of the table was a surprise addition—Jack's boss, Raines. The ATSA assistant director listened to the task-force leader but took no notes. From time to time Raines's gaze flicked from De Carlo to him.

"Thorne, your assistant director has vouched for you as a man with solid experience and ability," said De Carlo, a short man with a wrestler's build and a bald spot like a tonsure. He passed a file folder down the table to Jack.

"What's this, *Commissario?*" He flipped open the folder.

"I need more men investigating possible buyers of the uranium. That's a file on one of them, a Yamari exile named Ahmed Saqr. He's a fanatic, a terrorist who has associated with Vadim in the past. We believe he is in London."

Jack's heart plummeted. Reassigned. Exiled to London. Before he broke it, he dropped his pen on the table and wiped his sweaty hands on his trousers.

"Sir, with all due respect, I believe the Rinaldi woman is our best hope of finding Vadim."

"The woman may be his lover, but she has amnesia. The doctor's report says she remembers nothing of her time with Vadim, and they have no idea when she might remember."

"I have my doubts about the amnesia," Jack countered. "I think I can get through to her." After her reaction this morning, he wasn't too sure, but he had to try again. And soon. "She's the key, I know it."

Jack respected Raines and hated to have failed him almost as much as he hated failing his personal mission. He prided himself on his powers of observation, on being able to read people—but not Raines. Not the slightest clue to his impressions or thoughts betrayed him. Although Jack could keep his own features impassive, he had the eerie feeling Raines could see into his mind.

If the AD went along with reassigning him, Jack would quit and go it alone. Nothing would stop him from taking down his enemy.

And Sophie Rinaldi was the key.

He gripped his knees so tightly his knuckles turned white. He cast a glance at Raines.

Jack's ATSA boss cleared his throat. "*Commissario* De Carlo, as you know, I defer to you as head of this task force, but Jack Thorne's instincts about people are what make him invaluable. I trust his judgment on the Rinaldi woman. A few more days on that assignment might yield the intel we need."

A muscle jumped in Jack's jaw, and he felt sweat bead on his temples. The tension between the Italian and U.S. factions of the task force was typical. De Carlo didn't trust the ATSA officers. Leoni's laid-back approach didn't help. Nor did the elitist attitude of some in the *polizia* contingent.

Jack's next argument had to be logical, not emotional. He flattened his palms on his knees and sought calm.

When De Carlo hesitated, Jack jumped in again. "Whether she has real amnesia or not, she knows Vadim's secrets. He *will* try to kill her again. You can count on it. He has connections we don't know and he's ruthless. I can protect Ms. Rinaldi while I question her."

"*Boh.*" De Carlo waved off Jack's plea with the all-purpose Italian dismissal. "The woman is not important. She is safe while in hospital. Once she is well enough, we will return her to the States."

"But—"

"You have your new assignment." He gave a deferential nod to Raines. "However, I will give you two days to probe this Rinaldi woman. That is all. After that you fly to London. In the meantime, I suggest you study this file and the other data Interpol has provided to our computers."

Chapter 3

When the nurse looked in on Sophie at ten o'clock, she pretended sleep. They'd given her a sleeping pill, but she'd slipped it under her pillow. Sleep could wait. Time and pain-killers alleviated much of her pain, but in its place questions pounded in her head.

What had happened in the past four weeks?

Her head throbbed from the effort to remember.

But would there be memories she didn't want? Was she the lover of this man Vadim? And worse, did he really try to kill her? Or could the government man Thorne be lying?

Sophie frowned, then winced as the movement revived pain. But why? What reason could ATSA or this international task force have to make up a lover and an accident?

Could Elena Donati's relative be a criminal? A murderer and dealer in blood diamonds? She knew that term from the news. Diamonds were mined in war-torn African countries by slave labor. They were smuggled out and traded for arms. Could Sophie have aided him?

Her mind rejected the idea, but dread kicked that spiked ball around in her skull again. But what about the rest of her time in Italy? Did she locate family? Did she find Pinelli cousins in Rome or Rinaldi cousins in Florence? Did she bounce their baby on her knee or share their wine and pasta?

Finding her roots was part of finding herself, the main reason for her journey to Italy. After taking care of other people for most of her life, Sophie wanted a life for herself. But what?

Tears threatened to fall for the ninetieth time that day, but she willed them away and yawned. Sleep would overtake her, pill or not. Pain and those terrible accusations exhausted her. Odd, but berating her had seemed to take a toll on Thorne. Twice he'd nearly reached out to comfort her but stopped himself. He didn't want to care, but he did.

She yawned again. Gingerly she turned on her right side, her good side. She adjusted the wrapping on her injured shoulder and snuggled into the pillow.

Sophie was just drifting off when glaring light striped across her bed. The nurse coming in again? So soon?

Shadowy dark returned as the door closed. Rubber soles squeaked across the tiled floor. Beside the bed came quick, shallow breaths as though from exertion.

Something was wrong. Sophie tensed and started to turn.

She caught a glimpse of a male figure before a dark form blocked out the pale moonlight through the window shade. A soft thickness sealed her mouth and nose.

No! Fear spiked her adrenaline and gave her strength.

She thrashed and kicked, fighting through the pain, but could move only one arm. He swore but held her. Her muffled cries were lost in the covering that stole her breath.

Air. She needed air…

* * *

Jack exited the *vaporetto* and climbed the steps to the street. Water bus was the most efficient transport among the countless islands that were Venice. From the stop, he could see Ospedale di Lorenzo a block away, the hospital where Sophie was. He headed toward the golden-brick building.

He'd finished his boning up on the Yamari terrorist. De Carlo had given an inch and agreed to install a police officer outside Sophie's room. But the protection wouldn't start until morning. Jack would keep watch for the night.

As he arrived at the hospital's main entrance, Jack considered its security—or lack of it. The place had once been a damn palace, with entrances on all four sides, at least six staircases and a courtyard. Beautiful but not secure.

If Vadim were sending one of his thugs to finish Sophie off, he might choose daytime, when no one would notice an extra person in the halls. But Jack's money was on a late-night foray. He looked at his watch. Ten-thirty. The hospital corridors would be quiet and dim, the staff inattentive.

He climbed the entrance steps and hurried to the arched stairwell that led to the patient floors. As he neared the third floor, he heard more than one voice shouting.

Sophie!

Pulse revving, Jack took the last flight two steps at a time. He burst onto the corridor to see two people grappling outside Sophie's room—a nurse and a man with a black cap pulled low on his forehead. Two other uniformed staff ran toward them. The man knocked down the nurse and took off.

One woman spotted Jack and yelled to him, but her Italian was too rapid for him to catch even a few words. She waved her arms frantically toward the dark-capped man, who was hurrying toward another stairwell.

Jack peered into Sophie's room but saw only white uniformed staff around her bed. "Sophie? *La signora Ameri-*

cana?" he said, his tone urgent. Damn it, he ought to know more of the language!

Through the nurse's incomprehensible stream of Italian, he understood one word in English. *Okay.*

At that, he sped after the black-capped man. His quarry had a head start, but Jack knew the hospital layout. He heard the muffled stomp of sneaker-clad feet as the man pounded down the stairs ahead of him.

Jack hit the ground floor in time to see Sophie's assailant make it out the door. He recognized it as a side door away from the canal, on Ruga Brunetti. He raced after the man, who lengthened his stride when he glimpsed his pursuer.

Using his Glock was unwise in these narrow streets of homes and shops. Jack was at a disadvantage in dress shoes against a man in sneakers, and his high school track days were in the distant past. Regular jogging didn't cut it for flat-out sprinting.

The assailant could be Vadim's Cleatian bodyguard Petar. Right build. Right moves. Damn, he wanted this guy. But all he could hope for was to keep the man in sight.

Sweat stung his eyes, but his pace was steady, his breathing strong. He could keep the black cap in sight. He followed his quarry through a right turn. The man peeled left, and Jack followed him into a church plaza.

The race led across a bridge, then toward another narrow street. He raced behind the man to yet another bridge. This one arched higher than the others, and he could see only the black cap as he crested the bridge.

By the time Jack crossed, the assailant had disappeared. Three narrow streets diverged from the canal's edge.

Petar—if it was Petar—could've gone down any one of the three streets. Or into any building.

Dripping and defeated, Jack walked to catch his breath and to cool down. In his mind he spewed out every oath he knew and kicked himself for not being at the hospital earlier.

A few minutes later, cooled down and cooler-headed, he checked the street signs.

Great, just great.

He had no idea where he was, but he had to get back to the hospital fast.

Sophie could still be in danger.

The early-morning sun streaming through the window woke Sophie. She opened her eyes and recoiled with a start. A man sat in the chair beside her bed. When she recognized Jackson Thorne, she relaxed, her pulse slowing to normal.

He was asleep, his head lolling sideways against the high back of the sagging upholstered chair. Mussed from sleep, his hair gleamed like antique gold in the sun. In repose his harshness was muted. His eyebrows and eyelashes were a red-gold mix. The darker contrast created that fierce eagle stare she'd seen yesterday. Red-gold bristle covered his chiseled jaw. His mouth still looked austere but not stern or intense.

The light tan softened him, but not much. He didn't seem like a man who frequented tanning booths or lounged on beaches. A jungle or desert assignment, then.

She studied his strong throat and wide shoulders, impressive in such a lean body. Her gaze traveled to the golden hairs curling out of his shirt opening, then down his leanly muscled chest to his folded arms and the scarred knuckles.

The scars—how had he gotten them? Rescuing a hostage? Fighting a terrorist? And how would those tough and wounded fingers feel on her skin?

She must still be dizzy to have such thoughts about this man, of all people.

No wonder, after last night's scare. The attack had brought back the ringing in her head and the drilling ache in her shoulder. Painkillers and a sleeping pill had done their job. She felt better this morning.

Better enough to face facts. A man tried to kill her last night. Remembering her panic when she couldn't breathe, she tensed from head to toe, and fear tightened her throat.

Jackson Thorne must be telling the truth about Sebastian Vadim. At least the part where he wanted to kill her.

Why was the big question.

"Why what?" a deep male voice asked. Thorne straightened in the chair and scrubbed a hand over his eyes.

She hadn't realized she'd said it aloud. "I didn't mean to wake you. Have you been here all night?"

"Most of it."

"A nurse told me you chased the man. Did you catch him?"

Thorne shook his head. "He had a head start. I chased him long enough to get lost. Had to pay a water-taxi driver a month's rent to return me here."

If not for his scowl, Sophie would've thought the ATSA officer was making a joke. "You tried."

"Trying doesn't cut it. I was too damn late getting here. It's a miracle you're alive. What stopped him?"

"I'm not sure. I didn't take the sleeping pill they brought me and I was still awake. I don't think he was expecting me to fight him." Fear flooded back with a buzzing in her head and a spasm in her throat.

"Can you go on?" He stood and stared hard at her, as if willing strength into her.

She nodded, reaching for him with her free hand. He hesitated, then clasped it and held on.

His hand was tough and hard, like the man, but offered warmth and solid support. After a moment she felt able to continue. "I…I couldn't breathe. He held a pillow or something over my face. I pulled my good arm free and knocked over the IV stand. The nurses came."

"Did you get a good look at him?"

"No. It was too dark to see his face." She searched her brain for impressions. "He wasn't as tall as you but strong and fit."

"I'll vouch for fit." Thorne subsided into the chair again but kept possession of her hand. "You were asking why earlier. Why what?"

"Why does someone—Vadim—want to kill me?"

"If you can remember the last few days, we'll know the answer to that."

More than anything, Sophie wanted to remember. And not just a motive for murder. She wanted the last four weeks. She wanted her life back.

But remembering could be a double-edged sword. What if she'd been that man's lover? What could she know that was so bad he wanted to kill her?

Whatever had happened, she needed the truth.

"Officer Thorne, yesterday you said ATSA could offer me protection if I would help find Sebastian Vadim."

Jack watched her eyes as he had while she'd seemed to struggle within herself. She seemed damned sincere. After last night's attack, even that *polizia* prick De Carlo would have to admit she needed protection 24-7.

After his unprofessional loss of control yesterday, he'd expected her to refuse to talk to him. That she reached out to him today shocked the hell out of him. But no more attack dog. Kindness had a better chance of gaining her trust.

Reluctantly he slid his hand from her soft grip. He shouldn't get too used to how soft and silky she felt. "I was too hard on you. I apologize."

"It's okay. You have a job to do. But I was too upset to understand or accept what was happening. I don't know if I *can* help. I don't remember Vadim or *anything*. I want to remember, but I'm afraid."

He smoothed his rumpled dress shirt and dragged fingers through his hair. He'd have to move fast to convince De Carlo and Raines to leave him here. Sophie didn't yet trust him, but she seemed to acknowledge that she needed him.

He could work with that.

"I have to arrange some things. I'll get back to you later today." He started toward the door.

"But what if someone comes again?" A note of panic tightened her voice.

"There's a police officer outside your door. You'll be safe." There'd better damned well be a cop on duty today. Jack would alert the day staff to keep an eye out, too.

Her lips curved with a warm smile. "Thank you. A cop is good, but I feel safer with you, Officer Thorne."

He sure as hell hadn't done her much good so far, but hearing her say it eased his tension a notch.

He opened the door, then stopped and half turned. "Sophie, my name is Jack."

"Tell me about this man," Sophie said as she rode with Jack to Sebastian Vadim's mainland villa two days later. "Why do you want him so badly?"

Why do I— No, she meant why did *ATSA* want Vadim. He was jumpy and overreacting. Jack slanted a quick glance toward his passenger in the tiny Fiat.

Sophie's hair was clean and brushed so it floated in a glossy cloud around her shoulders. A female ATSA officer had taken pity on Jack and selected clothes from Sophie's luggage for him to take her. In the short pink slacks she'd called "cropped," a buttoned blouse and sandals, she looked like any young woman out for a drive.

With a few exceptions. The abrasions and scrapes on her face—but those were healing. The purple-and-red bruises were fading to yellow. Her shoulder bandage had been replaced by a green sling with hook-and-loop fasteners and a strap around her chest to immobilize the arm.

As if she'd asked him the weather, she gazed out the windshield at the lush green countryside. How did she maintain that ethereal calm? Even if she was faking the amnesia, two attempts on her life ought to have shaken her to the core.

And they had. He'd seen her tears.

"Did you hear me? Earth to Jack."

He checked the rearview mirror to see if their escort was staying with them. Behind them, in another unmarked *polizia* Alfa Romeo sedan, were Leoni and Assistant Director Raines. De Carlo was waiting for them at the villa. He'd grumbled but agreed to leave Jack where he was, guarding Sophie. For now.

"Sorry. I was concentrating on the traffic."

"A good thing." Sophie laughed, low music that sent tingles low in Jack's body. "In Italy, driving is a blood sport. And it's even worse on the *Autostrade*."

A dark green BMW passed them. It zigzagged around two trucks and took a sharp curve with two wheels airborne.

Jack saw that the next exit was theirs. Thank God. "Four lanes is a free-for-all."

"I asked about Vadim. ATSA is a terrorist-hunting agency. What do you want with a diamond smuggler?"

Did she really want to know or was she testing to see what ATSA knew? Either way, Jack saw no reason not to tell her the facts.

The events surrounding Roszca's arrest had been in the news. Very little was still classified. "Viktor Roszca is an international arms dealer. A few months ago he arranged the theft of weapons-grade uranium—four-point-five kilos, about ten pounds—from an old nuke dump in the former Soviet satellite of Cleatia. He was arranging an auction when ATSA arrested him. The courier vanished. We think he sold the package to Vadim, but we have no proof."

"I understand. But if Vadim is from Cleatia, how is he Mrs. Donati's cousin?"

"His mother was Italian. He grew up in both countries. He

learned his trade with the Mafia before graduating from local rackets to diamond smuggling."

Sophie heard the bitterness in Jack's voice and wondered. "Why hasn't he been arrested before?"

"He was tough to track. Too many aliases. He seemed to be at least a half dozen different people."

"But Sebastian Vadim is his real name?"

"Sebastiano Vadim, to be exact," Jack said, biting out the words. "He must've kept in touch with the Donatis under his real name. The villa's also listed under Vadim."

Sophie considered the possibilities. She already knew how dangerous he was. The man had aliases, Mafia connections, resources to add to his arsenal. Her stomach gave a flutter of fear. "And what about the uranium?"

Jack heaved a sigh of apparent frustration. "Vanished with the courier. What Vadim plans for it is anybody's guess. Four-point-five kilos could arm a dirty bomb or a small missile."

"It could fall into terrorist hands. I see." She contemplated the vineyard that came into view as they exited onto a two-lane highway. "And you think I know something about his plans. That's why he tried to kill me."

"His plans or about the uranium. Yes."

She fell silent as they tooled along the country road, her gaze on the scenery. Farm fields and vineyards thick with leaves and ripening fruit edged the road. The leaves of olive trees flashed green and silver, with wildflowers sowing color at their feet. So much beauty with such evil in its midst.

When they turned in at Vadim's villa, Jack saw Sophie sit up straight. She scanned the long driveway, the vineyard and the redbrick villa as if hoping for a breakthrough.

"Look familiar?" Jack said.

She blinked and sat back against the cushion. She stared so hard she must've roused the dizziness again. "No. Nothing. I wish it did."

The two cars pulled up to the manor house's entrance. Jack helped Sophie out of the little car. She was still shaky, and her bandaged arm limited her agility.

Before they'd left Venice, Jack had introduced her to his colleagues who accompanied them. He doubted her artless charm would win over De Carlo as easily as it had them.

De Carlo opened the heavy front doors of the house and stepped out, and Jack introduced him. In a formal Italian manner, the task-force leader bowed slightly over her hand. *"Piacere,"*—a pleasure to meet you—he said.

Jack noted that his eyes were cold.

"Piacere," Sophie replied.

Inside were three more officers with boxes of documents and electronic devices in their arms.

"Let's walk through the house," he said, taking Sophie's good arm.

"You're hoping something I see will trigger my memory."

"Yes."

"I hope so, too."

They strolled through a large sitting room and a dining room with tile floors, into the kitchen and out onto a shaded terrace. Fifteen minutes later, as they reached the back section of the main floor, she sighed. "I don't remember ever being here before." Looking tired, she eased down on a settee.

"Your things are upstairs in your bedroom. Can you manage the stairs?"

Hope bloomed on her delicate face. "Oh, yes." She looked around. "I saw the stairs when we came in, but now I'm all turned around. Where?"

His mouth compressed. "This way."

As they walked back toward the front hallway, she said, "Jack, I know you don't believe in my amnesia. Yesterday you said Vadim accused me of stealing. You made that up to trick me, didn't you?"

He winced that she'd read him so well. "I had to try."

She gave him a sad little smile. "And just now you were trying to trip me up about finding the stairs. It doesn't matter. There's nothing you or I can do to bring back my memory except keep trying."

"The doctors said your memory might return all at once or in pieces."

"Or never. Thank you for being kind enough not to mention that possibility." Her smile sagged. "I'd be grateful for one of those pieces anytime now."

They entered a spacious bedroom with hardwood floors, a large bed with a pale peach coverlet and a vase beside it. The flowers in it had died. No one had been there to replenish their water. The doors and woodwork, including the bed frame, were painted grass-green.

"The room is inviting. I wish I remembered staying in it." Sophie ran her fingers across the soft cotton coverlet.

Jack opened a wardrobe. "Your luggage is in here." He pulled out two red leather suitcases, one large and the other a carry-on tote. He slung them onto the bed. "They're a little damaged from searches. Slits in the lining, a few scuffs."

"If I recognized them, I might be upset." She lifted out dresses and skirts and tops, silk and linen, all expensive.

These were the boutique fashions Vadim had bought her. Had bought his lover, Jack reminded himself. There was no clothing of Vadim's in her room. That meant nothing. He must've made her come to him.

"How about the other bag?" He stood by, his gaze fixed on her, willing her to recognize something or to slip and prove his doubts right.

She opened the tote and gasped. "My purse. My folio of letters." She beamed at him. "You said they were here. Oh, thank goodness!"

A corner of his mouth twitched. He didn't seem to be able to resist her infectious smile. "Your passport's there, too. You must've had those with you on the flight from Florence."

One-handed, she pawed through the frilly underwear and the cosmetics bag at the bottom of the tote. "My camera? I could've taken pictures of my long-lost relatives."

"No camera." He cleared his throat, waited. "You don't recognize anything else?"

"Sorry. These things are lovely, but they aren't mine." She gestured at the clothing strewn on the bed.

"They *are* yours," Jack said. "Vadim bought them for you. Until your luggage is found, they're all you have to wear."

Sophie frowned as if ready to object, but a voice from downstairs summoned Jack.

He scrubbed knuckles over his jaw. A moment ago sympathy had cracked his determination, but he needed to remember what this woman was to Vadim. And keep his eye on his goal.

"See if you can pack this stuff. I'll come back to carry the suitcases downstairs. We'll be at a safe house in Venice for a while. You'll need clothes." He turned and walked out.

Sophie collapsed on the bed, her grandmother's papers crushed to her chest with her good arm. At least she had those and her passport. *Something* of hers.

Dizziness swirled in her head, and she closed her eyes. For a long time a knot had constricted her chest at not having an identity separate from those she took care of. Not having her memory or her life was drawing that knot tighter.

She wouldn't think about it. She couldn't let fear and worry suffocate her.

Her purse and passport proved that she *had* been in this house. Somewhere in her brain was there the knowledge that would help capture Vadim? Could she locate the stolen uranium?

If Jack wanted her to remember, she would try. He was hard and unsmiling and he wasn't telling her the whole truth.

But she could trust him to protect her.

The torment she glimpsed in his eyes told her he had deeper

reasons, personal reasons to find Vadim. And deeper emotions he kept in check.

Sophie stood and packed as best she could with one hand. The clothes were more expensive than she could afford but styles she liked. Did she choose them?

Finished with the packing, she looked around. On the bedside table was a marble statuette of a woman, about a foot high. She wore a long cloak and held her hands in a prayerful grip.

So beautiful. A religious icon, she thought. It looked very old. The attached base was cracked and had been glued.

Sophie felt the cool marble. One-handed, she could lift it only a few inches. Heavier than she expected marble to be.

Beneath the statuette was the business card of an antique shop. She turned it over. "Santa Elisabetta Rinaldi."

Tears gathered. Sophie crossed herself. Saint Elizabeth. *Rinaldi?* A Rinaldi family saint?

Where did she come from? Surely Vadim hadn't given it to her. Clothing, yes, because she had to have something to wear. The statuette was an antique, probably valuable. She would never accept such an extravagant gift.

She must've bought this with her new traveler's checks.

It was hers. But not the clothing. She wanted nothing from such a despicable man. She would return the clothes and luggage. Well, not return. She would donate them to charity.

Finding a Rinaldi saint. What would *Nonna* say? Her grandmother would tell her it was a miracle and to bring Santa Elisabetta home. She was certain.

Santa Elisabetta belonged to her. Why would the task force care?

Chapter 4

Vadim wished his cousin had never brought him the cursed uranium. This palazzo, obtained under a new alias for just such a contingency, was musty and dark, but it would serve. If not for Dobrich, he would be relaxing on the terrace of his villa instead of hiding like a rat in a hole.

Tapping his fingers on the windowsill, he gazed through the gap in the heavy draperies. He kept his back to his men as he sorted out the mess. Let them sweat a little longer. They had both failed him.

The whole debacle was Dobrich's fault, may he rot in hell. Had Interpol been following his cousin? Or had the Italians finally gotten evidence on the illicit diamond trade?

It had to be the former. Tracking the uranium would be the reason for the Americans' involvement. And Dobrich, with his toolbox full of radiation, had led them to him.

Perhaps the American woman was not as naive as he'd

thought. Could she have been sent to spy on him? Why else had she listened to his phone conversation?

Petar had reported that she remembered nothing. Amnesia made no difference. Memories returned. She must be eliminated before she remembered his and Ahmed Saqr's plans. The uranium had to be retrieved. His plans would go forth.

They must.

Ahmed had made a down payment on his purchase and demanded its prompt delivery. He would not understand if Vadim reneged. The Yamari fanatic would cry betrayal.

In that eventuality, Vadim would have a great deal more to fear than Interpol or the Americans.

He turned to face Petar and Guido. "Petar, you failed to silence the woman in the hospital," he said in Cleatian. "With her arm in a sling she fought you off. Is that correct?"

The wiry man's short hair stood up in tufts as though he'd been pulling it. He opened his mouth, apparently to object, but sighed and said, "*Dak,* you're right. I failed."

"And the American nearly caught you. Did he get a good look at you?"

"He did not. I was too fast for him to get close enough." His chin rose a notch. Petar had competed in marathons and was proud of his speed.

"Then I can take comfort in something."

The sarcastic tone triggered a flush up Petar's neck.

Vadim turned his wrath on his other man. "Guido, the uranium? Is it still hidden in the house?" he said in Italian.

The bodyguard's thick fingers worried his driving cap as he shook his head. "I don't know. The *polizia* still have the villa. I am told it's a task force of the *Polizia di Stato* and an American agency. I can't go inside yet. But I don't think they have found it. They continue to search."

"*Bene,*" said Vadim. *Good.* He could salvage diamonds from the ashes. "Getting inside could be difficult, but I will think of something."

Soon. He couldn't keep Ahmed waiting much longer.

If Sophie were silenced and the uranium recovered, all would be well. The terrorist would have his purchase. With one bomb he would destroy those he perceived as enemies— and Vadim's competition. A victory for them both.

"You have another chance to redeem yourselves." He switched to English, a language both knew. He glared at the two men, whose sweat soaked their dark shirts. Clearly they understood that failing him twice was not an option.

"The woman?" Guido asked.

"The *polizia* have arranged a safe house in Venice for her." He handed Petar the address on a slip of paper. "You will wait for them to arrive."

"If the task force sends more than one escort boat with her," Petar said, "a dose of gasoline could take care of the house and all inside it."

Vadim considered. Petar's penchant for arson surpassed his other lethal skills. It might work. "Be prepared for that contingency. But only if they do not have the uranium with them or if you obtain it first. Arm yourselves well. They must not escape. I have encountered the American operative guarding Sophie. He is dangerous. Take him down first. Then the woman."

By the time they left the villa, Sophie was tired but encouraged by having her handbag and the tote with its precious letters and the family saint figure. Her other meager possessions—medicine and her sandals—had left the hospital with her in a plastic bag. She didn't count the big suitcase of boutique clothing stashed in the Fiat's trunk.

Jack said nothing but appeared to be concentrating on coping with heavy traffic as they entered the *Autostrade*. Instead of a dress shirt with his khakis, today he wore a knit shirt the color of his eyes.

A naturally taciturn man, Sophie decided. He kept his

emotions walled up inside except for hints of intense anguish. Oddly his silence didn't bother her. His large presence and the musky scent of his aftershave both comforted and intrigued her. Relaxing, she settled in her seat.

When the sedan stopped, she opened her eyes to see docks lined with freighters and crawling with activity. She'd napped without realizing it. A printed sign announced the Port Authority of Mestre. So they were still on the mainland.

From there they climbed into an unmarked motorboat provided by the task force. Jack settled her into its cockpit. A canvas awning provided sun protection.

Another officer—a sleepy-eyed man named Leoni—handed Jack a sheaf of papers. "Here are the permits. You sure you want to try this without an escort? Venice canals can be a maze. And dangerous."

"Safer if no one outside knows. An escort might attract attention." He tossed the papers into the cockpit along with the bow line.

Sophie saw a map among the papers. "I can help navigate."

"Go for it. I'll be tracking you on GPS." Leoni threw up his hands and went to untie the stern line. "Give the *vaporetti* wide berth."

Jack slid into the driver's seat and turned the key. "You sure you can handle this? Are you okay?"

"Fine." She was still tired and a little groggy, but she wanted to do whatever she could. Anything that would clear up this fog surrounding her.

"I should've asked if you have medicine to take," Jack said as he spread the map on her lap.

"Something for pain if I need it. I have another medication to help me regain memory. Piracetam. It's probably not approved in the States." She smoothed the creased map and put a finger on their location. "Maybe it'll sharpen my map-reading ability, too."

Jack maneuvered them from the dock space and out into the *Laguna,* the waterway between the mainland and Venice. Shoving the throttle forward sent them cruising the six miles across the lagoon toward the entrance to Venice's Grand Canal.

"I'm glad we're going by boat," Sophie said. "This may be my only chance to see Venice. And remember it, I mean."

He cocked his head at her, but she couldn't interpret his official mask, a blank expression that hid everything.

She knew he lay in wait for a slip that would betray feigned amnesia. If only.

She pulled her guidebook from her bag. "A guided tour along the Grand Canal. I can pretend this is a gondola."

"Sophie, why do you think the injury wiped the entire trip from your memory?"

"You mean instead of just the moments before the impact?"

"Losing such a long span of time is unusual, the doctors said. What else does your brain want to push away?"

She wished she knew. Or maybe she didn't. The painful knot inside her tightened another loop of dread. "Maybe when I found my relatives, they were mafiosi. Or losing my luggage—"

"Or being taken in by a rich lover twice your age?"

They passed a barge loaded with containers and a regular transport traveling from Mestre to the floating city. Gasoline and engine exhaust mingled with the salt air.

A strand of hair blew in her eyes, and she brushed it away. "You're trying to trap me again, Jack. I was taken in by Vadim. That I believe. But I was *not* his lover."

"If you don't remember, how do you know?"

Sophie considered the photographs and videos she'd seen of her with Vadim. He'd seemed attentive and charming but no more. Not intimate.

For some reason of his own, Jack was leaping to a conclusion. Or his insistence on Vadim as lover was a tactic to trip her up. "Some things a woman knows."

Soon they arrived at the Grand Canal. The causeway from Mestre rose on their left and ended at an enormous parking lot. Only foot and boat traffic were allowed in Venice.

Jack guided the powerboat around a *vaporetto* at the train station dock on their right and slowed to follow the sinuous course of the canal inside the city.

Other boats jammed the canal with traffic. Motorboats ruled the waterways—private boats, work boats, water taxis and the ubiquitous *vaporetti*. The picturesque gondolas fought constant chop as their long oars propelled them more slowly along the canals. Sophie smiled at the sight of a brown boat marked UPS and at a robin's-egg-blue delivery "truck" carrying food to a market or shop.

"So where are we headed?" She hoped her question would sidetrack Jack from his inquisition.

The look in his eyes told her the change of topic was only temporary.

He handed her one of the other papers. "Here are the directions. We're going to an apartment in the San Polo district. The street's there on the paper. I checked the map, but don't let me make a wrong turn."

Fat chance, she thought as she perused the directions. This man never made a wrong turn. He was too controlled.

"It looks like we follow the Grand Canal as far as the Rialto Bridge." She traced their route with her finger. "Then we turn right on the Rio di Meloni."

"*Rio?* River? I wondered about that when I saw it. Aren't these all canals?"

"Right. Canals run through the city's hundred islands, but just the big ones are called *canale*."

"And you know this because?"

"Not from memory, Sherlock." She slid the guidebook from beneath the map and held it up as her source. Then her eyes widened in pleasure as she took in the scenery.

"Oh, look. One palace after another. Incredible! They seem

to dance on the water. I can't take my eyes away, but I need the guide to tell me what they are."

They passed a Baroque church and beneath a bridge. The Ponte Scalzi, Sophie told him. Then a Gothic palazzo with beautiful pointed arches, where she read that the composers Liszt and Wagner had once stayed.

As he asked questions and stared in awe, amazement swept through her. A new man, a laid-back and interesting man, replaced the grim ATSA operative. He still scanned the other boats as if trying to spot assassins, but he slowed the boat so she could enjoy the sights. His large, scarred hands rested on the steering wheel, and he turned his face to the sun. He enjoyed the moment as much as she.

She wanted to touch his angular jaw, to feel the strength in this hard man. What would it be like to feel his sinewy arms around her?

Sophia Constanza, you have way too much imagination.

The sling kept her from reaching for him even if she gave in to temptation. She kept her good hand on the guidebook and continued her commentary as they traveled the Grand Canal.

Fantastic palaces and famous architecture surrounded them, but Jack couldn't keep his gaze from Sophie's glowing face. Her espresso-brown eyes glittered with pleasure and her cheeks flushed pink with excitement.

How did she do it? She put aside all her trauma and anguish and threw herself into the experience of the moment. Her emotions were there, just beneath the surface, ready to light up or darken her beautiful face.

Maybe it was her youth—eight years younger than his thirty-five. But had he ever been that young, that free? If he had been, his light heart had been crushed five years ago.

He'd had her pegged as a sophisticate, a party girl. She was anything but. Her assertion that she hadn't been in Vadim's bed buoyed Jack's spirits more than it should. Why he cared made no sense. Mainly he was relieved for her—*if* she was right. Or truthful. That was it. Nothing personal.

So if she wasn't the party girl he'd pegged her for, was he wrong about the amnesia, too? Did she really not remember seeing Venice's fading splendor?

He hadn't seen it either. He'd been too busy. Too driven.

As he'd been doing since they left Mestre, he checked behind them. None of the same boats. Vadim's informants must have told him Sophie had left the hospital and gone to the villa. He must have something planned. But what?

There was no rush to get to the safe house. He cut the boat's speed further. Hell, he wanted to play tourist, too. If he were truthful, savoring Sophie's joy was half the reason. Checking out the side canals as they drifted along—in case he needed an escape route—didn't hurt either.

Jack pointed to an ornate building coming up on the right. "Venice seems to have palaces in every conceivable ornate architectural style."

"Byzantine, Gothic, Renaissance, they're all here. Venice was the link to both the East and the West." Her lips curved in an apologetic smile. "But I'm probably telling you things you already know."

"I had no time for sightseeing. Be my guide."

She emitted another breathy exclamation. "Oh, look, over there on the left. That's the Ca' d'Oro, House of Gold. *Ca'* is short for *casa*. When Venice was a republic, only the duke's palace could be called a palazzo. When the Ca' d'Oro was built, it was decorated with gold leaf and lapis lazuli."

They bobbed in the chop to admire the pointed arches and elaborate stone decorations.

Jack scanned the three stories of white-stone facade. "Where's the gold?"

"Gone in centuries of decay or stolen, I suppose. The book doesn't say."

"Like everywhere, restoration costs don't include replacing gold leaf. I'd like to have seen that." On both sides of the Ca' d'Oro rose church steeples. Bells resounded from one. On their side of the canal, vendors in the fish market displayed their freshly caught wares. "From the sublime to the smelly. What's next?"

"So you *are* interested in Venice." Grinning, Sophie turned the page in her guide.

He shrugged and pushed the throttle forward. The boat's pointed prow cut through the waves as they headed toward the next palace. "Who would not be amazed by this unreal place built on a hundred-plus marshy islands? Even if the city's sinking, it's mysterious and ingenious."

"It says here there are about two hundred canals and four hundred bridges."

"I must've crossed half of them the other night. Dead ends, odd corners, twists as intricate as the city's history."

"When you chased the man who attacked me?" A shadow of fear crossed her eyes, but she seemed to shake it off.

"And when I tried to find my way back. The two people I asked who spoke English told me to just go straight, but there is no *straight* in Venice."

"A nurse told me that on foot you can't get lost. If you keep walking, you eventually arrive at Piazza San Marco."

"All roads lead to St. Mark's? Maybe." He slanted her a skeptical glance. "I didn't *have* 'eventually.' I needed to get to the hospital fast to see that you were all right."

Her brow clouded again. "You're sure this apartment you're taking me to is secret enough to be safe?"

Jack reached across her injured arm to squeeze her right hand where it rested on her lap. Even that brief touch coursed heat through his blood.

He gripped the steering wheel with determination to keep his mind on the job. "*Commissario* De Carlo set it up through Venice police headquarters, the *Questura*. You'll be fine."

She seemed to accept his reassurance and turned her gaze

to the next building, oddly Oriental with arched arcades. "Ca' da Mosto is the oldest on the Grand Canal. Byzantine, from the thirteenth century."

Jack hardly listened as he checked around them. Her worries had brought him down. Back to reality, where he ought to stay, not sucked in by her flowery scent, her ingenuousness and the scenery. Still no sign of trouble, but he wouldn't relax again until they reached the San Polo apartment.

"Here we are at the Ponte di Rialto." Disappointment that their tourist break was at an end laced her words.

The Rialto was a building in itself, a stone span over the wide canal. Arcades with arched openings and carved cornices rose above the walkway to strengthen the structure.

As they passed beneath the bridge, a chill raked down Jack's spine. His hand went instinctively to his sidearm, but he shook off his nerves. Probably just cold radiating from the massive stone arch.

He pushed the boat's throttle forward as they left the bridge behind them.

When Sophie directed him to their turnoff on the right, Jack steered into the smaller canal and slowed again.

Not palaces but graceful town houses rose on both sides, houses in pastel shades, some with iron balconies and red-tile roofs. They were set back from the canal and interspersed with walkways and small squares.

Sophie tucked her guidebook in her handbag and traced their route on the map. "San Polo is a residential and merchant section." She pointed to a bar where people sat at tiny tables beneath striped umbrellas. "People come from all over Venice to the produce market and the fish market we saw earlier. The ground is higher, safer for banks and other businesses from the *acqua alta,* the high tide that sometimes floods the streets."

"Is all that in your guidebook?"

Sophie's soft mouth rounded and her dark eyebrows

winged skyward in shock. "No. I…I don't know how I know that. It just popped out."

"The doctors said your memory might return gradually."

She laughed. "Does that mean you believe me?"

Her low chuckle, although with a bitter edge, resonated in Jack's very bones, but he wasn't ready to concede the amnesia. "Just conversation."

"Wish I remembered something more helpful, like what secrets Sebastian Vadim might have told me."

He couldn't reply. The old grief and anger clawed inside him and stole his power of speech. His hatred had acquired a new dimension, one that included Sophie. The mere thought of Vadim's hands on her, of his involving her in dirty business, fired rage that could boil over without firm control.

"Are you all right, Jack?"

Sophie's gentle question freed him from his funk. One by one he relaxed his fingers on the steering wheel. "Fine. Just fine. Anxious to get you to the safe house."

She nodded, but her pleated brow said she didn't buy it.

Following Sophie's directions, he turned left, then right, then another left to an even smaller canal.

"There it is, Fondamenta Mariani." Sophie indicated the street that ran alongside the canal. The yellowish brick house at the end on the left was their destination.

Jack maneuvered the craft toward the finger docks in front of the house. He eased it into an open slip. A set of stone steps from the docks led up to the *fondamenta*.

"Wait here while I check on the house." Jack gathered up the bow line.

As he stood up, he heard a familiar ominous noise. *Thunk, thunk, thunk* of bullets slamming into the boat's port side. His pulse kicked into high gear.

He dived back into the cockpit.

"Sophie, get down!"

She turned white as paper but complied. She scooted down onto the cockpit floor. "Jack, what was that?"

No loud reports had shattered the neighborhood peace. The shots had come in rapid succession. His mind flipped through the possibilities. "Gunshots. A submachine gun equipped with a suppressor. Either an AK74 or an H&K MP-10."

Professionals? Doubtful. Their aim wasn't so hot. Or maybe Vadim's regular muscle with shiny new weapons.

More silenced shots zinged into the water beside the boat. Tiny fountains sprayed up at the lethal impact.

Where were they coming from? He couldn't take time to search. The safe house had been compromised. Without more caliber than his Glock, he couldn't risk a firefight.

Protecting Sophie was his priority.

"We have to get out of here fast."

He saw pain etch her brow and tighten her mouth. The contorted movement needed to hide below the console did that. If he'd accepted the escort, could he have spared her this danger? Probably not, but damn it, they'd have had backup. No time for recriminations. He had to deal with it.

Jack turned the key in the ignition to start the engine. He threw the boat into reverse.

Farther down the canal, another boat motor revved up.

The attackers?

A sleek black powerboat with silver lightning bolts streaming back from the prow surged toward them.

Jack straightened the wheel and shifted to forward. As he jammed the throttle ahead, the motor coughed.

Damn it, don't die.

He eased back slightly. The motor caught and evened out. Slowly he pushed the throttle forward. The powerboat sliced through the water back the way they'd come.

Jack kept an eye on their pursuers as he flipped open his cellular phone. Familiar profiles in the cockpit. It figured.

He punched the speed dial. When he heard Leoni's voice,

he barked, "Safe house blown. Bad guys shooting and in pursuit. Vadim's boys Guido and Petar. Do you copy?"

He zigged and zagged at each turn of canal and *rio*.

Other boat drivers cursed and waved fists at them as they sped by. The wake from the chase boat sent a gondolier scrambling for footing.

"I copy," Leoni said. "Got your position on the screen."

The black boat wasn't gaining, but Jack wasn't widening the gap between them. More bullets riddled the boat's stern, but none hit the gas tank. Yet.

He described the black boat to Leoni. Its distinctive markings ought to make it easy to spot. "They know these damn canals a hell of a lot better than I do. I can't shake them."

"If you can make it back to the Grand Canal, you can lose them in traffic." Leoni paused as if consulting the computer map. "Head south. I'm sending official boats to intercept."

"Roger that," Jack said and disconnected.

He glanced down at Sophie, still huddled on the cockpit floor. "You okay?" He had to yell over the roar of the motor.

Her face was a pale oval tilted up to him, but she nodded.

Jack gave terse directions, slid the map to her.

"What canal are we on?" she yelled back.

At the next turn Jack spotted a sign. "Rio dei Megio."

"Take the next left. Rio di San Polo leads back to the Grand Canal."

"Worth a try." He sped ahead and swerved around a water taxi. The boat's spray soaked the driver and his passengers. The man's fluent curses filled the air.

"Don't enter any side canals," Sophie called up to him. "Some of them are dead ends."

Jack sped along on the wider canal.

More shots hit from the stern. Fiberglass cracked and light covers shattered.

The thugs hadn't fallen back, and the heavier traffic wasn't inhibiting them. But the shots came from a pistol, not a sub-machine gun. Less obvious to witnesses.

Jack and Sophie's boat burst onto the Grand Canal.

A ferry-sized tour boat churning by forced Jack to wait.

On their other side, flower-decorated gondolas clustered at a palazzo blocked their turn. Formally dressed people in the slender boats hoisted wineglasses. A white veil floated in the breeze, and the bride wearing it blew Jack a kiss.

The black boat pulled up behind.

Guido stood up in the cockpit. He leveled a silencer-equipped pistol at Jack.

The bride screamed.

Chapter 5

From beneath the console Sophie couldn't see much of what was going on. When she heard a scream, she craned her neck to see. A woman in a bridal gown was pointing behind them in wide-eyed and openmouthed fear.

Sophie jumped at the *thunk, thunk* of bullets slamming into the teak decking behind the console.

Jack hit the deck between the two seats. He crouched low beside the driver's seat. His lanky body was almost folded in half. "I'm going to try something. Pray there's enough room."

Her shoulder throbbed and her head swam. Fear of Vadim's men so close dried her mouth. She struggled to focus.

Jack would save her. She had to believe that.

Save *them.* Vadim's men were shooting at him, too. She had made him a target. Guilt twisted inside her, but she reminded herself that protecting her was his job.

She had a clear view behind them as Jack propelled the

powerboat ahead. Their boat grazed the dock on one side and the tour boat on the other. Sparks shot up from either side, and wood against fiberglass screamed in protest. The wedding party shouted at them, but Sophie couldn't understand them over the motors' roar.

Seconds later they surged ahead of the tour boat. Jack had threaded the needle. Sophie could see the tourists and their guide, microphone in hand, gaping at them.

But she could no longer see the black boat.

"They're gone!" she shouted. Navigating from the floor was flying blind, so she started to push up into her seat.

Jack sat up and eased back on the throttle. "No, here they come around the other side!"

Sophie's head bumped the seat back as the boat surged ahead. Black spots bounced before her eyes, but she blinked them away. She'd be no good to Jack if she didn't stay alert. Staying low, she slipped into the seat for a better view.

"Still on our tail," Jack shouted, half standing, half sitting so as not to be a target, "but not shooting."

"Too much traffic," she said. *Vaporetti,* tour boats and every conceivable type of private and commercial boat crowded the Grand Canal and lined the docks. "Can you dodge around and duck into a side canal?"

Jack shook his head. "Got to lead them to the task-force roadblock, er, canal block."

Up ahead, on both sides of the broad canal, she spotted the distinctive blue-and-white launches of the Venice *polizia.* Task-force men and women in vests with *Polizia* on the back appeared to be monitoring the passing traffic.

"I'll get us out of the way. Hope the shooters keep going and don't see us."

Sophie crossed mental fingers as she gripped her seat with her free hand.

She watched as Jack zoomed around a slow barge. He hung a sharp left just behind a *vaporetto* traveling the opposite way and hugged its right side. They were then hidden by the water bus, three times as big a craft.

"Can you tell what they're doing?" Jack said as he fought the wash from the *vaporetto.*

Sophie winced as she twisted in her seat, but she ignored the pain. She spotted the sleek black boat continuing its same course. The fast reversal of direction must've confused their pursuers. "They don't see us. They're slowing and idling. Oh, Jack, if they look this way, they'll find us!"

He pulled back on the throttle and steered into a slip at a finger dock. With a taller boat in the next slip as cover, they could observe their pursuers by peering around the stern.

"They shouldn't see us here," he said.

Sophie watched, her breath backed up in her throat, and prayed the men wouldn't spot them.

The two thugs in the lightning-striped black boat apparently didn't notice that other traffic had been cleared from that swath of the canal. They stood and searched for their targets.

Official launches with blue lights flashing converged on them. Loudspeakers blared warnings and guns were drawn.

The gunman hesitated only a second before he fired at the police. Sophie could see smoke and sparks spitting from the silenced submachine gun.

Then the boat swung around. At the helm, the other thug made for a hole in the police circle.

The police fired back. The volley echoed off the surrounding buildings in a deafening barrage, and the stench of cordite filled the air.

Flames shot up from the black boat's stern. The two men turned around, terror on their faces.

Sophie recoiled in horror as she grasped what was about to happen, but she couldn't look away.

A volcano of fire and debris obliterated the black boat. Smoking fiberglass shards and other flaming debris rained over a wide arc.

* * *

An hour later Jack stood on the dock at the Palazzo Balbi. A plaque on its painted-brick facade announced that Napoleon had witnessed regattas from the balcony. Since the Balbi was now the seat of the Veneto regional government, officials readily allowed the task force access. Sophie was resting in an employee lounge inside the government building, a secure area.

He stared across the water to where the task force and salvage divers still worked. Their maneuvers barely registered in his brain. Instead he pictured Sophie's face.

She intrigued him. Hell, she drove him nuts.

The face of a Renaissance angel and a body built for sin. Wide mouth, lush curves and skin like wild honey. Not for the first time heat pooled in his groin. He sucked in a breath. Yeah, she was an erotic dream, but she was more.

Her injuries and her artless demeanor gave the impression of fragility, but today she'd remained cool under fire. She hadn't panicked at the flying bullets but read the map and shouted directions. She hadn't fallen apart after the explosion either.

She had to be exhausted and aching. She'd swallowed one of her pain pills when he'd found her a place to rest. Not once did she complain or berate him for leading them into a trap. Strength lay beneath the delicate exterior.

Exotic beauty, strength, fragility. Just thinking about her triggered potent heat he hadn't experienced since Miami. Not since—

Not in a long time.

The beast of hatred and guilt that prowled inside him left no room for softer feelings. Sometimes the pain was more than he could bear, but he couldn't let it go until he had Sebastian Vadim by the short hairs.

Justice depended on staying on track. He owed it to *them*. He owed it to himself.

Sophie was temptation he could ignore. Temptation he *had* to ignore.

In a secure safe house he would have other officers there as buffers. He wouldn't be alone with her.

If Sophie was faking amnesia, after the chase would've been the time to admit it, to pretend recovered memory. She did neither. Maybe the doctors were right. She really didn't remember.

If he was going to prod her memory, they needed a new safe house where they wouldn't land in a trap.

And it had been a trap. Vadim knew about the safe house. The suspicion of a leak tied a knot in Jack's gut.

"Hey, man, this Italian sun getting to you? You're sweating." Leoni climbed onto the dock from a police launch. He carried two plastic evidence bags.

Jack was sweating, all right, but not from the climate. "You don't know sun until you've spent a summer in Florida." He ignored the trickles down his temples. "What d'you got?"

"IDs on the shooters." He handed Jack the bags.

As Jack had thought, Vadim's agents. One bag held a charred Cleatian passport in the name of Petar Smryczk, and the other an EU driver's license for Guido Mazza. "Is there enough left of these guys for forensics to do a positive ID?"

Leoni shrugged. "With DNA maybe. I saw you discussing things with De Carlo. What gives?"

Jack's respect for Leoni had risen several notches since that first day. The ATSA officer might appear lazy and uninvolved, but a sharp mind hid behind his sleepy eyes, and he could move fast when necessary. His efficient organizing had lined up the official boats in the canal block.

"Debris from the boat looks like a gas can exploded," Jack said. "Could've been hit by bullets. Or they had the can stored too close to the motor."

"An extra gas can? If you'd made it into the safe house, they could've smoked you out with one hell of a bonfire."

A muscle in Jack's jaw knotted. "Vadim doesn't fool around." He knew from past experience.

Leoni dug a gum packet from a jean pocket and offered it. When Jack refused, he unwrapped a piece and popped it into his mouth. "De Carlo must see how important the Rinaldi woman is."

"He sees what he wants to see. He doubts I'll get information from her, but he'll go for protecting her. I have to check with him on a new safe house." The CO was putting Jack off on that. *Why* was the question.

"Did you warn him about a possible leak?"

"You'd think I'd offered him poison. He blamed the Venice *polizia* for assigning us a safe house known to locals. Guido Mazza had connections and could've sniffed it out. From De Carlo's attitude, I thought he suspected me."

"Like you'd set yourself up to be shot at." Leoni squinted against the sun's rays as he stared across the canal. The salvage boat was heading toward them. "We're about done here. And speak of the devil, here comes De Carlo."

The *commissario* might be height-challenged, but he didn't lack for arrogance. As he sauntered from the air-conditioned Palazzo Balbi, his gait contained a distinct swagger. After dispatching Leoni to write his report, he turned to Jack.

"Officer Thorne, the task force will not authorize another safe house. Too risky. You are better off hiding the woman somewhere away from Venice."

"What about backup?"

"The terrorist Ahmed Saqr has been located in England, in a South London flat. Vadim's phone records show multiple calls between his villa and the number there. Scotland Yard will hold off arresting Saqr so we don't warn off Vadim. I need all available officers to find Vadim and confiscate that uranium. Backup? *Non è possibile.*"

Jack had picked up enough Italian to grasp the man's last words. Even if he'd translated incorrectly, the control officer's stern look said Jack was on his own with Sophie. He had to ask anyway. "So I get no one?"

A thin smile cracked De Carlo's face. "Only the lovely Signora Rinaldi. Keep in touch with Leoni by *telefonino,* uh, cell phone, as you Americans say."

By the time Sophie climbed into the powerboat, she'd recovered from the effects of the chase. The prescription pain pill and a bottle of water had revived her so she could go on.

She would never get over seeing the terrified looks on those men's faces just before their boat exploded. She knew they'd intended to kill both her and Jack, but no one should die like that. A shudder quaked through her.

She had to do whatever she could to stop the madness, to find her memory of Vadim and his secrets. But being cooped up in a safe house would be unbearable if her laconic guard reverted to his initial cold-eyed demeanor. In unguarded moments, pain burned in his eyes.

He had secrets. Secrets he shared with no one.

Before the attack she'd glimpsed another man inside his hard shell, a man who could enjoy the beauty around him and laugh with ease. A man she could be comfortable with, a friend. She shouldn't, but she wanted to see more of that man.

"You okay?" Jack asked as he started the boat motor.

"Fine. Are we going to the safe house now?"

"The safe house isn't so safe after all. Vadim knows about it." He flicked toggle switches and examined dials.

"Oh. Of course." She wondered how Vadim had found it and them but said nothing.

"That's it? 'Oh.' Don't you want to know about that or where we're going?"

Sophie smiled at Jack's trademark scowl. He questioned everything. "I do. I suspect you don't know how Vadim knew about the safe house and you'll tell me where we *are* going soon enough."

"You always so amenable?"

His cynical tone said he wondered if she'd gone along

with whatever Vadim had asked of her. She wondered, too. Questions ate at her. Sometimes they crushed her chest with pain, the hidden answers ticking away in a memory time bomb. "Jack, I've given you my trust and I'll do all I can to solve the mystery of my lost memory."

He regarded her for a long moment, then nodded. "I'll try to merit that trust. I nearly blew it today." He lifted a hand as if to reach for her, but instead gripped the steering wheel. "We have some time before Vadim can regroup. As far as we know, the explosion eliminated his only agents."

"There, you've just used that word, *agents*. And you're an officer, not an agent. Explain your spookspeak, please."

His mouth quirked. She swore he almost laughed but couldn't see his eyes to be sure. A laugh was probably too much to ask.

"An agent isn't official, someone outside the government paid to do a job for an official operative, like me."

"Ah, an agent might be a spy inside a terrorist cell or a foreign government."

"That's it."

"Why are the FBI called agents then?"

He turned to look at her. He wasn't smiling, but his gaze softened. "You got me there. But they *are* 'special agents.' You'll have to ask a Feeb sometime."

"The very next time I meet a Feeb, I will."

As if wiping off a grin, he swiped a hand across his mouth. He slid the map to her. "Think you can direct us back to the mainland?"

"*Assolutamente!* If you trust me to do it."

"Go for it."

A hedged answer. Sophie wanted him to trust her for more than that, but she'd take what she could get. She hardly knew if she could trust herself.

She scanned the map. Ah. Jack wouldn't mind a tiny detour. She hoped. "Go back the way we came a little bit. We can follow a smaller *rio* south to the Canale della Giudecca. It leads to the lagoon."

They followed the Canale Grande to the *rio* she'd chosen. The narrow waterway passed a church on the left and then approached another palazzo.

One red-gold eyebrow shot up. "More sights to see, Sophie?" He cut the motor to an idle.

There were, but not this one. She felt the heat of embarrassment on her cheeks. "No, I didn't know about this building. Oh, but look at that staircase!"

Constructed of tan bricks and accented with white arches and balustrades, the spiral staircase curved up the side of the palazzo in an open tower. A sign on the dock said in five languages that the staircase was open to the public.

Sophie's gaze rose to the fifth story of the staircase. "Oh, look, a family up there. The children are waving to us." She waved back, but noticed Jack looked away, his mouth tight. His hands gripped the steering wheel with equal tension. Was he thinking about their ordeal earlier? Or did something about the family upset him?

"Got your guidebook? You might as well tell me about it," Jack said as he flexed his fingers.

His gruff tone meant the stern fed had returned. How would he react when he saw where she was taking him? She gave a mental shrug. Too late now.

After flipping some pages, she found the entry. "'Palazzo Contarini del Bovolo with a snail-shell staircase,'" she read. "*Bovolo* means snail."

"A major feat of engineering," Jack said.

"Engineering, *boh*. Venetians love decoration. It's way cool and beautiful."

Jack shifted to forward, and Sophie directed him to turn left. "Keep going straight. *Sempre diritto*."

"Now you sound like a native *Veneziano*. Go straight, go straight."

Sophie grinned. "Then you know we won't get lost."

Off to the right, above the buildings, she spotted a distinctive tower. If he saw the Campanile, he'd know where she was taking him. So far, his eyes stayed on the waterway.

"But they don't go straight. Not the streets. Not the canals," he protested. "Look at this canal, a jig here, a jog there. Nothing *diritto*."

The next sharp right made by the *rio* proved his case. When the boat pulled even with the massive gray-stone basilica set back in a broad square, Jack stared in disbelief.

"Piazza San Marco. Remember, all roads lead to St. Mark's," Sophie said. She held her breath as she waited for his reaction.

Jack did something she never expected to witness. Tiny lines formed around his blue eyes as they crinkled with amusement. His mouth twitched. A great fountain of laughter gushed from him as though it had been bottled up since birth. He tilted back his head and let the laughter flow.

Enjoying the deep timbre of his delight, Sophie, too, laughed at her joke on him. This interlude kept her fears at bay and gave her strength for what might come. She'd coaxed to the surface the man she could talk to.

She wished they had time to walk around the piazza. Lighting a candle inside the basilica might bring her another piece of memory, but she wouldn't ask.

As if he'd read her mind, Jack said, "We need to reach Mestre and a car before dark. It's getting late."

"Do you know? Have I visited St. Mark's?" She couldn't help the plaintive tone.

"Tell you what. When this is all over, I'll bring you back here. You can stay as long as you want."

Ignoring the twinges in her sore body, she turned to reach across the space between them. As she curled her fingers over his scarred ones on the steering wheel, she felt his strength and heat surge into her.

And more. A rush of awareness that surprised her.

She withdrew her hand. "Thank you. It's a deal."

He appeared to regret his offer, but merely nodded.

As the boat continued on, Sophie glimpsed the two gruff red lions that guarded the basilica's left flank. It was said that St. Mark's was the soul of Venice, and she felt the power of its spirit as her gaze followed its silhouette.

"Where are we going, Jack?"

"I thought you'd never ask. A place Vadim won't suspect. A place I hope will help you remember. Tuscany."

As they reached the car park in Mestre, dusk turned the sky myriad shades of pink and mauve. Driving west on the A4 *Autostrade* in the subcompact Fiat assigned to them, Sophie had to close her eyes against the glare of the setting sun.

Did she imagine it or did her hand still tingle from contact with his? Attraction to Jack Thorne? He did have the bluest eyes, a brilliant blue that seemed to burn from within. When he'd laughed, his deep voice had resonated through her.

She opened her eyes and stared at his hands on the steering wheel. He wore no wedding ring, but that meant nothing. "Jack, are you married? Do you have a family?"

His hold on the wheel slipped, and the car lurched to the right. He gained control fast and righted their direction.

"Jack?"

"No. I have no family."

The dispassionate and deliberate way he said it broke Sophie's heart. She yearned to know more, to know what had happened to him. But the amber light of the setting sun cast his features in a hard mask and stifled her next question.

A bump in the road jarred her senses. What was she thinking? She blinked at the lowering sun.

Sophia Constanza, this man is not for you.

Some past tragedy had wounded him deeply and had hardened over all softness. He suspected her of working with a criminal. Without her memory, she couldn't be sure of the truth. Of the woman she really was deep inside.

Of anything.

Even if her memory returned tomorrow, she had no time for a man. Figuring out a direction for her life took priority. An identity separate from other people who would depend on her, a life of her own.

And she certainly wouldn't choose a man like Jack. No strong, silent types for her.

Well, strong was good, but she needed a man who would share more than a few words with her. A man who would share his dreams and delights and disappointments.

Definitely not a man immured inside a thick shell. Definitely not Jack Thorne.

Chapter 6

Jack should never have offered to take Sophie back to Venice. Her wistful tone had yanked on his heart, and his mouth had opened before he could think. Once he had the information he needed, he ought to get far from this woman.

Personal involvement with her or any woman was impossible. Vadim would die one way or another. He would take no chances on the scum escaping into yet another alias.

Jack would forfeit his future, his life if he must. If the takedown resulted in a firefight with a righteous kill, well and good. In that case, even if Jack survived to continue in ATSA, he had no business putting another woman in jeopardy.

Danger in the job spilled over. The ones you loved could get killed in the crossfire.

Images of twisted metal and mangled bodies rose in his mind as if he'd come on the horrific scene yesterday. Hatred raked his chest and grief gripped his heart. Nothing would interfere with what he must do.

Not even a beautiful and vulnerable woman who touched him as no one had for a long time.

In the meantime, he would remain professional. Her flowery scent teased him, not perfume but a heady brew of shampoo, soap and Sophie. Her voice and low laughter were a siren song. Her dark mane invited touching.

Professional control was a tough job in the confines of a roller-skate-size car that crimped his knees up around his Adam's apple. Fate and De Carlo had thrown them together for the foreseeable future. Alone.

Jack gritted his teeth and drove. On the *Autostrade* the drive from Venice to Tuscany would take only three or four hours. Speed was not his aim. Disappearing was.

He stayed on the four-lane major highway as far as Padua, where he exited onto a secondary road. "There's a road map in the glove box. Think you can navigate through the mountains?"

The urban sprawl of Padua was disappearing behind them, and rolling green hills led into the central mountains.

"You bet." Sophie retrieved the map and a small flash-light. "After Venice, highways are a piece of pizza."

The exhaustion lacing her voice punched him in the chest. But her words lightened his mood. Lord, she always made him smile. "Pizza? I thought the saying was 'piece of cake.'"

"But we're in Italy, silly man."

Chuckling, he helped her open the map.

She quickly found their location. "So if we're headed to Tuscany, why take this country road? More sightseeing?"

He shrugged. No reason to hide his strategy from her. "Off major routes and away from cities, we have more options. Places to hide."

"Didn't you say we had some time?"

"There's no sense leaving a clear trail. Vadim's connections make recruiting more thugs, even a pro, easy. I want to make finding you as hard as possible."

He cut a glance her way. In the fading daylight he could

tell from her tight expression she'd grasped what he meant by *pro*. She seemed to collect herself, then suggested he turn right at the next intersection.

They wound through picturesque mountain villages, back and forth on switchbacks and narrow roads, but always heading in a southward direction.

In one town the central square contained a fountain and bronze statues. A fortresslike medieval castle dominated another. And each boasted a majestic church, some medieval, some Gothic in style.

As Sophie guided and commented on the sights, Jack could tell from the increased strain in her voice that they needed to stop for the night soon.

The day's drama had taken its toll on her. She needed rest. So did he, he had to acknowledge.

In the next village—one of many with *castello* in its name whether or not its castle was still standing—he said, "I see a restaurant ahead. We'll have dinner and ask about a place to stay."

Out of habit, Jack chose a parking place on a side street. Nobody should know the car, but he'd take nothing for granted. He pried himself out of the driver's seat, then opened the door for Sophie.

He noticed her moving more stiffly, the binding on her injured shoulder seeming to drag on her. Should he offer his arm in support? Remembering the awareness that had sparked between them, he kept his hands to himself.

The trattoria was small and basic, with a selection of menu items posted on a white board by the doorway. Outside, two young couples nursed espressos at postage-stamp-size tables. Inside the long, narrow room, diners at white-linen-covered tables lining the side walls turned to stare at the strangers. Family groups, couples, a few single men.

All appeared to be locals.

Ceiling fans stirred aromas of brewing espresso and spicy

foods that made Jack's mouth water. Their hostess, a well-fed woman swathed in a snowy-white apron, hustled toward them.

"*Buonasera. Per due, per favore,*" he said, requesting a table for two.

The woman's plump countenance widened in a broad smile. She launched into Italian too rapid and too wordy for Jack's phrase-book knowledge.

Without missing a beat, a smiling Sophie greeted the woman and apparently answered her question. A conversational stream flowed from one to the other as the woman led the two of them to an empty table in the back. Sophie helped Jack interpret the menu, and the hostess left with their order.

Jack realized he had to rely on her for more than map reading. "What was that long dissertation about?"

"Only that foreigners hardly ever stop in this village, and she was honored to serve us."

"That's not good. If someone asks, she'll remember us." They'd blend into crowded tourist traps. But staying in villages on Sophie's list might jog her memory. He had no choice. "Anything else?"

"She asked about my arm. I told her it was a car accident." Sophie spread a blue cloth napkin in her lap and looked up at him through lowered lashes as thick as a curtain. "I hope you don't mind my jumping in."

"Mind? Consider it your job. Without your fluent Italian, we couldn't hide away in remote villages. Good call on the car accident. Anybody should believe that, the way they drive in this country."

"And a car accident is sort of the truth."

Jack couldn't believe his ears. Was she downplaying what Vadim had done? She was too kind, too sanguine to run around alone. No wonder that bastard had conned her.

"It was no accident," he said, lowering his voice. "Keep that in mind if you forget the danger you're in and the criminal who put you in it."

A teenage waitress brought two glasses, a carafe of ruby-red wine and two bowls of steaming tortellini. She smiled shyly and said, *"Buon appetito,"* before ducking away.

"Mmm, just smell that dish! *Tortellini alla parmigiana,* pumpkin-filled with a light cheese sauce." Sophie spread her napkin on her lap. She stabbed her fork into one of the little pastas and popped it into her mouth. "Ah, homemade. Heaven!"

Jack stuffed pasta into his mouth and forced himself to chew before swallowing. The sauce glistening on Sophie's lips sent a different kind of hunger surging through him. Her rapturous expression and small moans of delight were too orgasmic for comfort.

She took such pleasure in everything. A woman with such gusto and emotion, what would she be like in—

He choked on his tortellini and coughed to clear his throat and his brain. *Don't go there.*

"I think you need wine to wash down the pasta. The waitress has brought us *un mezzo,* a half liter of their family Sangiovese. Will you pour?" Sophie slid her goblet toward him.

He hesitated but served them both. "But should you be mixing painkillers and alcohol?"

Fire crackled in her luminous dark eyes. "Ouch, jabbed by the dreaded Thorne! Ease up, Jack. I need protection, not a keeper."

He held up his hands in surrender. "I'm concerned about you. No offense meant."

His abject tone seemed to dismay her. She sipped wine, then sighed. "Sorry. I guess I'm just tired. But for your information, I've taken my last prescription pill. From now on, aspirin or ibuprofen will do."

Soon the pasta plates were cleared away and replaced by the main dish. The young server delivered the dishes, but the hostess hovered nearby, pressing her hands together in worry.

In Italian, Sophie thanked both women, and more. From her gestures, Jack inferred she was praising the new dish.

The blushing teen made a small curtsy and the hostess beamed. When they left, Sophie said, "The waitress is the *signora*'s daughter. She's just learning the family business."

The main course was slices of pork roast with a Parma ham stuffing. Sophie's sensuous delight in the food enhanced his own enjoyment of the savory dish.

The food and the full-bodied wine relaxed him, and he reflected on Sophie's earlier reaction. For the first time she'd spoken up for herself. He liked her biting retort more than her usual passive acceptance of events.

Except he could do without more to like about Sophie. For his own good. And hers.

Since his marriage ended, he'd kept his distance from women. His ex-wife's manipulations and sulks had kept him guarded. He'd felt no strong attraction to any woman.

But one look, one breathy sigh from Sophie made him as horny as a hormonal teenager.

Now look at me. Hell of a thing.

He concentrated on the pork and didn't come up for air until the salad and coffee arrived.

Sophie sat on the sagging bed and unzipped her suitcases. So much had happened that day, she welcomed time to herself.

After dinner the trattoria owner had directed them to her sister's bed-and-breakfast on the village outskirts. Jack paid for two rooms with an adjoining bath.

She unwound the silk scarf she'd wrapped the saint in. The figure was too heavy to lift out one-handed. Back at Vadim's villa, she'd had to tip it over and roll it into the tote. "I don't know who you were or why you're a saint, Santa Elisabetta, but I pray you'll watch over me and Jack."

She'd hoped the wine would loosen him up. No such luck. Then, after she'd snapped at him, he'd closed up like a steel safe. Most of the time she liked his take-charge manner, but that patronizing tone had rubbed her the wrong way. Something about Jack tempted her to try to shatter his hard-case shell.

Never mind that his rangy body, angular good looks and overpowering masculinity drew every female eye—including hers. He was a challenge. And a mystery.

Why he drew her so, she didn't understand, except for the occasional glimpses of grief that twisted her heart. And the warmth and humanity when he let down his guard.

Thinking about him curled awareness through her. And shocked her. Her injuries and bone-deep weariness had to be the reason for her susceptibility to him. And her relative inexperience.

She was no innocent, but raising her sister, attending some college classes and working as a nanny hadn't left much time for dating, much less sex.

Wanting to know more about Jack made no sense. He was protecting her, but she was only a suspect and a job to him. Given her circumstances, she could want nothing more.

So why did Santa Elisabetta seem to be mocking her?

After covering the statuette, she dug out her nightclothes and toiletry kit. The silk nightgowns in her Vadim-bought wardrobe would've been impossible to put on with one arm immobilized. One of the female officers had bought her pajamas with a shirt that buttoned in the front.

But first she needed a shower and a shampoo. That meant she needed help. She smiled.

Now she would see how hard Jack's shell was.

When she stood, the room spun in a crazy circle. Whoa, the dizziness wasn't done, she thought, sinking down on the bed again. She waited for the spell to pass, then tried again. No spinning, no light-headedness.

But the reminder of the concussion told her to take it easy and slow.

She kicked off her sandals, draped the cotton pj's over her good shoulder and carried the kit into the bathroom.

The bathroom was a typical European one, with white porcelain fixtures—a deep tub with a shower curtain, a bidet and a separate water closet. A wooden chair sat beneath the open window. The owner had provided fluffy green towels that matched the ceramic tile floor.

Sophie deposited her pj's and kit on the vanity. Her pulse pounded. What if Jack refused to help her? Drawing a deep breath, she knocked on his door.

He opened it immediately, as though he'd been about to enter the bathroom. "Are you all right?"

Sophie mustered up a smile. "Fine. Just tired and dirty."

"Oh. I thought… Never mind." One arched red-gold eyebrow asked what she wanted.

The moment spun out awkwardly, with her standing barefoot in the bathroom and his large frame filling the open doorway to his bedroom. His musky male scent mingled with the spicy food aromas that had permeated the restaurant.

He'd pulled the shirttail loose from his trousers and looked ready to undress. She'd probably beaten him to the shower. That and seeing his duffel bag open on the bed reminded her of how personal his protecting her was becoming. She felt her pulse throb in her neck, and her stomach clenched with anxiety.

Sophie forged ahead. "When I left the hospital, they told me a female officer would come to the safe house to help me with…personal matters."

Both eyebrows dived low into his trademark scowl. "Personal matters," he repeated in a puzzled tone.

"If I raise my arm before the joint heals, the shoulder could pop out again. I can't dress and undress by myself. I see no female officer, so I need an *agent. You.*"

His Adam's apple rose and fell as he swallowed hard. Was that a blush blooming on his tanned cheeks? No way. It was either the heat or her imagination.

Staring at the wall behind her, he scraped a hand through his hair. "Okay. How d'you want to do this?"

"I can undo the closures on the sling if you help me take it off."

First she unfastened the strap that held her arm tight against her body, then the other around her neck. The ripping of the hook-and-loop strips echoed like gunshots against the tiled bathroom walls.

Gingerly, as if afraid to touch her, Jack slid the sling off her shoulder and down her arm. As though yanked by an invisible force, he stepped back. He strangled the sling in his hands. Moisture beaded between his brows. "Look, maybe you should ask the B and B owner to do this."

"I told her we were husband and wife. How would it look if my husband didn't help me?"

His brows dived together into one. "Why the hell did you say that?"

"Italy is a very conservative country. She thinks we have to sleep in separate beds because of my injury."

"Sophie, we'd be nowhere if you didn't speak Italian, but from now on I need to know what you tell people. What they know might be key to our staying safe."

"Okay." She hadn't thought of that.

He stared at the sling as if he couldn't fathom how it had gotten in his hands. Smoothing it out, he placed it on the chair.

She opened the two top blouse buttons. When she reached the third, what she saw in Jack's blue gaze stilled her fingers. What had been exasperation turned to heat, bright and hot as lightning. Excitement streaked through her, and she reached for the sink behind her to steady herself.

"You okay?"

"A little dizzy." But not from the concussion. It was his touch that rocked her senses and tingled in her belly. "I'm pretty tired." That much was true. She turned her back to him and continued to open the blouse.

"Tell me how you learned to speak Italian like a native." His voice, raspy with strain, told her she hadn't imagined the sparks dancing between them.

"*Nonna,* my grandmother, came to live with us after my father died. She insisted. Living with the Donatis for six years helped, too."

"Your file says you were six, your sister two, when your father died. Your mother went to work, and your grandmother cared for you and your sister."

"Until she became ill. I was twelve." There were times when the pain of missing her grandmother hit her like a physical blow. *Nonna* had been more mother to her than her real mother. Sophie's blouse hung open, but she made no move to remove it.

"Who took care of you after that?"

"I did. Mom had a career by then, not just a job. I attended parent-teacher conferences for Anita and nursed *Nonna* until she died."

"That's a big responsibility for a kid."

His deep voice, resonant with concern, licked heat down her spine. Shaking off the melting effect, she began shrugging the blouse down her good shoulder. "I knew no other way. I raised Anita until she was in high school and too independent to listen to me. Then I went to work for the Donatis."

"Seven years. A long time to be a nanny."

He'd stepped closer behind her, close enough for her to feel his body heat and smell his sweat, honest sweat earned protecting her. He lifted the fabric and continued its removal. The glide of his long-fingered hand burned the bare flesh of her exposed neck and arm.

Her stomach did a backflip. She struggled to answer his question. "They needed someone who spoke Italian. I needed the work. The hours allowed me to complete some courses at CCNY—City College of New York. A degree will be a start toward my own life. I won't be only the woman who takes care of other people and never herself. What that will be is still a mystery."

She'd started in education. When she'd seen that as an extension of being a nanny, she'd thought of switching.

But to what?

"So you came to Italy to figure that out?"

"Finding my ancestral past is part of finding my future."

"You came to Italy to find yourself and lost your memory of the trip."

"The irony hasn't escaped me." He was the first person who hadn't considered her quest odd or foolish. How strange for this hard man to understand her.

A blouse button snagged in her hair. As he worked it loose, she felt his warm breath against the back of her head. His solid strength lured her to lean against him, but she gripped the sink again instead.

Together they slid the cotton blouse off her injured shoulder and down her arm. That left only her bra. Sophie plucked a towel from the pile by the sink and held it in front of her. She pasted on a smile and turned. "Thanks. I can do the rest. The bra has a front closure."

His eyes dropped to her chest, thankfully covered by the thick towel. As he forced his gaze up to meet hers, a definite wine-red blush suffused his lean cheeks. "What if you get dizzy in the shower?"

"I'll be okay. If I'm dizzy, I can sit on the edge." The desire flaming in his eyes ignited an answering heat low in her body. Her hands shook so she nearly dropped the towel.

"Roger." He executed an about-face that would gratify a drill sergeant. "That's it, then."

"When I'm finished in the shower, I'll call you."

On her last word, the door clicked shut behind him.

Hands on his knees, Jack bent over and dragged air into his lungs. The voltage between them had set him afire.

Touching her had felt as if he'd stuck his finger in a light socket. She blew his circuits. His blood sizzled.

Breathing her female scent, salty with sweat, had ignited a brush fire. Sliding his hand over her soft, warm skin and sifting his fingers in her luxuriant mahogany-brown waves had hardened him so he might need medical intervention to recover.

He heard the shower running and tried not to picture Sophie naked with water sliding down her wild-honey skin. At last able to breathe normally, he straightened. Checking in with Leoni would take his mind off Sophie. He dug in his pocket for the secure satellite phone.

Her skin was perfect, too soft to be real but for her injury. Peeling off her shirt had revealed healing scrapes and fading red-and-yellow bruises that reminded him sharply of the stakes. Deep within him tenderness and longing welled up. A longing he couldn't name or acknowledge.

When she'd clutched that towel in front of her and faced him, her shallow breathing and dilated pupils had told him she felt the flames, too. Sheer nothing edged in lace had covered her breasts. The slipping towel had plumped the creamy mounds and concealed only her nipples. He'd mustered Herculean strength not to toss away the towel and carry her to bed.

Not even a week since Vadim's Maserati had struck her. She had to wear the damn sling for five or six more days.

Six more days of torture. For them both.

Another reason to break through the amnesia fast.

Sinking onto the bed, he flipped open the phone and pushed the speed dial for Leoni. When the officer answered, he said, "Any news?"

"Yeah, Vadim walked up to the desk sergeant in the *Questura,* handed over the uranium tied in a big red bow and gave himself up. Case closed."

Jack nearly threw the phone across the room. "I'm in no mood for that crap. Any leads in the wreckage?"

"Zip. The boat was reported stolen the night before. There is one thing. We may've located the missing courier."

"Dead, I assume." Nothing else had gone their way.

"You psychic or something?" Leoni chuckled. When Jack remained silent, he sighed and cracked his gum. "A couple local kids found a body in the marsh not far from Vadim's villa. Looks like our boy ran into a bullet headfirst."

Another nail in Vadim's coffin. "Vadim doesn't like to share. Dobrich should've known that about his cousin."

"The dumb slug might not've had other options. Anyway, I'll let you know developments. How's the honeymoon trip?"

"How d'you think?" Jack growled. "Someday you'll have your guts in a vise, and it'll be payback time."

"It ain't your guts in the vise, buddy, but another part of your anatomy," Leoni said. "Like I said before, lighten up. Enjoy the scenery. Just don't touch."

Easier said than done. Jack gave his contact their location and his plan for the next day. "That it?"

"One more thing. Vadim's housekeeper was poking around at the villa today."

At that Jack narrowed his eyes in speculation. Although the task force had finished searching, they were keeping the villa under surveillance. "What d'you mean poking around?"

"Said she'd left some stuff there. Seemed bent, if you know what I mean, phony. One of the guys kept an eye on her."

"You think Vadim sent her to look for the uranium?"

"If he did, she came away empty. All she took was an apron and a dish."

They discussed the possibilities for a few moments, then Jack disconnected.

"Jack, I need your help. Please."

At Sophie's call, he dropped the phone on the floor. He hadn't noticed that the water had stopped running.

Chapter 7

"Jack?"

Her siren's voice tugged him toward the bathroom. He could no more have let her fend for herself than he could've flown to Mars in a Venetian *vaporetto*.

But what would he find? Sophie wrapped in a wet towel? Or in nothing? *Hell!*

When he opened the door, he entered a cloud of fragrant steam. In the middle stood a dark-haired Venus on a half shell.

He blinked at the mirage but realized she was mostly covered. Desire and dismay dueled in his struggling system.

Sophie had wound the bath towel around her upper torso. Her hair hung in glistening ropes over her shoulders. She wore yellow cotton pajama boxers that bared her long, tanned legs. And the shell was merely a white bath mat.

His hungry gaze climbed her legs' slender length until it reached the massive yellowing bruise on her left thigh.

Reality slapped him back to earth. He could do this. His

brain knew his duty even if his body didn't. He had a duty to right a wrong. She was only a means to that.

Add to that, she was still a suspect and under official protection. All kinds of tangles to trip him if he didn't keep tight control.

She needed care, not sex. "Your *agent* reporting for duty, ma'am."

"How do you like these pj's? The color matches my bruises." Grinning, Sophie managed a model-like pose with her good arm in an elegant gesture.

Even more like Venus. Jack clenched his teeth. At this rate, he'd need a dentist soon.

"Practical. Ready for the shirt?" Then she'd be covered. No more Venus mirages. His constant arousal would ease.

She held up a tube of cream. "The hospital gave me this liniment to promote healing. I can't reach very well. Could you rub it on for me?"

Rub it on her? On her bare skin? Jack's body thrummed with tension. She was asking him to stroke her bare flesh, all warm and rosy from her shower. Everything male in him saluted.

He repeated the task over and over in his head. *She needs liniment. Only liniment.*

He helped her arrange a second towel in a turban to confine her wet hair. She turned her back, and he opened the tube. The cream had a slight medicinal odor, not enough to mask her unique scent or block his reaction to it.

He squeezed cream onto his palm and took the plunge. He stroked the white liniment along the elegant line of her back and into the scabs and bruises on the soft flesh.

Sophie kept her hands on the sink. She stood quietly, with occasional murmurs and sighs. The sounds of desire? No. More likely his ministrations were hurting her.

"Tell me if I press too hard."

"I'm okay."

"No punishment is too harsh for the low animal that did

this to you. With this crime, he has compounded his debt. When I get my hands on the scum-sucker—" He clamped his mouth shut, afraid he'd said too much.

As his massage reached her sore shoulder, Sophie turned.

Her shallow breathing and the lure of her half-parted lips shifted his pulse to high gear. With his palm he circled the shoulder and massaged down her upper arm. When his hand brushed the outer curve of her breast, she inhaled sharply.

His blood rushed south. Need fisted into him.

Enough.

He'd touched her as much as his system could tolerate. He should step away from the temptation of her creamy skin, her trusting eyes and her vulnerability. She revived protective and possessive instincts he'd buried long ago.

He couldn't step away. His feet were nailed to the floor. Capping the tube, he held it out.

Sophie could barely breathe. Sparks tap-danced over her skin where he'd massaged. Flames of arousal ignited in her groin. She ached to know how he tasted, how that grim mouth would feel against hers, how his hard body felt against her.

How could she want this man? He was all wrong for her. The time was wrong. *She* was wrong.

She reached for the cream. "Thanks."

He didn't release the tube but covered her fingers with his long ones. He didn't speak, only stared at her with an intensity that strangled her breath.

Pupils so dilated that barely any blue showed, his smoldering gaze made her skin tingle and her thighs tremble. If he kissed her—

No, not going to happen. Mustn't happen.

Pulse raging in her ears, she dragged her gaze to their joined hands. The scars, his growling fury at Vadim, a debt… "Jack, are these scars the reason you hate Vadim? Is he responsible?"

"Sophie, don't," he said on a shaky breath.

Before she could speak, he rocked his mouth over hers, and

she went liquid with want. His lips seared hers, first with gentle nips and then with thoroughness. He took his time, molding his mouth to hers. His tongue slipped inside, plundered and stole away her feeble resistance.

She was dizzy with contrasting sensations. The surprise of his firm yet soft lips, the scrape of his whiskers. The heat of his mouth, redolent with garlic and wine, the rasp of his callused fingers on hers. The intense male energy yet equally intense control that limited their contact to mouth and hand. She clung to his mouth as the kiss went on, urgent and needy and thrilling.

When he ended the kiss, it was as though someone had thrown a switch. His mouth left her and he released her hand.

The tube of cream fell to the floor.

Jack bent to retrieve it. He placed it on the sink. "I shouldn't have done that. I apologize."

Heart drumming loud enough to wake the town, Sophie ducked her head. "Don't be sorry. I'm not. But it shouldn't happen again. This…we…" She fluttered a hand in mute explanation as she picked up her pajama top.

"Yes. If I'm to keep you safe and help you remember, I don't—neither of us needs the distraction."

As if by mutual consent, he helped her finish dressing without speaking. Once the pajama shirt was around her, she dispensed with the towel. They worked on the sling and tightened its fastenings until her shoulder was secure.

She thanked him and said good-night. After gathering up her toiletries, she stepped into her bedroom.

She'd intended to ask for help with her hair, but having his hands on her any longer wasn't wise. For either of them.

He'd kissed her because he'd wanted to, but she guessed that wasn't the only reason. "Jack, you never answered my question about Vadim."

Her statement stopped him in his doorway. He held his

wide shoulders as rigid as a statue's. "No. I didn't. Good night, Sophie." The door closed behind him with a firm click.

A few minutes later, as she sat on the bed combing the tangles from her hair, she heard the shower running.

Sebastian Vadim closed his mobile phone and dropped it in his suit coat pocket.

He smiled as he sipped his morning coffee. The greedy housekeeper at his villa had proved resourceful enough that he didn't begrudge the extra euros he'd sent her. His other contact had just given him the last piece of information he needed to finish this business.

Once he had the package, he would arrange its delivery to Ahmed. Then he would slip away.

He hated to leave Italy, but the situation forced him to relocate and create a new identity. He might return to Cleatia, but only temporarily. He preferred somewhere more civilized, perhaps Paris or Madrid.

He left the breakfast dishes for the maid he'd hired and strolled into the palazzo's sunny courtyard. Petar and Guido had been worth little. Their deaths hadn't cinched the noose around him. The police had no one to question and no clues to his location.

The loss of his men had left a void, however. He had to hire people. This time he took no chances with careless amateurs. Contacting the Sicilian had required bowing and scraping, but time was of the essence.

The aria from *Aida* floated up from his pocket. This had to be the response to the other call he'd placed earlier. No one else would have the number of this new mobile phone.

He flipped it open and greeted the caller. *"Pronto."*

"The don said I should call you, *dottore.*" The caller's voice rang with the familiar Sicilian accent Vadim disdained.

The respectful address mollified him, increased his confidence in the deal. Low-class or not, this man was supposed to be the best. He'd better be. His price had been exorbitant. "I know who you are. You have your money and my requirements?"

"*Sì*. Eliminate the man and woman. Bring you the package."

"That's it. You must be extremely careful. The package is not to be damaged."

"I understand. And their location?"

"As of this morning, they left the small village named Castelbuorno, north of Bologna. My source says they're headed south toward Florence. There is a bonus if you complete the job quickly."

"*Nessun problema*." No problem.

Satisfied, Vadim disconnected. Strolling amid the blooming roses, he plucked a blood-red bloom. He knew well the reason Jackson Thorne was part of this so-called task force. Thorne hated him for his well-deserved retribution. Vadim's fingers curled around the delicate petals.

Five years ago Thorne had thwarted his plans and paid a price. Not a big enough price. Vadim would not be thwarted again. He tightened his fist, crushed the rose to bits.

This time Thorne would die.

In the morning Jack was still reeling from their kiss the night before.

While he helped Sophie dress, neither mentioned it. The red sleeveless dress she chose buttoned in the front. Good, the less he had his hands on her the better. But the garment's hem ended at the knees and didn't cover enough of her legs for his peace of mind.

Not that it mattered. Their sleekly toned image was burned into his brain.

The usually ebullient Sophie thanked him in a subdued tone and avoided his gaze. The kiss had affected her, too.

Better they stick to business. He knew it. So, apparently, did she.

Later, when Jack steered into eastbound traffic on A14, Sophie said, "I thought you were avoiding major highways."

"Vadim probably expects us to head to the Tuscany coast, the tourist areas. We'll go this way for about a hundred clicks, then south on secondary roads."

Most of the route lay away from populated areas, and spectacular scenery rolled away into the distance. Cypress and other trees lush with early summer leaves dotted emerald hills. Distant peaks loomed, craggy and purple.

Entranced but tired, Sophie leaned against the headrest. She'd tossed and turned in her bed. Well, not really. Her injuries had prevented too much movement. But she'd lain awake for what had seemed hours wondering how to talk to Jack after that incredible kiss. His hunger and need had scalded her, and together they'd combusted like Roman candles. Afterward, their shared denial had burned almost as hot.

Even now.

She felt the tension emanating from Jack in waves, like the terraced vines marching over the adjacent hillsides. She was no less tense. And not wholly because of their hot kiss.

This morning, when he'd helped her put on the red sheath, something had flickered in her mind.

Sebastian Vadim.

A ghostly image, out of focus. Holding her hand in an intimate gesture. She gave an involuntary shiver. Had she been the man's lover after all?

"You okay? Your shoulder bothering you?"

Jack's voice startled her from her reverie. She must've made a sound or spoken.

Telling him what she remembered was out of the question. Disturbing and too close to what he'd first thought of her. "No. Just admiring the bell tower over there above the tiled roofs of that village. And I'm tired. Talk to me."

"Talk to you. What about?"

"Since the task force has a file on me, my life is an open

book. Yours, Jack Thorne, is so closed the pages are glued together. Tell me your story."

A muscle jumped in his jaw. "Not much to tell."

"The Anti-Terrorism Security Agency is new since 9/11. What did you do before?"

"U.S. Marshal Service for seven years. I came on board ATSA five years ago."

She scooted around so she could tuck one foot beneath her. "U.S. Marshal. And how did you get into that?"

His hands lay lightly on the steering wheel. "My dad was a small-town cop. Fieldton, Indiana. After college I wanted more than arresting rowdy teenagers. The USMS suited me."

In safe territory. She knew why he relaxed. "All I know about the U.S. Marshal service is from *The Fugitive*. They transport and guard prisoners."

"That's one of a deputy marshal's jobs. Court security, protecting juries and witnesses are others."

Now she was getting the picture. "Protecting people. I see. I'll bet you were the guy who defended the little kid against the playground bully."

His eyebrows shot up as if in surprise that she'd figured him out. "I never could stand guys who tried to look tough by picking on others. The strong should protect the weak, the way I see it."

Protecting was what Jack did, Sophie thought. Although he wanted information from her, he was protecting her, as well. An admirable man, a quiet man sure of his strength and honor. A man of many layers, one of them pain-filled.

"What made you move to ATSA?"

He lifted one shoulder, but it was more muscle tightening than shrug. She'd hit a nerve again. "Lots of reasons. I needed a change. Wanted to get out of Miami. 9/11. ATSA was a new agency doing a crucial job."

None of that touched what she really wanted to know.

"Miami? I've never been there. I couldn't go far from my family in New York. Until now."

"You had responsibilities."

"Did *you?* You said before that you have no family. Is there an ex-Mrs. Thorne?" *Someone who hurt you so deeply you keep it all inside?*

His jaw worked, and the amber brow dived into a scowl. Finally, as though each word were torn bloody and writhing from the depths of his soul, he said, "I had a wife and son. They…they died."

Sophie's senses went numb with shock. *Dead?* That was the last thing she'd expected him to say. Tears stung her eyes. "Oh, Jack, I'm so sorry. You must miss them terribly. What—"

"Here's our exit. I'll need you to watch the map again."

When she saw the jaw muscle leap, she knew he'd closed the book again. Her heart twisted with sorrow for him.

Now she understood why he was so grim and closed. Why he hadn't waved to the children on the snail staircase. In fact, he'd deliberately looked away from them. Seeing little ones must bring back the terrible tragedy.

Memories.

His plagued him with grief and perhaps guilt. Hers were deadly, except they were locked in her brain.

Which was worse—remembering horror or not being able to?

What happened in Miami? An accident? Did what killed them also scar his hands?

And what did it have to do with Sebastian Vadim?

Jack's tension finally eased as the Fiat chugged into the Tuscan hills. Sophie had ceased grilling him, thank God. Her exclamations on this gorgeous vineyard or that adorable farmhouse had even elicited a smile or two from him.

They bought lunch from a produce vendor—bottled water, a crusty loaf of bread, apples and a wedge of pecorino, a sharp cheese from sheep's milk.

By the early evening they approached one of the villages mentioned in her grandmother's letters.

"Before we arrive, I need you to understand something." Jack braced himself for an argument.

Sophie tilted her head and gazed at him expectantly. Trust shone in her espresso-brown eyes.

Despite the twinge in his conscience, Jack forged ahead. "We have a fine line to walk. We want to awaken your memory. But we don't want to announce our presence."

Her dark hair swung onto her shoulder as she shook her head. "So what are you telling me exactly?"

"Too much contact and conversation with locals will make them remember us. We don't want to attract attention."

"But talking to people, asking questions, might lead me to Rinaldis. Finding family might trigger memories. Don't you want me to remember?" Desperation edged her voice.

She was right, damn it. But he'd take no chances with her safety, for ATSA or his personal aims.

Curbing her natural gregariousness would be hard. But her naive curiosity and warmth charmed people. People who would remember her.

He felt her disappointment in palpable waves, but there was no other option. "Your memory is key, but so is your life. By now Vadim must have people on our trail. You have to talk for us both, so I need your word you'll limit conversation to getting a room and ordering a meal. Don't chat."

"All right."

Her wistful expression and crooked smile twisted something in his chest, but he kept quiet.

The narrow, steep roads challenged his skills enough without distractions. An Ape—a three-wheeled miniature truck—approached at breakneck speed. Squashed into the tiny cab over the single front wheel, the corpulent driver saluted cheerfully as he nearly clipped them. No wonder Italy didn't export those damn vehicles. Unsafe at any speed.

A while later she said, "I get the feeling you believe me now. About amnesia, I mean."

Jack reflected on the past few days. He had no hard evidence, only his observations. And the reality of Sophie. Had his attraction to her swayed him? He didn't know, but for now he'd hold his cards close to the vest. "What if I did?"

"That would be something, anyway." She turned her gaze to the forested hillside beyond the passenger window.

The village sat in a verdant valley ringed by vineyards and narrow roads snaking into the surrounding hills. As in the previous one farther north, businesses and the church faced a town square. The sun-kissed reds and golds of the ancient brick structures looked grown from the Tuscan soil.

The single small inn's location on the square didn't entirely suit Jack's low-profile requirement, except for parking in back. Pale yellow, with arched windows, a wrought-iron sign and red-tile roof, the building glowed the same Mediterranean gleam as the rest of the village.

The innkeeper assigned them connecting rooms, but the bath was across the hall. Somehow the arrangement seemed safer, less domestic. Less prone to temptation. The intimacy of tending Sophie in their shared bathroom had strained Jack's nerves to the snapping point.

After settling in, Jack decided he approved of the room location. His window had a clear view of the small square.

Two women chatted with the fruit and vegetable vendor at *Fruttivendolo Conti* as she closed up shop. The butcher swept the pavement by his doorway. Boys kicked a soccer ball around the fountain. No obvious strangers in sight.

That evening he and Sophie walked to the restaurant, *Trattoria da Paolo,* across the square. The host, Paolo himself, greeted Sophie like long-lost family and brought them his family's best Chianti. He seemed to remember her, but Sophie replied only in monosyllables.

Over aromatic spaghetti with a porcini mushroom sauce,

she informed Jack that Paolo said she'd taught his young daughter to make an origami bird. She had no memory of the man or the village.

This woman who could converse with the wall restrained herself per his orders. Hunched over her plate, she seemed more ethereal and fragile than ever.

The waiter brought her marinated grilled chicken and his *bistecca fiorentina*—a huge cut of T-bone—both grilled.

Jack didn't know what to say, so he picked up his knife and fork. He didn't wear emotions outwardly. Or handle others' emotions comfortably. Sophie's laughter or tears were never far beneath the surface.

But not temper.

She hardly ever stood up for herself. Her casual obedience and subdued acceptance confounded him. He almost wished she'd rebel and converse away with everyone in the place. Almost.

Unwarranted or not, guilt turned the grilled beef from tender to tough in his mouth.

The next day, Sophie felt as if lead weighted down her Gucci sandals as she trudged across the square from the bar where they'd just eaten lunch. She was tired and her shoulder ached. Quiet blanketed the square as shops began to close for siesta.

She sighed as they approached the inn. "You'd think there'd be at least one Rinaldi alive in this town."

That morning they'd searched town and church records for Rinaldis. The only ones they'd found had lain in the cemetery. The elderly priest had informed them the last Rinaldi family had moved away twenty years ago.

"Give it time, Sophie. Rest a while. Then we'll walk around and see if anything looks familiar."

"Sounds like a plan." She forced a sanguine tone but had little hope. So far in this town, no scent or object or person had fished out a memory from the deep pool of Sophie's brain. She had only a few glimpses of her missing memory, and Vadim's face tainted those.

This morning, unwinding the silk scarf from the saint statuette had triggered the sensation of him kissing her hand. *Did he do more than kiss my hand? Could I be wrong that he wasn't my lover?* Anxiety made the *panini* she'd eaten for lunch grow heavy in her stomach.

"One more night here ought to be safe enough," Jack continued. "Putting off bending myself into a pretzel to bounce around mountain roads in that damn can suits me fine."

Relief washed over Sophie like a balm. Her bruised body could use the day, too.

The siesta's peace was broken as a refrigerated truck clattered into the square. The words *Vianello e Figlio* and cartoons of lambs, pigs and cows decorated its sides. With a squeal of brakes the meat truck stopped as its driver consulted a clipboard.

"No noise-abatement laws here, I guess," Jack said, shaking his head at the disturbance.

She was about to comment when she saw a small figure in bright yellow dart past them. The girl, about three years old, ran from the fruit-and-vegetable shop. Dark curls bobbed and chubby legs pumped as she chased a gray kitten back and forth.

The meat truck began backing toward the butcher shop.

Unaware, the toddler pursued her pet as it darted back and forth.

Directly in the path of the truck.

Chapter 8

Sophie stiffened. Adrenaline pounding her pulse in her ears, she started toward the child. *"Attenzione!"*

The truck's clattering and grinding drowned out her warning.

The girl scurried back and forth after the kitten.

Before Sophie could take a second step, Jack raced across the square. His long legs ate up the distance.

Distracted by a blowing leaf on the paving stones, the kitten put on the brakes as the child reached it.

Jack scooped up girl and cat together. Two more strides removed them all from harm's way as the oblivious truck driver kept backing toward the butcher shop.

Sophie exhaled her pent-up breath. Dizziness threatened, and she had to steady herself.

Jack marched up to Sophie and handed off the wide-eyed little girl to her like a football. Sophie clutched the child with her one good arm, and when she saw his face, she nearly dropped her.

Color had drained from his cheeks. His tan looked gray. When he turned away, his hands were shaking.

"Fabiana! Mi bambina!" Shrieking with terror for her baby and waving her arms, the produce vendor ran to them.

As soon as little Fabiana saw her mother in such a state, her chubby face puckered and tears filled her blue eyes. She joined the panic, crying for her *mamma*.

Sophie handed her over, and the woman clutched the child so desperately that Fabiana bawled harder.

The kitten yowled and clawed its way to freedom. It tore across the square to home and safety in the *fruttivendolo*.

All the while the woman babbled her thanks to the kind *stranieri*—foreigners—who had saved her daughter's life. Amid tears and smacking kisses on her daughter's cheek, she called Jack her hero. She began to settle down, but when people came out of other shops to investigate the commotion, her hysteria mounted again.

She wailed. The child bawled even louder.

Jack stood apart, gray-faced and stiff as the paving stones underfoot.

Sophie's heart bled, but what could she do for him? Nothing at the moment. Calming the child came first, poor baby. Her only injuries were a few claw scratches. Fabiana's face grew redder and redder with every exclamation from her mother's mouth. She gasped for air, close to hyperventilating.

Sophie shooed away the spectators and, crooning soothing words, escorted mother and child back to the shop.

She glanced back to see Jack trudging along behind them. His mouth was tight, his eyes not cool and assessing but filled with the weary dullness of a grief-stricken parent.

"You okay?"

Jack stopped short of closing his door on Sophie.

They'd just returned from the *fruttivendolo,* and he ducked into the sanctuary of his room. Rude, he knew, but he needed time alone to regroup. He reeled from the near calamity. Judging from her words, she knew that.

Stepping aside for her to enter, he said, "I'm fine. Why wouldn't I be?"

A knowing but sad smile blossomed. She closed the gap between them and wrapped her good arm around him. She pressed her cheek to his shoulder.

She fit him perfectly, the exact height for her head to fit beneath his chin. He kept his hands away from her, his body rigid so he wouldn't succumb to the pleasure of her body against him. He damn near didn't breathe so he wouldn't inhale her scent. An impossible challenge.

"Saving that child was heroic. I could see it hit you pretty hard." Her voice muffled against his chest, she held him tightly. "I was terrified. I shudder to think what could've happened."

He didn't want a hug. He didn't need a hug.

Damn it, what was she doing? Her warm tears wet his shirt. He felt her tremble. Ah, the aftermath of danger.

The woman had deep strengths, for herself and for emergencies. When Vadim's men had chased them, she'd hung tough, hadn't fallen apart then or afterward. Today, when the child and her mother had needed help, Sophie had taken charge. No shock for herself, but plenty for a little one. And a huge, warm heart that included everyone.

He melted. How could he deny her? What the hell. If she needed comforting, he could handle that. Careful with her sore shoulder, he curved his arms around her.

They stood quietly, wrapped around each other. He could feel the fine bones of her spine through the thin T-shirt, the plump fullness of her breasts against his chest.

Getting the stretchy cotton over her head that morning had made him sweat until she'd finally tugged it down over her barely covered breasts.

He was sweating again.

Gradually her tears dried and her trembling stopped. Her

scent and her softness seeped into him, giving the comfort he'd denied. One part of Jack hardened, but his muscles relaxed and the band around his chest eased.

Sophie tilted her head to regard him oddly, as if considering what to say. A few remaining tears beaded her thick lashes. One fell, trickling down her dampened cheek to the slight indent by her mouth.

He shouldn't touch—any more than he was already. But that single tear pulled his finger up to swipe it away. Her cheek felt unbearably tender, a damp petal. And her mouth— he ached to run his finger across her full lower lip, to kiss her again. To do more than kiss.

What had Leoni said? *Enjoy the scenery, but don't touch.*

On a deep breath Jack dropped his hand and stepped back.

Sophie did not. Her hand went to his forearm. "That awful scare must've reminded you of your son."

Seeing that little girl in danger had stabbed him in the heart. Fear had galvanized him. No parent should suffer the senseless tragedy of losing a child.

"I don't need reminders." He cleared his throat and crossed the room, away from her touch.

No more consolation. No softening. He wanted to relish the sharp, fresh pain, to stoke the ruthless, relentless need for revenge.

"I didn't mean you could ever forget." She pivoted and grasped the doorknob. "If you ever want to talk, I'm here."

He should let her go. Hell, he should push her out the door. But he said, "What was all that babbling the mother did before you calmed her down?"

A tender smile dancing on her lips, Sophie released the knob. "I didn't understand everything Chiara said. That's her name. She spoke in fast-forward, and the Tuscan accent changes the *c* and *ch* sounds. What I gather is that Fabiana got up from her nap and slipped past Mom. Probably to follow the kitten.

"Chiara blames the butcher—he's her brother-in-law—for

not coming out to supervise the trucker. She called him some colorful names. Creative ones, involving the animals whose meat he sells, and definitely insulting."

"You were amazing, the origami and all." He'd stood by in mute shock while Sophie had distracted the child by making an origami swan with pink and green tissue paper from the fruit display. The project had calmed both mother and daughter. And intrigued Jack. "You're a natural teacher."

Sophie laughed. "Maybe. I learned origami from an art teacher. I used to do crafts with the Donati kids when we couldn't go to the park. We made all kinds of things."

"You just proved my statement. Natural teacher."

She shook her head. "A variation on nanny. Not in my plans."

"Isn't there some saying? 'Life is what happens while you're making other plans.'"

"When I get my memory back, maybe I'll know."

Before he could respond, she slipped out the door.

Their afternoon tour of the town and environs produced no memories for Sophie. As dusk approached, they returned to the inn to change for dinner.

Jack took the time to check in with Leoni. He reported their location and that they planned to move on the next day. "Any developments?"

"Not much. Vadim owns several properties under his various aliases. Some in Italy, some in Cleatia, one on Cyprus. We're tracking them down, but it's slow going. The Cleatian authorities don't want to cooperate."

Jack could almost hear Leoni's shrug. He made himself comfortable on the bed. "And the courier Dobrich? Autopsy results yet?"

Sophie knocked on their connecting door and opened it. He waved her in, and she crossed to the window. In preparation for dinner, she'd changed from cropped pants into a short skirt, something she could manage one-handed. The scoop-necked top was the same. He should be glad she hadn't needed his help, but he was no saint.

When she sat to observe the square, he had an excellent view of her trim legs. She would people watch, and he would Sophie watch.

"Funny you should ask," said Leoni. "Damaged spleen, low blood count, lungs shot. Doc said radiation poisoning. If they hadn't shot him, he'd have died in a matter of days anyway."

"He opened the package."

"That's my take on it. Makes sense. He didn't know what he had. After his boss was picked up, he was on his own, curious. And you know what they say about curiosity."

Jack emitted a long, low whistle. "If radiation was released, whoever has the package now could be in trouble."

Wide-eyed in alarm, Sophie stared at him, but he mouthed *okay,* and she returned her attention to the square.

"Vadim's no dummy. He would've had it secured again."

"I hope you're right."

They ended the conversation. Jack related Leoni's update to Sophie.

She nodded absently. "You might want to look at this man sitting outside the trattoria. I don't think he's local."

He joined her at the window and immediately knew what she meant.

Thirties, short dark hair slicked back, black polo and shiny trousers, predatory look. Drinking a glass of something, he sat apart from the other patrons, who glanced nervously his way from time to time.

The fine hairs on Jack's nape rose. "Definitely not local. Not a tourist."

He had *hit man* written all over him.

The distance fuzzed the picture, but Jack snapped three shots with his cell phone. Leoni could ask the techs to enhance them enough to ID the guy. Fifty euros said he was known to the *polizia*.

"Look, there's Chiara, Fabiana's mom, leaving the trattoria," said Sophie. The woman glanced furtively at the stranger, then jogged across the square. "She's coming here, to the inn."

Jack kept his eyes on the stranger. At the man's waist, beneath his shirt, bulged a distinctive shape. Armed. Unusual in Italy.

Excited voices rose from downstairs, then louder as the speakers mounted the stairs. There was a frantic pounding on Jack's door. *"Signore! Signora!"*

"What is it?" Sophie rose from her chair and wrapped her good arm around her injured one as if for security.

Jack opened the door to Chiara and the innkeeper, who were talking in chorus. He stepped back and motioned Sophie forward. He listened to the excited exchange, punctuated with expansive hand gestures, but he understood little. Only the words *stranieri*, foreigners, and *pericolo*, danger.

When the rapid-fire conversation began to run out of ammunition, he could stand waiting no more. "Sophie, explain."

Her eyes were bright, but her cheeks had paled. "Chiara says she was delivering peppers and mushrooms to the kitchen when the waitress ran in all nervous. The man out there was asking if any foreigners were in town. She says he's a Southerner. That seems to be the local term for Mafia."

He looked out the window.

The Southerner he preferred to call "Slick" sat sipping his drink and browsing the square with a hard gaze. The waitress, her eyes round as plates, brought him a pasta dish.

Good. Still there. Would be there for a while. "What did the waitress tell him?"

Sophie relayed the question to Chiara, who stood wringing her hands. Her eyes were still puffy from her earlier fright. Another volley of words, and Sophie said, "She told him he was the first stranger she'd seen in weeks."

He was impressed, but somebody would blab soon. Slick was here for them. But he wanted to calm her. "Good, then maybe we're okay."

"Wait, Jack." Not calmed, she gripped his arm. "He described us—a man and a woman with her arm in a sling. *He's looking for us!*"

He nodded and turned to the gaping innkeeper and Chiara. *"Grazie mille,"* he said, thanking the women and shaking their hands.

To Sophie he said, "Please tell the innkeeper we're checking out."

After Sophie translated, the innkeeper dashed downstairs to prepare their bill. Sophie and her new fan exchanged cheek kisses, and then Chiara left.

"Chiara says Paolo will keep the Southerner occupied with food and a full wineglass."

"Good, but I'm taking no chances. Get your bags."

In a few moments, bill paid and bags packed, Jack hoisted his duffel on his shoulder and entered Sophie's room. "Ready?"

She lifted the red tote from the bed. "I'll carry this."

"You sure you can handle it?" He lifted the larger one.

"It's light."

He snorted in disbelief. "The thing weighs a ton. What's so heavy?"

Sophie gave him a wobbly smile. "Shoes, makeup. Stuff."

There was no time to argue. If she'd healed enough so she could carry it, he'd let her. They made their way through the labyrinth of corridors to the back stairs that led to the parking area.

As darkness descended on the small town, Jack drove the Fiat into the hills. He remembered the roads well enough and headed for a crossroads where he turned farther south.

Since they would get no dinner, Sophie divided what was left of the pecorino and fruit to eat as they drove.

He crunched into an apple as he chewed on what had just happened. "Sophie, those people in that town saved our lives."

"Yes. Yes, they did." Her voice caught with emotion. "Chiara and Paolo and even Paolo's little waitress."

He'd admonished her not to chat, not to get involved in people's lives, that calling attention to themselves was dangerous. As it turned out, their safety depended on that same involvement.

Was he too by-the-book, too harsh in his approach?

To everything?

Sophie's soft appearance gave the impression of fragility, but inside she was stronger than he was. And the more time he spent with her, the more he liked her.

The more he wanted her.

When the mountain road widened for a scenic turnout, he pulled over and stopped. The sickle moon shed little light, so the scenery below lay unseen in its ebony blanket.

"What's wrong?"

"Nothing. Before we go any farther, I need to check for electronic bugs and tracking devices. Everything has been swept, but Vadim found us somehow."

He got out, leaving the engine running and the lights on.

Sophie watched as Jack began removing their belongings from the compact Fiat. She grabbed her tote from the backseat and lugged it onto the pavement.

From his duffel he withdrew a device that looked like a fat ballpoint pen. When he pressed a button, a tiny antenna extended from one end and a green light glowed.

"What's that?" she asked, intrigued. "Spy stuff?"

"An RF detection unit. RF for radio frequency. If we have an operational bug, the light will blink red. The faster it blinks, the closer the detector is to the bug."

He lay on the ground and ran the detector beneath the car chassis. Nothing. Then he passed it over and around his duffel. He opened the bag and jabbed the penlike device inside. Still nothing.

"You shouldn't have to be precise with this detector, but I'm taking—"

"No chances. And I appreciate that." As he finished with

his duffel and moved to her big suitcase, Sophie's nerves flitted like fireflies on a summer night.

If Jack saw the marble saint, would he think she'd stolen it from the villa? It belonged to her, but he'd seen it on the nightstand and didn't know that.

Maybe she was worrying for nothing, but she'd keep Santa Elisabetta hidden. Once her memory returned so she knew what secret of Vadim's she held in her brain, she'd tell him.

She remembered some things now, but nothing helpful. Impressions of Vadim kissing her hand helped no one. She shuddered in revulsion. *What did I do?*

"We're almost done. Just this." Jack reached for the tote handle.

"Oh, can I do it?" Sophie gushed. "This is so cool. A real spy gadget." Managing to bat her eyelashes, she gazed up at him. She hated such feminine ploys as phony and obvious, but this was an emergency.

Jack looked at her oddly. Either he thought she had something in her eye or he was on to her. But then he shrugged. "Sure, why not? Nothing to it."

After a demonstration, he stepped aside.

Sophie passed the bug detector over and around the tote. She unzipped it and swept inside. "Nothing." She indicated the green light, steady and bland.

"That's that, then. No bugs." As they repacked the car, he said, "We'll head for a town you didn't visit before. Maybe Vadim knows what was in your grandmother's letters." Sighing in frustration, he bent his long body into the driver's seat.

Sophie slid into her seat and opened the map. "I suppose I could've shown them to him. I can't imagine why he'd care or remember. At the time, I mean."

"But the letters are only one possibility. There could be a leak."

* * *

Twisted mass of metal. Grotesque in the orange dawn. The small face. Upside down and too still. So much blood.

Pain and rage a jagged boulder inside. Must reach him. Save him.

Cascade of glass. Sharp. Stabs. Ignore them. Red shards. Dripping. A crimson lake. Red and more red. Nothing but red. Only blood—

Jack jerked upright. He dragged in a rasping breath. His gritty eyes stung from his own sweat and tears. Breathing deeply to calm his racing heart, he focused on the pale dawn lighting the open window. Tuscan June nights were comfortably cool, but not when past terrors came back to haunt a man.

Too much was happening to exhume all the pain. The small child yesterday. Sophie's gentle probing…

Sophie.

She lay beside him in the bed. On her side, she curled her free hand beneath her cheek like a child. The pj placket gapped open above the sling strap, affording Jack a view of the inner curve of her lush breasts. Nothing like a child.

He returned his gaze to the encroaching dawn.

Late last night, when they'd dragged into the hill town, there'd been only one room at this bed-and-breakfast. He offered to sleep on the floor, but Sophie insisted they share. So she'd slid beneath the sheet and light blanket, and he stretched out on top in gym shorts and a T-shirt.

Perfectly respectable.

Right.

The first part of the night he was too aroused to relax. He watched her fall asleep and half hoped she would roll into his arms and let him hold her. She didn't. Finally exhaustion had closed his eyes.

Sophie ought to have more rest. Another chat with Leoni before they hit the road was essential. The hour was early. So

Jack lay back on his pillow, found it soaked with sweat and flipped it over to the dry side. He adjusted his position to face his bed partner.

Inky lashes, long and curled, fanned beneath Sophie's eyes. If only he could see past them, past her eyes, into the brain that hid the information he needed.

Or did it?

She was hiding something from him. He sensed it. Did she remember and not want to tell him? Or was there something in her tote?

Last night she'd carried the bag herself, guarded it from him like a treasure. She'd insisted on scanning it herself with the bug detector. He'd begun to trust her, but now he wasn't sure.

He didn't know about her or how Slick had found them. He didn't know much, but he would go with what he suspected.

No more cat and mouse with a hit man. No more chances with a leak. Was somebody in the task force feeding info to Vadim? Jack's cell was secure, but was Leoni's? Could he trust Leoni? Or De Carlo?

Contacting them to find out meant more risk to Sophie's life. Not an option.

From now on, he and Sophie hit the road on their own. No more contact with Leoni or the task force.

He slid off the bed and padded out barefoot in search of the bathroom.

Sophie wrenched her good arm into the stretchy yellow T-shirt and worked the garment into place. Thank God for Lycra. She panted like a marathon runner from the strain, but she'd dressed by herself. Even the bra. Her injured shoulder had healed enough in a week that she could manage a limited range of motion.

Dressing and undressing she could handle alone. No more unnecessary intimacy.

Now why did that give her a pang? Wasn't sleeping in the same bed with him too close for comfort? Comfort, yes. The reality of his large presence weighing down the covers cocooned her in a feeling of safety and security she hadn't felt since waking in the hospital.

But close meant body heat and masculine breathing and muscles that invited cuddling. Not that Jack would ever…

Enough of that, Sophia Constanza.

She perched on the bed, picked up her hairbrush and began working at the knots. She'd always prided herself on her long, thick hair, but managing this rat's nest required two hands.

The scents of coffee and minty soap entered the room with Jack. His hair wet from a shower and shiny as new taffy, he strode in carrying a tray laden with steaming mugs and a basket covered with a white linen napkin.

Never mind the food. With his loose-limbed gait and freshly shaven chin, he looked good enough to eat.

He set the tray on the blue-painted bureau. "I found coffee and pastries. Hard-boiled eggs, too."

"Tante grazie," she said, tossing down the hairbrush. "I could devour it all."

His coffee mug stopped halfway to his lips. His blue eyes browsed her length—with heat, if she wasn't mistaken—as he took in her T and flowered capris. "Sophie, you're dressed."

Was there disappointment in his tone or merely surprise? She poured milk into her coffee and stirred. Not until she'd stuffed an almond pastry in her mouth and swallowed did she trust herself to respond. "My shoulder's much better."

"It's been a week. The doctor said ten days." A scowl pleating his forehead, he swallowed coffee and regarded her.

"I won't overdo." She demonstrated with a tight, circular arm motion. A sharp twinge made her wince.

Jack uttered an inarticulate growl. "Good thing you don't

have to conduct an orchestra or drive our demon car. Let's get the sling on that arm."

Sophie grinned at his deadpan humor and felt a warm curl in her belly at the obvious concern in his voice. She submitted to his care as he adjusted the sling's fastenings. Letting this man protect her, take care of her, put his hands on her and…and… Well, whatever, she was becoming way too accustomed to the intimacy.

"I want to leave off the sling. I can remember to keep my arm still, and wearing it is like painting on a bull's-eye."

He placed his hands on her shoulders and massaged gentle circles. "Vadim's goon did use the sling to describe you. You're sure?"

The concern for her in his words and on his furrowed brow made her smile. The feel of his hands nearly melted her bones. *"Assolutamente.* Besides, the sling is much too hot. I roast enough with all this hair down on my neck. A French braid would get this mess off my neck, but I can't reach high enough for that yet."

She felt Jack's hands go dead-still on her shoulders.

"What is it?"

He cleared his throat. His hands flexed, warm and strong. "I know how to make a French braid."

Chapter 9

Sophie wheeled so fast she sloshed coffee from her mug onto the woven rug. "You can *what?*"

A ruddy hue crept over Jack's cheeks. "I can do a French braid. I used to braid my wife's hair."

Her heart squeezed at what the admission must've cost him. Jack never talked about his wife. And yet he looked more embarrassed than grieved. Five years was a long time to keep a memory in sharp focus, even a painful one.

What throbbed like an abscessed tooth was the death of his son.

Sophie pasted on her most dazzling smile and winked, opting for humor to ease his discomfort.

She dug around in her kit for a scrunchie, then handed it and the brush to him. "A man of hidden talents. A French braid, *per favore,* Signore Giovanni."

As he stroked the brush through her hair, a low growl or possibly a chuckle rose from his throat. "Giovanni?"

"Italian for Jack or John. If you're playing hairdresser, you need a Continental name."

She stood as still as she could as he lifted her hair and worked the brush again and again down its length. Each tug of the bristles, gentle or not-so-gentle, felt like heaven. When he gathered her hair into sections and began braiding, she wanted to lean into him.

Lost in his ministrations, she felt as boneless as a kitten, but behind her she sensed Jack was as rigid as the automatic pistol he kept out of sight. "Did your wife have hair like mine?"

There was silence as though he were deciding whether to answer. In the distance, a church bell rang nine times. Nearer, a car engine ground and ground, refusing to turn over.

"Blond. Not as thick."

So much for relaxing him. Detective Rinaldi was interrogating a hostile witness. "What was her name?"

Another pause. A long-suffering sigh. "Tonia. She liked me to braid her hair, said it felt good."

"I can vouch for that," she murmured, barely able to speak.

Mint soap, aftershave and body heat mingled with the sensual feel of his big hands tugging at her hair and sliding across her scalp to radiate a shivery tingle from her head downward.

One final tug, and his hands settled on her shoulders. "All done. I should've offered sooner."

Without his support, she would've melted into a warm puddle at his feet. Shaking off the sensual haze, she let him turn her to face him. "Thanks. I won't be constantly wind-blown this way."

The smoky look in his blue eyes said having his hands in her hair had unsettled him, too. His voice was husky when he spoke. "Sophie, you've been a trouper through all this."

"Oh, yeah, having my hair braided is such an ordeal." Her attempt at humor fell at her feet as he pushed a stray wisp from her cheek.

"You know what I mean. The canal chase with shots flying.

Our charging from town to town. Your injuries have to drain you, but you don't complain or—"

"Wimp out?" She executed a stiff shrug. "I have no choice. Getting back my memory and finding out what really happened is as important to me as it is to you. Not to mention the little matter of the uranium. But thank you."

She flattened her hand on his chest and rose on tiptoe to kiss him. She intended only a light brush of lips, but the magnet that pulled them together wouldn't let go. She clung to his mouth and savored the warm muscles beneath her palm.

"Sophie." His arms wrapped around her, and he deepened the kiss with a moan that said he couldn't help himself. His tongue swept against hers, all sultry heat and need.

She tasted him—dark roast coffee and salty male—and heat spiraled up inside. His embrace ignited her senses and stole away reality. Her nipples rasped against the bra's lace. She leaned into him to assuage a growing ache. His rampant virility against her belly declared his matching need.

His lips left her mouth to nip at her temples, her earlobes, and to make his way down her neck. "Sophie, I shouldn't...we shouldn't. But..."

"I know." When his lips found her hard nipple poking the shirt's soft knit, she rubbed against him with a feline purr.

His mouth covered hers again, hot and hungry, no longer hard but determined. He made her pulse sing as arousal bloomed inside her like a profusion of roses.

She went liquid with want.

For years she'd floated along in occasional superficial relationships, so how could this man—this hard man, this determined man, her staunch protector—create these deeper feelings? How could such intense desire be possible? And a connection beyond their bodies her soul yearned to explore?

Desire and connection she—*they*—couldn't act on. There could be no relationship without trust. He didn't trust her and she didn't trust herself. Her pulse clattered like the metal turnstile at the Forty-second Street and Times Square station.

No, I can't. We can't....

"Jack," she murmured into his mouth. She placed a trembling hand on his freshly shaven cheek.

When he raised his head, his eyes were unfocused and his mouth glistened with their kisses. His hands slid away from her, and he stepped back. "You're right to stop. A minute more, I'd have had you naked. I apologize. I took advantage."

The desire still swirling in Sophie's belly ebbed. Feeling slightly insulted, she twitched her hips and stalked to the window. "We have more reasons to stop than Italy has grapevines, but you taking advantage *isn't* one of them. I kissed you first."

Jack rubbed a hand over his nape. "If you say so. But I shouldn't have gotten carried away. It's been a long time for me, and you're a beautiful woman and…"

She couldn't help but smile at his discomfiture. He ran down like a windup clock. The poor man really didn't know what to say.

The notion that he didn't hop into bed with every other woman flicked her pulse again. "So chalk it up to proximity and hormones? Thank you for the compliment anyway."

"Besides, I should know better. ATSA has regs against sex with witnesses or suspects."

She was tempted to ask which she was but reflected that she knew the answer. "Speaking as both a witness and a suspect, I agree. And I have my own reasons. I need to find my memory and myself. Everything else is on hold. Even sex with a hunky, strong man who happened to share my bed."

Now it was his turn to smile. He looked like a small boy begging an extra cookie. "Hunky?"

"Don't let it go to your head." Afraid this mutual admiration society might lead them in a circular path back to the bed, she began gathering up her toiletries and clothing.

When she glanced at Jack, he was scowling into his coffee mug. "Good we cleared the air on that subject."

The professional ATSA-officer shell was in place. Sophie could take a hint and pretend they'd put an end to the sizzle humming between them. "Too true. I'm glad we're straight on that. Sex on this road trip is *so* not a good idea."

Denying their feelings was the rational thing to do. He knew it. She knew it. So why did she have this hollowed-out ache in her stomach?

After packing, they headed farther south. They maintained a zigzag pattern for two days, stopping in remote villages and contacting no one.

Once he figured he'd ditched their tail, Jack intended to make a clockwise circuit of Tuscany before going to Florence. Maybe they could get lost in the city.

Before that, he needed to contact somebody in ATSA, but not anybody connected to the task force.

He watched the rearview mirror, but the winding mountain road seemed to contain only locals and a few tourists. On a rare straightaway, he passed a German camper camouflaged with folding chairs, bicycles and canoes. Produce trucks, the tiny three-wheeled Apes, tourists and commuters headed to the larger towns of Montepulciano or Arezzo jockeyed for position.

On the third day, as they drove into a small hilltop town for lunch, Sophie read to Jack from the guidebook. "'Chiusi was once a powerful Etruscan city.'"

Before Rome became dominant, Jack remembered, the Etruscans were Italy's first major civilization. Noting the sleepy Piazza del Duomo that spread before the cathedral, he snorted, "What, back in the seventh-century B.C.?"

"There's an Etruscan labyrinth beneath the piazza and Christian catacombs outside town. Etruscan tombs pepper the hillsides around the city, and the National Etruscan

Museum is…" Her voice trailed off as Jack pulled into a parking space before a restaurant.

"What is it?" he said. "Are we being followed?"

She shook her head, flipping her braid onto her shoulder. "I've been here. I remember this town. I went to the Etruscan Museum." Her eyes widened as pleasure spread across her features like dawn.

"You remember something."

"I remember this town."

Hope bloomed inside him. "It wasn't on your itinerary."

"I was driving around after leaving Arezzo. The Etruscans fascinate me." She shrugged in elaborate Italian fashion, and her white smile nearly blinded him. "Jack, I'm remembering!"

He wanted to wrap her in his arms and kiss her senseless, but he said, "We've lost Vadim's thug for now. After lunch we can investigate the museum. Maybe you'll remember more there."

The longer they stayed in one place, the easier for Slick to find them. But it was worth the risk.

A tiny frown dimmed her beaming countenance. "It's so frustrating. I grasp pieces of memory, images of places and people, but nothing hangs together. I don't remember anything about the villa or the car hitting me or even that day."

He squeezed her hand as he helped her from the car. "You'll get there." According to the doctors, she might never remember the impact of the car hitting her, but the rest should return. In time.

Time was a problem. Every day he didn't find Vadim meant his enemy had opportunity to flee farther away or dig deeper into cover.

They found the Etruscan Museum on the Via Porsenna and paid the modest entry fee of four euros each.

Sophie could barely contain the anticipation that bubbled

inside her like champagne. She picked up a folded map of the many Etruscan tombs outside town and tucked it in her pocket.

Her memories were buried in her brain like in those ancient stone vaults dug into the Tuscan hills. Now that returning to Chiusi had unearthed this memory, maybe others would find their way from the labyrinth of her mind. She squirmed inwardly at the memories of Vadim she'd already glimpsed.

Once she remembered the rest, Jack's protection would end. And so would the attraction. What was between them arose from the necessary closeness, the isolation.

He was a man she'd never have met otherwise. His reluctant caring and fierce dedication touched her heart. She would never forget him even if another blow to the head wiped clean all other memories.

But they had nothing in common. When the danger ended, they would walk away from each other.

Tell yourself that's what you want, Sophia Constanza.

At a terra-cotta exhibit spotlighted by the sun streaming in the adjacent window, Jack pulled her aside into the shadows. "Across the street. See him?"

Sophie spotted the man slouching in a shop doorway. He looked up and down the street. The same slicked-back dark hair and black shirt. The man the two of them called Slick.

Her pulse jittered, and she edged closer to Jack. "How did he find us?"

Jack shook his head. "I don't think he has. Our route took us south, and Chiusi's not off the beaten path. A logical place to look for us. See, he's checking out every passerby and vehicle."

"What do we do?"

He took her right arm and steered her deeper into the museum exhibits. "We stroll around like the tourists we are and look for a rear exit."

They headed toward the museum's centerpiece. She recognized the frieze with the meticulously painted male figures in wrestling holds. It took centuries of time to wear away and fade the frieze's brilliant blues and reds, but one second's glimpse of the hit man dulled Sophie's excitement. She barely gave the naked wrestlers a glance.

Moments later, in an obscure corner, they found an exit. A guide with the museum's distinctive badge stood in the open doorway, beneath a No Smoking sign. She puffed on a cigarette. Her fluttering hand coaxed the smoke outdoors.

Jack curved his arm around Sophie's shoulders. He whispered, "Tell her you're not feeling well and need air."

As they approached the guide, Sophie sagged against him. She needed only a moment to convince her to let them go outside through the back exit.

The woman shot Jack a furious look as she shut the door behind them.

"What did you say to her?" Jack asked. They hurried from the courtyard onto the back street. Summer heat rose in shimmering waves from the baked paving stones to steam him in his heavy jeans and polo.

Sophie couldn't help the nervous giggle that erupted. "I said I was pregnant. I don't know the Italian for morning sickness, so I just said I was nauseous."

He rolled his eyes. "And she blamed me."

"Naturally." Relieved to have something to smile about, Sophie winked at him.

Then a thought halted her feet. "Do you think the...hit man or whatever he is knows our car?"

"It's a good bet. We'll rent a new one." He stopped in front of a *fruttivendolo* and nudged her between the displays and out of sight. "I don't want to drag you all over town looking for a rental agency, but I'd rather leave the car on the residential street where we left it."

Sophie withdrew the Etruscan tombs map from her pocket. "On the back is an ad. The car agency's in the Piazza Dante."

Both amber brows winged upward, and Jack grinned. Not

a twitch of lip or a small smile but an out-and-out grin. He framed her cheeks with his big hands and kissed her. Hard.

The world tilted and evaporated into the ether. Sophie wanted more, but he broke the kiss as quickly as he'd begun it.

"Sophie, ah, Sophie." He shook his head as if stumped for more words than her name.

She swallowed as the world reappeared. He looked at her as no one ever had before, deeply, as though trying to see into her soul. "What? That piazza's only a few streets over. I remember from the guidebook. We can walk there."

"You're sure?"

"I'm not as fragile as I look."

"No. I can attest to that. But you had a concussion only a week ago."

She slipped her hand in his arm and urged him in the general direction of the Piazza Dante. "A concussion affects the head. My legs are fine."

Grinning again, he said, "More than fine."

Sophie's heart did a backflip. Jack flirting with her? She was *so* in trouble.

Two hours later they drove out of Chiusi. Jack had hoped for a vehicle with more room and, damn it, just more.

No such luck.

All the agency'd had was another Fiat identical—still no horsepower or air—to the previous one except in color. This subcompact was black. Nondescript, but the color absorbed the more southerly Italian sun. Damn thing was a tin sauna.

After renting the car, they'd bought emergency supplies at an *alimentari,* a delicatessen-type shop. Then they'd transferred their belongings and abandoned the government-issue Fiat. It would probably be towed, but not right away.

He would have to notify the task force. Eventually.

Armed with a Chiusi street map, Sophie directed Jack on a circuitous backstreet route out of town and northwest on a narrow secondary road. He hoped their mafioso counted on them continuing south on Highway 71.

The route curved back and forth as if the road builders had simply followed the hills' contours or the tracks of meandering Tuscan cattle. In an Alfa Romeo or a Maserati, Jack would've enjoyed the hell out of the drive. Driving faster would send air in to cool them.

But in the Fiat, he groaned every time he shifted.

A few miles into the countryside he noted a blue Fiat a few car lengths behind them. He couldn't see the driver, but the man's bulk made his gut tighten. There was little other traffic. Jack had seen one man on a bicycle. That was it.

"He's behind us, isn't he?" Sophie said, her voice tight.

"Looks like Slick. I'll head for the *Autostrade.* Four traffic lanes should give me room to maneuver." And plenty of witnesses to make him think twice if he intended to shoot.

"How did he find us?"

The Mafia hit man had more tricks than expected. Did he have an accomplice who'd followed them? Jack had spotted nobody. The possibility scraped his nerves raw. "We'll figure it out later."

With the breeze dancing little tendrils loose around her face, Sophie turned halfway to peer out the rear window. "He's just following, not trying anything. What does it mean?"

Before Jack could answer that he had no clue, he saw the answer. Dead ahead.

Where the road turned, a red motorcycle, a Ducati, lay across the right-hand lane, and a man bent over it, one arm cradling the other as if he were injured in the spill.

"Oh, that man is hurt," Sophie began. "But if we stop—"

"If we stop, they have us." Adrenaline pumping, Jack shook his head. "A fake accident's an old ambush deception, to make the victim stop. Our Mafia boy has accomplices. But how the hell did they get in front of us?"

"What'll you do?"

"I'm going around." He downshifted in preparation for speeding around the stopper. "Get down as low as you can in case they start shooting."

Sophie slid to the car floor, as she'd done on the Venice powerboat. Jack caught that her movements were more agile than before and no pain tightened her mouth.

"Hold on," he said, glancing in the rearview mirror. The blue car was closing the gap. Jack accelerated at the same time he swerved into the oncoming lane to pass the spilled bike. He ignored the sweat streaming down his temples.

The motorcyclist waved frantically at him. When he didn't stop, the man drew a pistol from somewhere and fired at them.

Jack stomped on the accelerator. The little Fiat groaned but gradually sped up.

Behind them, the muzzle of a pistol jutted from the blue car's driver window.

Thunk! Thunk! Thunk! Bullets slammed into the fenders.

Just don't let them hit the tires. As he'd done in the boat, Jack zigged and zagged, hoping to throw off their aim.

He was just approaching the turn when he saw the second shooter kicking his motorcycle to life.

"Now they're both after us. Stay down, Sophie."

"Are you okay? You're not shot?"

"Fine. You?"

"Peachy." But her voice hitched on the last syllable.

Jack urged the whining Fiat into fourth gear. Hanging in the left lane, he gunned it toward the turn. The odds were against meeting oncoming traffic.

From the left a green Ford Fiesta pulled out of the roadside brush.

Oh, hell. Jack zipped over to the right lane and into the turn. The Fiat fishtailed, tires squealing. He yanked it into the turn and kept going.

Encouraged, he crossed mental fingers that the Fiesta's arrival would confuse the thugs. He glanced in the mirror.

No such luck. The Fiesta's driver joined the others in pursuit. Jack pounded on the wheel and swore.

"What happened?"

"Another car. There's three of them." He felt like a character in the movie about Butch and Sundance. *Who are those guys?*

He made it around the turn, but his pursuers were gaining speed. He was not.

Thunk! Thunk! Bullets hit the trunk.

He swerved around another turn.

Sophie rolled with a thump against the car door.

Inside him rage boiled—and fear that he couldn't protect her. He tamped down both, centering his mind and drawing from the experience he needed.

"Sorry, but the curving road is the only thing keeping them from catching us."

"I'm okay." She was holding her injured arm tightly against her. "Do whatever you have to do."

The road took them up hills and down the other side, still with the three vehicles in pursuit. The Fiat careened around one curve after another like a drunken donkey.

Another stopper entered from a side road just before another sharp curve.

Fear for Sophie grabbed at his throat. If he braked now, they'd kill her. "Aw, damn it to hell!"

"What now?" She pushed up on her knees to peer out the passenger window. *"A farmer?"*

The new stopper ahead was no Mafia accomplice but no less effective. The wooden wagon pulled by a team of horses blocked his lane and half of the left. Behind it lumbered a second team pulling a wagon.

Jack checked the lay of the land. Vineyard. Opposite, another dirt road. Boulders flanked both roads. "Hold on, Sophie. I might be able to make hay out of this."

He veered left, keeping the tires barely on the pavement. The rear fender kissed the boulders with an ear-splitting screech. The Fiat passed directly in front of the plodding horses.

The big animals shied and stomped. Three more steps and they halted and tossed their heads. The wagon driver dropped the reins. He waved both meaty fists at the rude motorist.

Jack eased the Fiat back onto pavement and zipped on around the curve. "I think that did it."

"What did you do?" Sophie crept back into her seat.

"The two wagons were loaded with men and tools from the day's labors in the vineyard on the other side. Now the wagons are blocking the entire roadway. Those Mafia bottom-feeders can't bypass the boulders. They'll have to wait for the horses to calm down and finish crossing before they can chase us." He rolled his shoulders in an effort to relax the tension.

"You're a genius!" She searched the road behind them as she tucked curls behind one ear. "I see no sign of them."

"We're not in the clear yet." A glimpse of her glowing face had him gripping the wheel tighter so he wouldn't reach for her. Damn, he didn't need this. "Look at your map. What detours can we take to throw them off?"

"The map from the Etruscan Museum shows more detail than the road map. I see several dirt tracks that lead to tomb sites. We could—"

His heart bumped when he checked the rearview mirror. "Hold it. The creeps are back. I see the motorcycle."

"No. *Oh, no!*" Sophie's trembling fingers crumpled the map.

Chapter 10

Sophie's chest tightened with fear. This chase was worse than racing through the Venice canals.

Jack covered her hand with his. "We'll get out of this. I promise. If what I have in mind works, we'll have a place to hole up for a few hours."

Downshifting, he pushed the little car to its limit, but he managed to pull ahead. A series of S-curves in the narrow road blocked them from view of their pursuers.

"Now where do I turn for one of these tomb sites?" Jack said, steering through another curve.

Just what she longed for, a place to hide, a safe place. The feel of his warm strength on her skin reassured her.

She drew a deep breath and shoved away her panic. "Take the next right. Then there's a dirt road on the left just after a small shrine." Fear had swabbed her mouth dry, and she managed only a whispery voice.

"Thank God the bike's small and not a monster that could

power rings around us. They're not close enough to shoot. We have a good chance of fooling them."

No sign yet of their pursuers, but Sophie knew they must be gaining. Her heart crowded into her already tight throat. *Faster, faster,* she urged the intrepid Fiat.

Jack hung a sharp right onto the side road.

"There, up there's the shrine. See the flowers?"

Beside a natural spring someone had built a stone pillar topped with a crucifix and a picture of the Virgin Mary. Roses and wildflowers bedecked the pillar's base.

Thirty feet farther along, barely visible, a narrow dirt track disappeared into a thicket.

"Got it." Jack braked and yanked the wheel left.

Dappled emerald shade embraced them as the Fiat bumped and bounced onto the rutted dirt. Jack saw a cleared place to one side. He pulled over and cut the engine.

Over them arched a cool canopy of native pines and beech trees, and behind them spread thick shrubs. The familiar scents of heather and juniper drifted on the light breeze. Deep shadows shielded the black car.

"We're hidden. I'll give it a few minutes before we go on to the tombs." He dug his 9mm from beneath his seat and checked it over. "Stay here."

Sophie held her breath as she watched Jack. Swinging open the door, he levered his long body from the car. He pushed the door almost shut. Thigh muscles shifting under worn denim, he crouched over and edged along a sprawling juniper to where he could see the paved road. A spear of sunlight glinted off his pistol, and he lowered it.

Sophie held her breath and listened. The hum of motors increased to a roar as the three Mafia vehicles drew near. Slowly the noise diminished to a hum.

The cars and the motorcycle passed them by!

She slumped in relief, her pulse thumping in her ears like a drum solo.

A moment later Jack returned to the car. She watched as he examined the rear, where the bullets had hit. Then he clambered back into the driver's seat. "Car seems all right. No sign of gas leaks. But our suitcases have new ventilation."

"Oh, you did it! You fooled them. They're gone." She wanted to throw her arms around him and kiss him, but no. There was that scowl. "They *are* gone, aren't they?"

"For now. They could turn back when they don't see us."

"Or they could think we took the other road."

"Miss Optimist. If they come back, we could be trapped here." His gaze softened and his big hand cupped her cheek.

Her insides turned to warm risotto. She smiled, savoring the contact and a whiff of male musk and sweat. "Or we could be safely hidden."

"If we leave, they could split up and find us again."

Sophie opened her mouth to object, then closed it. Their shade-camouflaged car was cozy, intimate. Jack was beside her, so close that his heat, his scent and his chiseled jaw made her dizzy with longing. "You think we should stay, too."

As he traced a finger across her lower lip, small flames flickered to life within her. "We're out of sight," he said. "Untraceable. And I need to make a call. Got to know how those guys found us."

His words broke Sophie's sensual trance. She considered. "How did they get ahead enough to set up an ambush? We didn't choose this route until—" Sudden realization had her sucking in a breath so fast she coughed.

"Exactly. The car-rental agency." Jack handed her the phone. "Check if anybody came in asking about us."

She flipped over her map to find the phone number. When a woman answered, she began to explain in Italian. But the agent cut her off, blasting Sophie's ear with a shrill narrative before she disconnected.

"Whoa, what was that about?" Jack took the phone from Sophie's hand.

Her brain whirled from the woman's hysteria. She blinked and tried to make sense of the jumble of words. "That was one of the rental agents."

"The woman. Her soprano aria nearly cracked the phone."

"She said that right after we left two men came in and asked about the Americans and where they went. Remember we asked about a back route? When her partner didn't answer fast enough, they beat him. The police came, and the man's in the hospital." Tears welled in her eyes. "Oh, Jack, they hurt that poor agent because of us. *Because of me.*"

"Don't blame yourself, Sophie. Vadim's hit men beat the agent. You didn't."

She blew her nose on a tissue from her bag. "The two men we didn't know must've seen us enter the agency."

"And the timing explains how the ambushers got ahead of us. We bought food and had to move our luggage. We gave those dirtbags more than enough time to get in place."

"What do we—"

"Shh," Jack said, holding up a hand. "I hear engines."

Sophie pressed the damp tissue against her lips. She could barely hear the cars over her thundering heartbeat.

The whine of the bike, like an oversize mosquito, registered first. Then the lower timbre of the small cars' engines.

They zipped past, a mini parade that came and went.

A tidal wave of relief washed through her. She grabbed Jack's hand and held on tight. "They didn't stop. Maybe they didn't see this road."

"If luck is with us, they think we've headed for the *Autostrade* or Siena." He rubbed his thumb across the underside of her wrist.

The rough pad abraded the sensitive skin, but she didn't want him to stop. "What do we do now?"

"We have a look at the end of this superhighway." Grinning, he started the engine.

But rather than roll ahead, the Fiat's wheels thumped like a rabbit with a swollen foot.

"Flat tire. They looked all right before," Jack said, shifting to neutral and yanking on the emergency brake. "Maybe there's a spare."

Sophie got out of the car with him to look. Scents of rich loam and wild herbs told of wooded seclusion. Overhead the sun played peekaboo among the branches of overhanging oak trees and pines.

"Correction—tires, plural," she said, pointing. Both rear rims sat on the ground with black rubber pooled beneath them. "Guess it took a while for them to deflate."

"Damn it, there won't be *two* spare tires. We're stuck here." He scrubbed his chin and scowled at the dirt track that led deeper into the woods. "We have enough provisions in the cooler you convinced me to buy, thank you very much. Task-force emergency kit with blankets and a tarp are in the trunk. How do you feel about camping out at an Etruscan tomb?"

So relieved to be safe—for now—and pleased to have with her the regular guy instead of the grim officer, Sophie felt as giddy as a five-year-old at a carnival. She flipped her braid over her shoulder. "Well, sir, that depends on the accommodations. And the company."

"You don't suppose these tombs are haunted?"

"I'd rather have Etruscan ghosts than Mafia hit men."

And she'd be alone with Jack in this leafy bower. Why did she have to be so aware of him?

Her lost memory frustrated and terrified her. She was afraid for her life, but she trusted him to keep her safe. He was brave and caring and wounded.

Or did her feelings for him rise from more than their situation? Did fear sensitize a person?

She didn't have a clue, but she did know that his every touch, his every look, aroused her. At first he'd built an invisible shield between them, but he'd gradually lowered that barrier so he touched her constantly.

And she wanted more.

They'd found safe harbor from Vadim's thugs—just what'd she'd wanted. But was she safe from temptation?

Which was frying pan and which was the fire?

They transferred necessities into Sophie's tote. Jack carried the emergency kit and the cooler, while Sophie trudged along with her tote. With the statuette in the bottom, the bag dragged on her right arm like an anvil, but no way was she leaving Santa Elisabetta behind.

The track led uphill on deep twin ruts and ended abruptly at a whitewashed stone wall at least twenty feet high. New wooden stairs climbed about ten feet to three rectangular openings in the wall.

There was a cleared space to the side. Only a wild cuckoo's song broke the silence. A faded sign said *Parcheggio*—parking.

"This clearing'll do for a campsite," Jack said, trying to sound cheerful. His mind still heard the fear in Sophie's voice though she'd masked it with flip words.

He'd begun their journey protecting a witness who could lead him to Sebastian Vadim. But Sophie hadn't remained merely a witness to him. Saving her now had little to do with Jack's main objective and everything to do with Sophie.

She was vulnerable with a tough core and sexy with a natural naïveté, too intriguing a female for his well-being. Being with her slam-dunked him so he didn't know up from down.

A toxic mix of fear and desire churned in his stomach. He wanted this gig done, Sophie's memory back, Vadim brought down. Where the hell was the slimy diamond smuggler?

To Jack's shock, he realized he'd hardly given a thought all day to the man he'd hunted for five long years. Add a shot of guilt and fury to the acidic cocktail. Damn it, he—

A glance at Sophie beside him, pale with fear, brought him up short.

Stuff it. Sophie needs reassurance.

He turned to place a hand on her arm. Anxiety flickered in her beautiful brown eyes before she averted her gaze.

The sensation of soft skin over firm flesh seeped into his hand and stirred his blood. "I hate like hell putting you through this. I've done a piss poor job of protecting you."

She threaded her fingers with his. "Oh, no, you've saved my life four times at least. Three times while we've been on the run, including today. And the day Vadim ran me down."

He cringed inwardly. She shouldn't think of him as some sort of hero. A hero would've saved his family from a monster. "How do you know about that?"

"Officer Leoni told me. He said you chased Vadim and shot at him or else he'd have run me over to make sure I was dead or shot me." She smoothed her fingers across his scars.

Sparks flared at her touch. He huffed a noncommittal reply, then said, "We all chased Vadim that day. Not just me."

"You were the first. Don't deny it. I have confidence in you. I just can't help being scared."

"Hey, I'm scared, too." With sweat-damp curls framing her face and her clothes disheveled, she looked cuter and sexier than any woman should. He wanted to pull her into his arms and kiss her again, but he'd violated the no-touch rule too many times already.

She gave him a limp smile. Sadness swam in her luminescent eyes. "You're my rock, Jack, the one solid reality in my Swiss-cheese world. I have these big holes in my memory. Sometimes I feel like I'm walking in a barren desert, nothing for miles around me. Occasional mirages shimmer in front of me, but I can't make sense of them or connect them. You're the only support I have to keep me from running off screaming. I feel safe with you."

Touched more deeply than he dared let on, he swallowed.

He lifted their joined hands and kissed hers. "I'm trying my damnedest to deserve your confidence, lady. Now let's go see what's in those tombs."

Only skeletons of spiders and scorpions. And living ones that skittered away from the flashlight's beam. That was all that remained in those tombs.

Sophie shuddered, glad to be sitting beneath the stars that night instead of beneath the rectangular carved-stone ceiling of an Etruscan tomb. They'd spread blankets on the grass at the clearing's edge, and Jack had strung the green tarp overhead to keep off the dew.

The musty stone crypts were interesting, but less than the one-star accommodations of their makeshift camp. The three tombs were room-size, in cross shapes, with benches carved from the curving walls. The guidebook said that the benches had held the urns of ashes. Tombs on the regular tourist circuit still possessed frescoes and carvings, and later ones had sarcophagi, but these had only bare stone walls.

Cold stone walls, she remembered. The June night was blessedly cooler than the day but not cold. After a sponge bath in a freshwater spring behind the tombs, she'd donned slacks and Jack's sweatshirt for warmth and her sling for support, since she would be sleeping on the ground.

If she slept.

At every rustle in the ivy-draped blackberry bushes beside her she jumped, fearing Vadim's hired hit men had found them. Her awareness of Jack didn't relax her either.

He sat on a boulder far enough away to talk privately on his phone, a secure satellite phone—a sat phone, he'd called it. Apparently he meant to stay secure from her as well as from anyone else. She couldn't help feeling a twinge or two at his not trusting her, but she understood.

He'd shared something at least, she consoled herself. He'd failed to reach his assistant director and then called another colleague Stateside. She watched his expression and hoped for clues to what he was hearing. Did the task force find Vadim? Did they plug the information leak? If only.

He jabbed fingers through his short hair. The gesture of barely controlled anger was her only clue. Otherwise, his erect posture and his stone face, limned with shadows in the fading light, revealed nothing more than rapt attention.

Patience, Sophia Constanza. Jack would tell her what he could afterward. And she had things to tell him. Rummaging in the cooler, which had escaped bullet holes, she organized a picnic supper.

"Why have the idiots not eliminated them and brought me the package?" Sebastian Vadim's bellow blasted his new so-called assistant up against the drawing room wall. "Why am I surrounded by incompetents?"

The Sicilian don had sent this man, saying he would be totally loyal to his employer. He'd better be. His name was Ugo, which meant intelligent—a mother's futile wish, Vadim supposed, for the man was anything but.

Vadim didn't have access to all his funds, courtesy of Interpol and the Italian *polizia.* His mouth tightened at the thought. Ah, well, he would permit Ugo to remain, to please the don, but one man couldn't perform mundane chores such as going to the market as well as protection and…other duties. Vadim would have to dip deeper into a bank account the officials didn't suspect.

He deposited his shopping bag on a table. "Answer me, Ugo," he continued in Italian.

"Peggio così, signore," Ugo said. *Unfortunate.*

He was a squat man with square hands that hung loosely at his sides at the moment. Except for a wry mouth, everything about him was square—square chin, square shoulders, a flattened brush of brown hair. "Tomasso will find them. The don has contacts between Firenze and Siena. You will see."

Vadim flopped into an armchair. There were too many shadows in this gloomy room. He turned on the table lamp. "Tell him they must split up and canvass every small town that has an inn or even one or two rooms for tourists."

"*Sì, signore.*" Ugo started to leave, but turned back. "There is one more item, *signore*. A man came to the door. He said his name was Pucetti."

Vadim sat at attention. Pucetti was the artisan who had secured the uranium tube inside the statuette. Did he want more money, the greedy bastard? "What did he want?"

Ugo frowned, the effort required to remember the visitor's purpose apparently monumental. Then his thin seam of a mouth widened in a grin. "Ah, he left a message. *Un minuto.*"

Vadim tapped all ten fingers on the chair arms while he watched this worthless man search the pockets of his scarred leather vest, the pockets of his yellowing dress shirt and the pockets of his shapeless brown trousers.

Ugo held up a white sheet of paper folded in quarters. "See?" He crossed to hand the paper to his employer. "He did not trust me to relay the message. You were not here, so he wrote it down."

Vadim accepted the paper and laid it on his lap. This man should not witness any reaction he might have to the message. He would read it in private.

"You are dismissed. Take the bread and cheese to the kitchen as you go." He waved a hand in the general direction of the shopping bag.

After Ugo departed, Vadim unfolded Pucetti's note.

I beg your pardon, but I must convey bad news. I entrusted some of the work on your package to my assistant. He is my nephew, my sister's son, and you know how that is. He mixed the wrong sealant for the base. And I am not certain about the lead casing. It may not hold such heavy—

Vadim crushed the paper in his hands. He leaped to his feet. *"The seal will not hold?"* Various scenarios played in his head, all of them disastrous.

Ah, but perhaps he'd read the words too hastily or Pucetti's poor handwriting had misled him. He smoothed out the paper and peered at the inked scrawl.

He sank into the chair again. No mistake. A weak seal on the lead casing could permit contamination. The rest of the note rambled on with apologies and an offer of a refund.

He crumpled the note again. Refund? *Dak,* Ugo would bring a refund in person.

But not the refund Pucetti had in mind.

What should he do about the weak seal? He couldn't tell the men searching for the marble figure or they would quit. How long would the seal hold? Had it already loosened?

Since this quest began, he'd read about radiation. Without direct contact, the danger was less. But handle the deadly genie, let it out of the bottle, and… He shuddered, remembering all too well what had befallen Dobrich.

If the genie remained in the bottle, all might be well.

Perhaps not for the others. He smiled. Not for that irritant Thorne. And not for poor Sophie. Ah, such a waste.

But he, Sebastian Vadim, would be ready with protection.

"This better be good. I was about to break for lunch. Hey, Thorne, too much *vino* and rigatoni send you home early from your task-force junket?"

Jack closed his eyes in relief that he'd reached someone he could trust. "I'm still in Italy. I need your help, Byrne."

There was a pause during which Jack pictured the officer picking himself up off the floor.

He and ATSA Officer Simon Byrne weren't friends. Jack barely tolerated the other man's iconoclastic and cocky demeanor and he figured Byrne felt the same about him. On the recent mission Jack had headed in the Caribbean, Byrne had proved invaluable. Jack knew him to be scrupulously honest and straightforward.

Finally Byrne spoke. "Shoot."

Byrne emitted only grunts of acknowledgment as Jack explained his situation. "If I rent another car or find us a safe house, I risk exposure again. Vadim could track us by my credit card." Which was nearly maxed out. "I can't contact anyone in the task force until the damned leak is plugged. I'll do whatever it takes to keep Sophie safe."

A long, low whistle pierced Jack's ear. "Sophie, huh? Sounds like this deal's not just professional."

Jack gritted his teeth. Yeah, in more ways than one. "Will you help me or not?"

"Man, when you need help, you don't mess around. Roger. The car and the safe house are as good as done."

"Can you reach the AD or get on the leak somehow?"

"Not the AD. The mystery man is underground on some top-secret op. I got the task force on my screen. Their files are encrypted, need-to-know basis only."

"So I'm sunk."

"Not yet, ol' buddy. My personal tech goddess is right here. I might have to sweet-talk her into cracking their code. I'm putting you on hold."

The receiver hummed, and Jack thrust tense fingers through his hair. He hated counting on long-distance help, but had no choice. If anybody could penetrate the task force computers, Byrne's tech-officer fiancée was the one.

Personally Jack couldn't see the two making it—Janna the straight arrow and Byrne the rebel—but they seemed happy. Opposites attract—like him and Sophie. But that was sure going nowhere.

"Okay, Thorne, I had to promise—hell, you don't want to know what I had to promise—but Janna's gotten us in. Recent report here says Vadim's still at large, but they've narrowed the search to northern Italy."

Thank God the bastard hadn't left the country. "Copy that. What else?"

"Figuring out who's shipping info to Vadim'll take time. I'll have to get back to you."

"Negative on that. If you find out, it's better if you inform Matt Leoni. He'll clean house. Search for mention of my name, maybe on the road protecting our witness. That might lead you to the leak."

There was a long pause, then muffled sounds like a hand over the receiver. "Um, Thorne, is there something you haven't told me?"

Suspicion grabbed Jack in the gut. What was going on? "Negative. What's up?"

"They've alerted the Italian police to bring you in, by force if necessary." Byrne's tone had shifted from jovial to suspicious. "Report says you've gone rogue."

Jagged-edged fear and anger raked Jack's chest and squeezed his throat. He wanted to toss the phone into the bushes and Byrne with it. "What the hell? Just because I haven't checked in?"

"In three days. Yeah, that's part of it. Wait a minute. Here's more. De Carlo dug into your background. Who's he?"

"The task-force CO, an Italian *commissario*." Jack's chest ached with dread. The control officer hadn't wanted Jack on the team from the day he'd saved Sophie. "Go on."

"Seems he found a connection between you and Vadim, only our boy was calling himself Renzo Adrik at the time. De Carlo asserts you've gone after an old enemy on your own. What did Vadim do to you, Thorne?"

The name Renzo Adrik slugged Jack hard. He'd chased that will-o'-the-wisp for a year before he'd realized the name was an alias.

"I'm no rogue. I'm not going after Vadim alone."

And wouldn't unless he had no choice.

Gripping the phone, he dug deep for control. "I'm protecting Sophie and helping her regain her memory. Byrne, I'm still asking for your help."

Chapter 11

When Jack's call ended, Sophie watched him stalk off into the woods. Judging from his rigid shoulders and clenched fists, the purpose wasn't a call of nature.

What terrible news had the colleague told him?

She fretted, running over possibilities in her mind until Jack returned a few minutes later. His scarred hands hung loose at his sides, but he wore his official mask.

"Will your friend help us?" she asked, trying to sound upbeat and not anxious. She'd spread their food on napkins on the blanket and gestured to him to join her.

He nodded, grabbing the wine bottle and opener. "I could use a drink."

"Can you tell me what he said?"

He remained silent until he'd opened the bottle and poured the dark red wine into plastic cups. He handed her one and gulped down his own. He poured more.

"Byrne's arranging for another car and a safe house. We

can go there tomorrow. He'll see if he can trace the leak in the task force."

The vise tightening all her muscles released its grip. "Oh, Jack, that's wonderful!"

"Yeah, wonderful." But his tone and expression belied his words. He peered at the supper displayed between them. "This that Tuscan grilled chicken?"

So he wanted to change topics, did he? Okay, for now. "Yes, and there's salad and bread. I bought plastic utensils but forgot plates. I'm afraid it's a communal spread, like in medieval times."

She placed the salad container and the loaf of crusty bread beside the chicken. The mingled aromas of herbs and garlic tantalized.

They ate in silence for a few minutes. Small creatures scurried in the underbrush, stirring the scent of wild mint.

Sophie watched Jack tear at the chicken, a poor substitute for Vadim. His amber brow beetled, a sign he was working out something in his mind.

Finally she could stand it no longer. The chicken was delicious, but she could eat no more until they'd talked. She had to make him trust her enough to tell the rest. "That Swiss cheese I told you about? I've filled in some more holes."

He regarded her over a chicken leg. The marinade glistening on his lips tempted her to lick it off. "You remembered? What?"

"Maybe the day's excitement shocked my system so that memories popped up. I was washing in the spring when images that are more than mirages came back. Kind of film clips. Not everything. I remember Rome and some sights in Florence."

"Any Rinaldis or…what was the other family?"

"Pinelli." A sigh of disappointment escaped her. "No, that's still a mystery. But I also remember some of my time with Vadim."

At that, he dropped his food and wiped his mouth. His blue eyes bored into her like lasers. "If anything critical filled those holes, you wouldn't dole it out piece by piece. Tell me anyway."

"I remember the lost luggage and having my credit card cut up in the restaurant. I had Vadim's number and called him. You know the rest. He took me in. We went shopping in Venice and to the *lido,* the beach."

"At Jesolo." He scrutinized her as though searching her mind. "What about...*him?*"

She desperately wanted Jack to believe her. She wanted his trust—and more. "Vadim was generous, courteous and kind. Yes, he kissed my hand a few times, and I kissed him on the mouth. Once. That was merely a thank-you. That's all. He never hit on me. He was my host, not my lover, and I know nothing about his business."

Relief and something else flashed in Jack's eyes before he shuttered his expression to skepticism. "You filled most of the holes. What's still empty?" He picked up his wine again.

"Memories are coming back to me in chunks, but they don't include the day I was to fly home."

"The day he tried to kill you."

She sagged, wishing she could give him what he wanted. What he needed. "Right."

To her surprise and relief, Jack reached across the blanket serving as their picnic table and laced his fingers with hers. "Remembering that much is a good sign. The doctor said you might never remember the actual attack. If you've recovered this much, more of that day will return, too."

"Thanks for that. I can't prove I wasn't part of what Vadim was doing or that he wasn't my lover, but *I know.*" The great burden of guilt, heavy as the stones in one of the tombs behind them, fell from her shoulders and smashed into dust.

"I began to believe in the amnesia a few days ago. Mostly because of your distress about what you might've done. I believe you now."

The warmth in his clear gaze sent her heart tumbling. "You don't know how much I needed to hear that." Emotion clogged her throat. She slipped her hand from his and reached for the foil to cover the leftover chicken.

Wordlessly Jack took care of the salad and bread. When they finished putting away the food, he poured them both more wine. He reclined on the blanket, propped himself on one elbow and gazed up at the stars.

"This hide-and-seek with Vadim's thugs," he said, "there's something odd about it."

"What do you mean?" Pleased that he was sharing his thoughts with her, Sophie sipped her wine.

"I don't want to scare you."

"Get real, Jack. It's way too late to avoid that."

"Roger. No whitewashing. Vadim could've had his men blow us away at any time. Today Slick and his thugs shot at the car but not in the windows. Not to kill. It's like Vadim wants you kidnapped, not killed."

"He tried to kill me before. Why is it different now?"

"An excellent question. I'm working on it."

Before he drifted away from her in his thoughts, she had more to tell him, too.

"There's one more thing you should know about." Sophie reached behind her for her tote. Tipping the bag on its side allowed her to roll out the statuette. "This figure is Santa El-isabetta Rinaldi. She appears to be the only family I've found in Italy."

His eyebrows rose. "This was in your bedroom."

"There was a card with it from an antique shop. I probably bought her with a traveler's check."

She levered the little saint upright. She sucked in a breath at what she saw. "Oh, no, a bullet must've struck her. I saw the hole in the tote but didn't think anything was damaged."

She turned the marble icon so Jack could see the chip.

He peered at it and pushed on the base. It slid sideways. "The base is loose. You can get that fixed in the States. Looks like it's been repaired before. She's old."

Sophie surveyed all sides of the little saint before she nodded. "No harm done to the sculpture at least."

One side of his mouth twitched toward a smile. "Why did you keep this from me?"

She sighed as she slipped the saint back into the tote. "I was afraid you'd think I stole it from the villa."

A laugh sputtered from Jack, spraying wine onto his shirt. He mopped at the droplets as he sat up. Mirth crinkled his eyes and softened his harsh features. "*This* is all you've hidden in that tote? Your family saint?"

She straightened. Indignant, she tilted up her chin. "She's precious to me, all I have of my ancestry. And my *nonna*'s letters, they're in the tote."

"Sophie, Sophie, I should've known." He scooted closer and cupped her chin. "I was seeing everything through my own lens, a glass that distorts even the innocent."

She felt the wine-scented puff of his breath on her face and gazed into his eyes, as blue as the summer sky. If he kissed her, she'd forget what planet she was on, let alone ask what she wanted to know.

She pulled back, breaking the spell. "So now you trust me?"

His index finger traced the shape of her jaw, lighting tiny fires as it went. "There aren't too many people I trust. But yes, Sophie, you I trust. Why?"

She drew a deep breath, then dived in. "Do you trust me enough to tell me what else you learned from your phone call?"

The rising half moon filtered lace patterns through the oak leaves onto Sophie's face. The pale light didn't stop Jack from recognizing the challenge on her features.

"I saw your anger when you disconnected," she said. "You walked away to calm yourself. What is it?"

He searched for a solution in his empty wineglass. When nothing magically appeared in the residue, he set it down. "You might as well know. When I cut communication with the task force, De Carlo put out a call to have me brought in."

"Brought in? Like a criminal?"

"Exactly. He thinks I've gone after Vadim on my own." He felt he'd fly apart if he remained still another moment. He pushed to his feet and paced in their patch of moonlight. "He called me a rogue officer."

"*Vendetta,* the Italians say. Now why exactly would he think that?"

He would tell her the least he could. "He dug into my background and found I have history with Vadim. He put two and two together and got ten."

"But your friend agreed to help anyway. You told him about the leak you suspect, about why you aren't checking in?"

"I spelled it all out. He believed me, thank God. He'll do what he can to clear up this mess." He flexed his fingers, stiff from tension, and stared up at the moon. "Until then, damn it, I'm a wanted man."

He heard the swish of Sophie's shoes on the rough grass as she crossed the clearing toward him. When she took one of his hands in her soft one, sparks that had nothing to do with static electricity arced from his palm to another, more responsive body part.

Cursing his testosterone, he observed their joined hands. His scars stood out white as bone in the moonlight. Twins of the scars on his soul. Hell of a maudlin thought.

"De Carlo's not far off, is he?" she said, yanking him to attention. "I'm guessing that getting Vadim is more than a job to you. What did he have to do with the deaths of your wife and son?"

A jaw muscle he felt twitch was the only betrayal he allowed of the powerful emotions storming inside him. How could he tell her without exploding into a million pieces?

He jerked away and wheeled toward the woods. "You don't want to go there."

"Oh, but I do. Your vendetta makes this mess a wheel

within a wheel—a complex mess with circles of danger. If I'm in the center—the bull's-eye—I want to know everything."

Not much riled Sophie usually, he'd come to understand. She went along to get along, even when she shouldn't. But on this she wasn't backing down.

He shook his head. "I don't talk about it." He couldn't. The prospect of telling the story made his chest ache and every muscle in his body tense.

"Maybe you should. Holding in all that grief is eating you alive." He could hear the choked-back tears in her voice. "I care about you, Jack."

For a moment he stood silently contemplating the gloomy darkness surrounding them. Should he face the deeper shadows within him? Could he? *Moment of truth.*

Sophie knew he'd decided when his shoulders rose and fell in a shuddering sigh.

When he turned around, she saw all the pain and anguish he'd held at bay etched on his face and in his eyes. He was such a strong man, so tall and leanly muscled, not handsome but so very male.

Hating to see him suffer, she wanted to take the two steps between them to wrap her arms around him, but his rigid stance stopped her.

"Grief? You think I haven't grieved for them, for my son?" His jaw clenched as he sought control. "No, what I harbor in here—" he thumped his chest hard with a fist "—is more primitive and more savage. If you'd ever had a son murdered in cold blood, you'd know."

"Murdered," she whispered. By Sebastian Vadim? A child? Jack's pain became her pain, his anger hers, an anger so powerful that her lungs seemed filled with ashes. All at once her legs felt too weak to hold her, and she went to sit on the blanket beneath the tarp.

"You would seek vengeance at any cost," he continued, his focus inward. "You'd nurture your hatred, sharpen its claws and focus it until you could hunt down the murderer and destroy him."

She blinked back tears. "Tell me what happened."

He glanced up, seemingly surprised to hear her voice. He came to the blanket and sat on his heels opposite her. "I've never told anyone the whole story. I don't know if I can."

"Take your time. I'm here."

"Five years ago, when I was a U.S. deputy marshal in Miami, a gang sold a jewelry wholesaler some stones that were illegal diamonds from West Africa."

"Blood diamonds, mined by captives or slaves and sold for arms," Sophie offered.

"Sebastian Vadim's specialty," Jack said with a bitter laugh. "These had been cut somewhere in Europe and smuggled into the States by boat. One of the gang members flipped to the cops. They nabbed the gang and the diamonds. The ringleader was the owner of the boat, but he vanished."

"Vadim."

"Except he was using an alias, Renzo Adrik. When the case went to trial, I was assigned to protect the main witness."

"The gang member who went to the police?"

He nodded. "Vadim-Adrik got a message to me that if I didn't give him the witness, he'd hurt my family."

"Oh, Jack!" Just thinking about it made her heart ache.

His shoulders were hunched, his hands fisted on his thighs. She could see him fighting for control. "Tonia and I were separated. She and David were living in Fort Lauderdale," he said, his voice gravelly with emotion.

"David. Your son's name was David?"

"He was three, would've been four the next month. I saw him as often as I could, but Tonia and I'd been growing apart ever since he was born. She was…high-maintenance. And she said I was never there." He uttered a strangled sound that could've been a bitter laugh or an anguished cry. "She was right. In more ways than one."

Sophie wanted to ask how but felt it was better to let him tell the story his way.

"I arranged for protection, but Tonia balked at agreeing to anything I said. She and I were divorced, quits, but I loved my son."

Quits. Not just separated, but the marriage was over. Sophie tried to ignore the little bubble of relief inside her. A selfish reaction, not admirable or compassionate.

So his son's death was the true source of his grief and anger. Yes, protecting the weak was what Jack was all about. "Tell me about David."

"He was…a gift, a terrific kid, smart and happy. He threw his whole little being into everything." A wistful smile played over his mouth. "Whenever I was with him at bedtime, I had to read a Bob the Builder, only he pronounced it 'Bob the Bidder.' I was teaching him to play catch, but…" Sucking a ragged breath, he bent his head.

When he looked up, tears filled his eyes. "While the witness against the diamond gang testified on the stand, Tonia took David and slipped past the cop on duty."

"Where did she go?"

"She must've been driving to her mother's in Tampa. It was raining, one of those brief Florida squalls that seem like the whole sky is dumping on you. Reconstruction of the crash indicated she'd skidded off the road into a stand of palms. The Camry rolled over and over and landed upside down in a drainage ditch."

"An accident?"

"No. She was a careful driver. She'd've pulled off to the side and waited for the rain to clear. But there was no paint from another vehicle, no second set of skid marks. The cops knew about Adrik's—Vadim's—threat, but he was gone. There was no proof he called me or that he even existed. In the end, the crash was listed as accidental."

"Maybe it was." But she didn't really believe her hopeful words.

"I know better. He called my cell phone again. To ensure I knew they'd been forced off the road. Murdered."

Sophie's heart sank at the thought of what he'd endured. At what he still endured. A cloud covered the moon, so she could barely see him, but she heard him sniffing back tears.

He passed a hand over his eyes and inhaled a ragged breath. "I should've convinced Tonia to let the cops protect them. I should've been with them. God, they were innocent— murdered because my job put them in a monster's way." He coughed, cover for a sob. Or a howl of pain.

Sophie felt the grief and guilt emanate from him in physical waves. In his eyes, he'd failed to protect the ones closest to him. Atlas's burden was a pebble in comparison.

She squeezed his other hand. He held on, as she had done ages ago, it seemed, in the Venice hospital. That this strong man allowed her to see his pain, to see him weep, humbled her. "How did you find out?"

"When the squall stopped, a passing motorist spotted the wreck and called police on his cell phone. I heard the call in the courthouse. Got to the scene—hell, I don't have any idea how I got there. I must've driven, because ambulances and fire trucks were just pulling up when I did. I reached the car first. The doors were jammed, but I saw…oh, God, I can still see him."

He pulled away from Sophie's grip and pounded his fist on the dirt beside him.

Sophie imagined the horror he'd met and how frantic he'd been when he couldn't do anything. She blinked back tears. "Tell me. Get it out."

"Tonia was dead. Because it wasn't a head-on collision, the air bag didn't deploy. Her head hit the windshield as the car rolled. But David…David was in the back, hanging from his child seat, upside down. Blood was dripping…so much blood…but his eyes…followed me."

Sophie could barely breathe. "He was alive."

"I had to reach him." He held up his hands, curled in helpless supplication. *"I had to."*

Darkness concealed the jagged scars on his fingers, but suddenly Sophie knew how he'd gotten them. "You broke the window with your fists."

"I don't remember. The EMTs said I did. Blood was everywhere. His, mine, I don't know. Loose objects in the car had slammed into David, cut him bad. I touched his cheek. He was warm. And real. And then the life went out of his eyes. After that the EMTs pulled me away."

Sophie felt the tears bleed down her face, a red-hot stream of pain and anger. Grief for Jack's loss scalded every nerve ending.

From somewhere she dredged up what she hoped were words of comfort. "He saw you and felt his father's touch. He knew you came for him."

"Too late." His voice raspy with pain, he seemed to tear the words from his soul. "I carry his picture so I can make myself remember him laughing instead of dying."

He twisted off his knees and stretched out. "We should get some sleep. Got to meet a guy with a car in the morning." He folded his arms, then turned on his side away from her.

End of conversation.

Sophie got that. She unfolded their extra blanket and spread it over them both before she lay down. Only inches from Jack, she longed to spoon against his hard body, but she sensed he needed space and time alone.

She comprehended the savage hatred that drove Jack the father. "Was joining ATSA part of your…quest?"

Silence. She wondered if he slept, but then he said, "I told you my other reasons for going to ATSA. The main reason was that I'd have better resources for finding Vadim."

Hello. She just realized…. "Five years. Your search took five years." Five years of hell.

"He operates under so many aliases, moves around. When Interpol connected his aliases for the task force, I got myself assigned here. One way or another, Sebastian Vadim will die. If I have to, I'll kill him myself."

"Justice? Or vengeance?"

"In this case vengeance *is* justice. Sebastian Vadim understands vengeance. The diamond-smuggling gang would've been convicted with evidence from the witness I was protecting. Vadim didn't want the creep freed. He wanted revenge. Later I heard the guy'd been shanked in jail."

"Shanked?"

"Stabbed to death with a makeshift knife."

Sophie shuddered at the brutal image. She had no doubt that Jack would kill Vadim with any weapon he could, his bare hands if necessary. He blamed himself for putting his family in danger.

She understood, but vengeance had its price. Too high a price. "If he were my son, I would never give up until his killer paid. Vadim is wanted for many crimes. You said he murdered the uranium courier or had him killed. The task force will find him. He'll be punished."

"A trial and *prison?* Not good enough."

Sophie's stomach clenched as she grasped Jack's intention. "If you get back on the task force, what then?"

He twisted around to face her. Shadows hid his face, but the live-coal force of his hatred and resolve seared her. "He'll resist capture, and force will be necessary. In a firefight, he'll go down. Legit if possible. If not, I'll do what I have to do."

"You're walking a fine line between necessary force and murder. If you cross the line, the consequences—"

"Damn the consequences," he said, his voice low and gravelly. "Don't you think I know? Vengeance is my only reason for living."

"Killing him won't bring them back." She scraped at her

brain for arguments. "Is it worth giving up your life, the possibility of a new family, for revenge?" It sounded crass, but it was all she could come up with.

"No family. Even if I come out of this clean. I'll never again allow my job to put a woman—or a child—in harm's way. *Never.*" He slugged his big body over, turning his back to her, like pulling a curtain.

"But Jack—"

"Go to sleep, Sophie."

More argument would accomplish nothing tonight. She hadn't told him anything he didn't already know. His career and his freedom—and oh, God, maybe his life—would be forfeited if he killed Vadim outright. She bit her lower lip to keep from blabbing on and to hold in a sob.

Jack was a good man. Underneath his guilt and hatred remained an honorable and dedicated man, a man who could laugh and joke and who had love and loyalty to give. He kept that man under tight control, but she'd glimpsed him. That man deserved better than ruining his life for revenge.

If only she could remember that last day at the villa, if only she knew Vadim's hideout, she would try to keep Jack from crossing the line. She would help the task force apprehend Vadim.

But too much of her memory remained a blank screen.

Guilt made him think revenge was his only reason to live. She longed to show him he was wrong. But all she had to offer was herself.

And why not?

Between them flamed awareness hotter than she'd ever felt before. Every touch flared sparks within her, every look ignited flames. He wanted her as much. Simple, right? At first, maybe, but no more.

He appeared harsh, but that was his natural reserve and his dedication. His vulnerability wrenched her heart and his wounded soul called to hers with a power stronger than sex.

She'd have to keep herself under control or she'd fall in love with Jack.

No way did she need a man who locked his emotions inside. She needed no man at all before she found her own strength.

Love? No, she couldn't. She wouldn't. But…

He felt so deeply and focused so totally. Would he concentrate as fully on a woman in bed? Would he lose control in lovemaking?

Imagining Jack's hair-roughened chest against her skin, his mouth on her breast, his rigid length seeking her, made Sophie's skin itch and a pulse throb between her legs.

She was *so* in trouble.

Chapter 12

Jack opened his eyes. His hand closed around the grip of his 9mm. He drew it slowly from beneath the blanket edge and listened.

A light breeze shivered leaves and stirred scents of loam and green things. Nearby an owl hooted. In the distance, another answered.

No bad guys in the woods. He exhaled and laid down his sidearm. The luminous dial of his watch read one o'clock.

He hadn't expected to sleep, but exhaustion must've done the job. When he turned on his side, sharp twinges in back and hip muscles protested a night on lumpy ground and days of crimping his legs into a sardine can disguised as a car.

Settling again, he knew he wouldn't sleep. In the woods the night was darker than the tombs dug into the hill, but in the clearing the moon shone silver on the grass.

And on Sophie sleeping beside him.

She was facing him, on her right side, the blanket over her sling-bound left arm and tucked around her feet.

Even without the moonlight he'd recognize the curve of her hip, lush and round and womanly, not Popsicle-stick thin. And if he couldn't see her, he would know her by the rhythm of her breathing and the scent of her skin.

God, he'd told her everything. Too much. But she'd perceived his pain. In their situation, he owed her the truth.

Tonight she'd absorbed his grief and cried along with him. And he'd bawled like a baby. Damn it, he hated tears. He hated the choking feeling, the weakness.

He needed strength—*she* would need strength from him.

Sophie shifted in her sleep and then sighed, a soft murmur that jazzed his pulse.

Imagining Vadim touching her, taking her, had twisted a jagged knife in his gut. Her reassurance that she'd never been in the creep's bed withdrew that particular dagger. Relief had swept over him in waves so strong she must've noticed.

Man, he wanted her. He'd been with a few women since his wife, but those had been just for sexual release.

With Sophie, he wanted more.

Impossible. A man with no future and no right to endanger another person could expect only brief passion.

Passion that would block from his mind and soul the damned beast that drove him. Oblivion, respite, release, if only temporary—*oh, God, to forget in her arms...*

She was intuitive, smart and sensual—a woman who experienced life with all her senses and reacted without artifice. She should never play poker because all her emotions were hanging out there—happy or sad, curious or exuberant. He ached to know if she tackled sex with the same gusto.

He brushed a curl from her cheek. The thick mane had come loose. Repairing her braid in the morning was the only way he ought to touch her. Heart stumbling with desire and regret, he withdrew his hand short of contact.

"Afraid I'll bite?"

"Afraid I'll wake you." True, as far as it went. Uptight about her reaction to his meltdown was more like it.

"Too late. This rock under my hip already did the job." She edged closer to him and placed her right hand over his now-sprinting heart.

Was she offering sympathy? Damn it, pity was the last thing he wanted from her. "Look, about earlier—"

Her fingers on his lips stopped his words. "Jack, chill. You needed to let it out. Honest emotions are healing. I always feel better after a good cry."

The smile in her voice eased his coiled nerves a notch. He kissed her cool fingers. "Now you're reading my mind." God, he hoped not. His thoughts might singe her hair.

"Let's see if you can read mine." She pulled his head down and sealed her lips to his. Sweet and insistent, her tongue slipped inside his mouth and blotted out all coherent thought.

Jack cupped her rounded butt and dragged her closer, let the taste and the scent and the feel of her course heat through him, unchecked and unrelenting.

She clung to him, setting flame to the hot coals that had been smoldering since he'd first seen her.

Never had he wanted a woman the way he wanted her, now and hard and deep....

When she broke the kiss, he gasped for control but ached to ignore the alarms in his head, to ignore everything but her and the inferno they created together. "Sophie, ah, Sophie."

"Yes, I know," she said in a breathy whisper.

And then she was tugging his shirt from his jeans and running her soft hand over his bare chest.

"We shouldn't." But all the reasons they shouldn't floated out of reach like her memory mirages. All he knew was Sophie—her sweetness, her vibrant spirit, her softness.

"I know and I don't care." She had never felt this heart-slamming hunger from a kiss, this rush at the musky scent and heat of his hard body. He was as sexy as he was severe and stern. And vulnerable beneath his protective shell. Knowing he'd allowed her to see the inner man kicked her in the heart. "Make love with me, Jack."

He smoothed a hand over the swell of her hip to the heat between her thighs. Heat surged through her in ripples of desire. When she scraped her nails over his nipple, he moaned and stripped off his shirt.

She tugged at the snap on his jeans. "I want to see you, all of you."

He grasped her hand and brought it to his lips. "Don't or this'll be over faster than you can blink. I'm so hard I can barely breathe."

She sank back into the shadows. "Protection. We have no protection."

Jack produced a foil packet from his kit. He shrugged with an apologetic and very appealing grin. "Leoni slipped them in my bag. Just in case."

She grinned in return. "Thank him for me."

"I make no promises beyond tonight. You're sure?"

"I want no promises, only tonight," she lied, knowing in her heart she wanted more, much more. "Hold me, love me. Give me a new memory to brighten the darkness around us."

"No regrets," he said.

"No regrets." When she saw heat leap in the dark centers of his eyes, she ripped at hook-and-loop fasteners. "This will go a lot easier if you help me out of this straitjacket."

He slid the sling away. She wriggled out of her jeans. He helped her pull off the sweatshirt.

When he saw she was wearing only a skimpy pair of blue lace panties, no bra, he sucked in a breath. The cool night air puckered her nipples. When he palmed her breasts, the sensation zinged through her body.

"Ah, Sophie, rose-brown nipples, perfect breasts. So beautiful. *You're* so beautiful," he murmured as their bodies fitted together, skin to skin.

"You're beautiful, too." She reveled in the feel of him against her, the coarse hair on his chest rasping against her nipples, his thighs hard as boards against hers and his rampant sex thrusting the harsh denim against her belly.

Stripping away her panties, he found her with his fingers. She gasped, arching her back at the exquisite sensation. He stroked and circled and explored. She sighed and nibbled and kneaded. They kissed, hot and hungry, until neither could wait a second longer.

He kicked off his jeans and boxers, and when she wrapped her soft hand around his aching arousal, he thought he'd lift off to Mars.

She shimmied beneath him and wrapped herself around him like a ribbon of fire. Without her clothing, she was a miracle of soft curves and silken skin.

He sank into her tight, pulsing heat as blood thundered in his head and flames enveloped him, and she writhed against him with urgent pleas.

Lost in the wonder of this woman, in the perfection of their joining, in an intensity that transcended sex, he wanted the incredible rush to transport him forever, but the tide of his climax pulled at his belly and licked at his spine.

He held on until he felt her first spasms clenching at him and heard her call his name, and then his body seized up and he convulsed with her in a wrenching wave of white-hot pleasure.

The next afternoon Sophie peeled garlic in the safe-house kitchen as she watched Jack outside talking on the sat phone to his ATSA colleague. Byrne was the name, she thought.

That morning a tow truck had arrived at the tomb road with a new car, an Opel Corso, another subcompact. The driver had handed over the keys and a sealed packet, then had driven off with the bullet-riddled Fiat in tow. Among other items, the packet contained money and directions to a farmhouse in the hill town of Giordano, just south of Florence.

Farmhouse, Sophie scoffed. Maybe once but no longer. Someone with a decorator's eye had bought the stone dwelling from the farmer. With truckloads of euros they'd transformed it into an elegant country retreat, complete with new tiled floors and a modern kitchen.

A mix of antiques and clean-lined modern furniture gave the rooms a relaxing ambience. Palm trees, as incongruous as a vineyard in the East Village, grew on either side of the red front door, similar to the *Under the Tuscan Sun* house.

Jack had told her it belonged to Byrne's fiancée's parents, their future retirement home, so neither ATSA nor the task force knew about it.

The caretaker, Silvio, who lived just down the road, kept the house ready for occupation. He'd just finished weeding the flowers when she and Jack had arrived. Sophie had smelled wine on the red-faced man's breath as they'd shaken hands.

She set the garlic aside on the slate counter beside the new peas, fava beans and asparagus. Experimenting, she rotated her shoulders—both of them. No twinges in her left shoulder as long as she didn't try to lift it too high. She was fine.

Next she began to chop the leeks and peppers. She'd probably bought too much in the Giordano village market, but fresh spring vegetables were hard to resist. Sautéed in olive oil and tossed with chopped tomatoes and ziti, they would make a wonderful dish to accompany the remaining grilled chicken. She'd also purchased fresh bread and half a cream cheese tart with orange marmalade and sliced almonds.

She crossed herself and aimed a glance skyward. "See, *Nonna,* all your efforts with me in the kitchen paid off."

Outside the mullioned kitchen window, the sat phone to his ear, Jack paced in the small garden. In a navy polo shirt that clung to his muscled chest and wide shoulders, he looked so sexy and strong that heat curled in her stomach. His rugged features set in a stony expression, he punctuated his conversation with jabs of his free hand.

Maybe not bad news, but no good news, for sure.

If only she could remember the crucial day at the villa. All she seemed to be able to think about was last night.

Making love with Jack had been incredible. After the first time, they'd slept in each other's arms. The second time, he'd lifted her astride him, insisting that he was concerned about her shoulder pressed to the hard ground. The night—no, *Jack*—had been romantic and sexy and magical.

She warned herself that her aching need for him was just lust. Big-time lust, not the other L word. The heady connection, the euphoria—all that emotion was because of being thrown together in the midst of danger. What she felt couldn't be love.

It couldn't, shouldn't be. But it was.

She'd fallen in love with Jack.

Her heart swelled with tenderness. She wanted to dance a jig and weep at the same time.

Making love had been amazing, not like the few hasty, lukewarm couplings she'd experienced before. Their bodies and needs meshed as though they'd been made for each other.

In every other way, they definitely hadn't been made for each other.

She was an emotional open book. He kept his feelings locked behind a stone mask—except for anger. And hatred. Besides, they wanted different things.

She was bound to find her memory and herself, not to be responsible for others until she was ready for a family of her own. He was bound in his grief and revenge and saw no future for himself, let alone a future with her or any woman.

So she couldn't let him know her true feelings. She would cherish whatever short time they had left together. She would make the most of it. For them both.

She sighed, longing to comfort him, to help him end this

chase in a way that somehow maintained his pride and assuaged his guilt.

But what could she do?

She had no idea.

A few minutes later Jack entered the kitchen and lounged, one hip against the counter, not close enough to touch her but close enough to snag some peas.

Today he'd backed off and kept his distance. He touched her only by accident. He talked to her only when necessary. A professional mask kept his emotions hidden.

Romantic and magical had vanished with the dawn.

Were his worries about being a pariah occupying his thoughts? Was it his focus on killing his enemy?

Or was their lovemaking, the attraction between them, a one-night fling? Had he gotten from her what he wanted and now it was over? The suspicion cut deep, piercing her heart with a blade sharper than the one she stabbed into the peppers.

"Smells good already," he said. His gaze focused on the vegetables, not on her, as he stripped the purloined peas from their shells.

"Thanks. What did you find out?" She hoped her voice didn't betray her hurt. She grabbed a pepper and whacked at it with enough force to sever the cutting board.

A barely perceptible tightening of his mouth was the only indication he'd noticed. "No news on the leak. Byrne has a contact on the inside who's working on the problem."

"Someone in the Venice *polizia?*"

"Interpol. And he shook loose some agents from Interpol to round up the hit men. I should know more in a day or two. Then maybe De Carlo'll clear me."

He bared his teeth in a thin-lipped grimace no one would call a smile, then popped the tiny green pearls in his mouth.

She set down the knife before she did real damage. "But it's hard to wait and do nothing."

"I'm treading water and sinking lower all the time." Pain

clouded his eyes before he shuttered them. He cleared his throat, apparently chagrined at revealing his frustration. "I have work to do."

He turned and marched into the dining room.

Sophie noted his masked expression as he seated himself at the table with his laptop. Earlier he'd installed its small satellite dish on the roof.

She returned to her dinner preparations and turned on the faucet. Through the window she observed a flock of birds streaking over the undulating green hills terraced with vines and olive trees. She couldn't see Florence but knew the city was tucked into a valley not far away.

Farther away dangled the solution to helping Jack. Whatever the reason, his torment roadblocked the bridges they'd gradually built between them. Persuading him to abandon revenge meant an upward slog steeper than these Tuscan hills.

Jack booted up the computer. Simon Byrne had given him the codes to enter the task-force site. Maybe he could find the damned leak and clear himself so he wasn't shut out of the endgame. He logged onto Internet 2, the secure high-speed pathway only academics and government agencies could use.

He stared but saw nothing on the screen.

Saw only the hurt in Sophie's eyes when he'd walked away from her in the kitchen.

Damn it, last night had been fantastic, the best sex of his life. The best…hell, it had been more than sex. Sensual and soft, she'd given herself to him with total abandon. Her scent, the incredible feel of her smooth, glowing skin and her giving passion were imprinted on his DNA.

He'd never lost it like that—and he wanted more. Much more. He desired her still. More than before. If that was possible. He wanted to rip off that sexy sundress Vadim had bought for her, damn him, and drag her down on the kitchen floor and drive into her right now.

And if he did, the release he found in her arms, like last night, would give him only brief respite from the fire in his blood. There was no forgetting what he had to do.

He cared for her, sure.

A lot.

Forced closeness and his protective instincts. Natural enough, even the tenderness and warmth. That was all it must be, all it could be. He had no right to involve someone else in his life or in his cause.

Besides, he couldn't give Sophie what she needed. Showing every emotion—joy or sadness or passion—was alien to him. Talking about it scraped at his nerves with hundred-grit sandpaper. She crowded him too much about the maelstrom of feelings he couldn't begin to sort through.

No, he ought to leave her alone. She was safe here at this farmhouse. She was better rid of him.

He was better off concentrating on finding Vadim and killing him. If Byrne couldn't clear Jack, if the task force kept him shut out, he'd have no choice.

And there was something he was missing, a connection he ought to make, an anomaly. Emotion always interfered with analytical thinking. That's why he was missing a vital clue.

He deliberately shut out his hatred for Vadim and his scrambled feelings for Sophie and keyed in the task-force password.

"Dinner was great," Jack said. His chair scraped against the brick-colored tiles as he pushed away from the table. "Five-star rating. Leave the dishes. I'll clean up later."

Leaving an openmouthed Sophie behind him, he strode through the French doors. He inhaled deeply, but the scents of white and yellow blossoms edging the brick terrace, whatever the hell they were, didn't settle his Mexican-jumping-bean nerves. Neither did the wind's racket in the palm fronds.

He'd hurt Sophie again, damn it. She'd tried to start conversation during dinner. She'd asked about his work, about the computer search that had found zip.

God, she'd even wanted to know more about David. He'd cut her off every time.

She'd gone to such trouble to prepare a gourmet dinner, and he'd barely tasted a blasted thing. He'd just shoveled in food until he could get away.

Damn it, he couldn't hear the gentle sound of her voice without feeling sparks ignite in his chest. And lower. He couldn't stand being around her without touching her, without craving her.

Hell, he had to stop. He had more important things to think about than a woman who made him wish for a future that didn't exist.

Light from the dining room illuminated rectangles across the terrace. Sophie's shadow crossed back and forth in front of the windows as she ferried dishes to the kitchen. Maybe she would stay there and leave him the hell alone.

Fat chance.

When she opened the terrace door, he turned his back so she wouldn't see the hunger in his eyes.

"Jack." Sophie's soft hand warmed the skin of his forearm. The sound of his name on her lips soothed what he didn't want soothed.

"Look, I apologize. I'm not very good company tonight."

Her arms slipped around him. "The task force, finding Vadim, it'll all work out. I'm not foolish enough to tell you not to worry. I understand. But it's a beautiful night, and there's a big, soft bed upstairs. I'll be waiting for you." She rose on tiptoe to brush a kiss on his mouth.

Even that light touch of lips zinged heat downward, and he ached to pull her close. Instead he hardened his resolve and stiff-armed her from him.

"You *understand?* You couldn't possibly understand what I'm feeling." He shot his gaze upward to the star-filled night so he couldn't see the shock in her cappuccino-dark eyes.

"Then why don't you tell me instead of keeping that fuse burning?" Her voice went from soft to a razor edge.

Ignoring the warning bells in his head, he glared at her with the same ferocity that had cowed captured terrorists and made scumbag witnesses wet themselves.

She didn't back down. Only inches away, she smelled of flowers and spices and she gazed at him not with fear but purpose. No more amenable Sophie who gave in when pushed. Cool compliance gone, she glowed with defiance and challenge, with such intensity of emotion that he felt the heat.

Instantly his body responded. Blood pooled in his groin, and he ached to possess her. To have her elegant legs wrapped around him, to bury himself inside her, to—

He sucked in a deep breath to clear away the unwanted needs. It didn't work, but he couldn't take his eyes from her.

In the depths of her eyes he saw sympathy.

Sympathy he didn't need, didn't want. *He wanted her.* "Tell you? I can't, I—" How could he express the war waging within him?

Not in words, for damn sure.

He yanked her hard against his chest and crushed his mouth to hers. Instead of fighting, she molded herself against him and encircled his waist with her arms. Lust jolted through him. He went from fury to fevered urgency in a sizzling flash.

The lightning-bolt impact of Jack's kiss slammed Sophie's pulse to a violent pace and struck wildfire in her very core. His kiss was untamed, harsh, full of demand and desperation, and her heart sang with joy. *Not a simple fling.*

All at once Jack shoved her away.

"Don't think you can distract me with sex." He fired each word from between clenched teeth.

She reeled, breathless from the onslaught, tossed asea by his senseless accusation. "Distract you?"

The skin drew taut with tension across his cheeks, and his eyes flared with blue fire. "You can't soothe away my flipping problems by luring me to bed. It won't work. I'm no crying child to appease with origami."

"No, Jack, I didn't—"

"Honey, you can't help trying to kiss and make it all better. Those maternal instincts are too strong. You're a natural." He raked his scarred fingers through his hair.

Where had this idea come from? She shook her head to jar his off-the-wall assumption into some sense. Anger at his arrogance heated to a boil.

She poked his chest with her index finger. "Jack, you are so wrong. About me. About everything. If you think I'm offering myself to you to soothe your wounded soul, you're *pazzo da legare!*" She folded her arms and glared back at him with matching heat. "*Pazzo* means—"

"I don't need a damn translation for that one, thank you very much." He turned on his heel and stalked away. "I'm going for a walk. *Alone.*"

Hugging herself, she shivered in spite of the warm night air. Tears burned the backs of her eyes.

"Gee, that went well."

She watched his long-legged stride carry him into the gloom. A natural? Was she fighting her own nature? He couldn't be right about her. Could he?

"I'll be waiting for you," she whispered.

Chapter 13

Sophie stayed up as late as she could, trying to occupy herself productively but mostly pacing and watching for Jack. Then she lay awake in the master bedroom's king-size bed. He hadn't returned when she finally fell asleep.

The next morning she came downstairs to find the dishes done, as promised, and the man hunched over his laptop and his coffee. He looked as though he hadn't slept at all.

He'd dumped his duffel bag in another bedroom, but that bed hadn't been mussed. She'd looked.

She started to ask if he was all right, but the rigid set of his shoulders warned her to leave him alone. He needed to work things out in his mind and heart.

In the kitchen she poured herself some coffee and popped slices of the wonderful crusty bread she'd bought into the toaster. Humming, she pulled eggs from the fridge and began to organize an omelet.

Outside, a small engine coughed to life as Silvio started

mowing the grass. Sophie waved and the portly man waved back. The mower's path resembled the curvy hill roads.

A little morning libation before work. Unusual. Although Italians enjoyed their wine, they frowned on intoxication.

Turning, she peeked at Jack over her coffee mug. He was bent even lower over the keyboard.

Trying not to notice her.

She'd figured out last night that he walled himself off from her because he cared for her but didn't want to. Ah, well, she had the same problem and her own issues, but without the torment raging inside her that he had.

During those hours she'd waited for Jack, she'd found a direction for self-discovery. He'd set her up on his laptop with a guest password, so she conducted a search for Santa Elisabetta Rinaldi.

On three different Web sites she'd found two dozen Saint Elizabeths from everywhere—Saint Elizabeth of Prague and Saint Elizabeth of Hungary and Saint Elizabeth the Recluse among them. Only three had been Italian. None a Rinaldi.

She wasn't giving up. There were other Web sites and more lists. She'd search again today. The next day if necessary.

Jack's gibes about her natural bent picked at her brain. Was he right? Or did she nurture and teach because there was no other choice?

The talents of her mom and her sister—the ambitious ad exec and the teenage artistic slacker—shone no light on her soul. Searching her roots brought her to Italy. Santa Elisabetta would guide her, would give her a sign. She hoped. Anyway, Mom would want the history of the family saint.

Her brain strain hadn't filled the remaining gaps in her memory either. Even if she remembered that last day, there was no guarantee she knew where Vadim might be or what he'd told her or anything helpful. And she was no closer to stopping Jack from ruining his life.

There was nothing she could do for now.

All she could do was give Jack space.

She managed to tempt him with her cheese-and-vegetable omelet, but he barely spoke to her. He spent the day working on the computer or talking to his contact on the sat phone or walking the hills, his gait restless and charged with turmoil.

When Jack wasn't using the computer, Sophie returned to her search for her family saint. Later, she sat in the sun with a Donna Leon mystery from the house's extensive library, but she couldn't concentrate, so she relived her recovered memories of Italy and hoped for a breakthrough on the memories still hiding somewhere in her brain.

No luck. With the saint or with the memories.

In the evening, he wouldn't let her cook but insisted they walk to the village trattoria for dinner.

As usual, Sophie translated and chatted with the villagers while Jack observed.

Boh, she got it. Surrounded by strangers, he didn't have to talk to her over a meal.

On the return to the house she noticed that the day's puffy cotton-ball clouds had left, driven out by charcoal-rimmed monsters. The air pulsed, alive with electricity. Maybe Jack wouldn't go out.

She was wrong. He left her at the door.

The wind fretted and tossed, rattling the palm fronds like dry bones. It shrieked under the stone house's eaves.

Around midnight, raindrops as fat as ripe plums splatted against the windows in a syncopated rat-a-tat. Lightning forked and cannon volleys rolled over the hills.

Sleepless and tense with worry, Sophie curled up on the chaise by the bedroom window to watch for Jack's safe return.

Jack stared at Sophie with aching eyes and a leaden heart, imprinted the image on his brain so he would have her goodness to sustain him.

She slept with her head propped on the chair arm, a light blanket across her legs. The bedside lamp haloed her dark hair in gold, but her face was in shadow. Beside her on a tiny round table stood her saint statuette, keeping watch over her while she watched for him.

Warmth curled in his chest and spread outward, leaching the chill from his wet skin.

How late did she sit there until even the lightning and thunder couldn't keep her awake? He was a thoughtless jerk who didn't deserve her worry. Half the night he'd spent in the shed garage talking to Byrne on the sat phone.

She'd left towels by the kitchen door for him. He didn't deserve that kindness either, but he'd sure been glad to see them when he'd dragged in. He'd left his sopping T-shirt and sneakers in the utility tub and dried himself with one.

He rubbed his dripping hair with another now and stared out the window at the storm. Jagged bolts speared the ground right outside the house. He'd made it to the house just in time to miss being fried. The exploding thunder shook the house and vibrated Jack's bones.

Italy sure as hell knew how to stage a sound-and-light show. Emotional and extravagant, like the Italian character.

Like Sophie.

Looping the terry length around his neck, he stared at her, ached to hold her, to spend his passion inside her welcoming body.

Hell.

He should head down the hall before he woke her.

During his solitary treks he'd made some connections he hadn't before. Byrne had told him a snitch had a line on Saqr's plans for the uranium. His other news set up his next steps to get to Vadim. And they didn't involve Sophie.

She was safe here. He should leave her the hell alone. He turned to go.

"Are you all right?"

Her soft voice glued his bare feet to the wood floor. "No lightning strikes."

She tossed aside her cover, and he recognized the yellow pj's he'd helped her into their first night on the road. The cropped top and low boxers revealed her warm-honey skin and killer legs. Her hair fell in sensuous waves across her shoulders. His Venus.

No, not mine. He couldn't let himself even think it.

She left the chaise and padded barefoot over to stand at the foot of her bed. "The gods wouldn't dare. You'd probably heave lightning bolts back into the sky."

He winced at the truth of her assessment. The concern and tenderness in her eyes shattered his good intentions.

His treks had cured his indecision, but they hadn't cured him of Sophie. He'd tried to concentrate on his enemy, but inevitably thoughts of her had shoved the others aside. Soon he would have to leave her, but now…

A scalding sea of fury and desire swirled in the vicinity of his heart. Every muscle in his body strained with tension. What if she refused him? "I said some things…."

"So did I. It doesn't matter." Arms inviting, she took a step toward him.

In two strides he reached her and held her close, breathed her unique woman scent, the fragrance of her skin, of her hair.

God, she felt good. Fantastic.

He tunneled his fingers through the dark luxury of her hair and drank from her lips. He could never get enough of this woman. "I tried, but I couldn't stay away from you."

"I know." She skimmed her hands up his belly. In her eyes he saw the same fever that burned in his soul.

Jack was harder than the stone walls, but he couldn't, wouldn't take advantage. Gritting his teeth against his pounding need, he held her away from him. "Sophie, I can't give you more than sex."

"I know that, too. I'm not looking for long-term. First I need to make a life for myself. If all we have is now, why not? *Spogliati.*"

"What's that? Throw caution to the winds? Go for it?"

She gazed at him from beneath lowered lashes. "*Spogliati* means *take off your clothes.*"

His blood-starved brain needed a moment to process. As her words made sense, amusement bubbled up like champagne. He sputtered a laugh.

She tackled his jeans snap. "You're getting me all wet. See?" As demonstration, she took a step back.

The wet denim had soaked the fabric to transparency. Damp cotton molded to her gently rounded stomach and outlined the dark triangle at the apex of her thighs.

His stomach twisted and coiled with need. He stripped off his jeans and boxers, and his arousal sprang free.

Lightning strobed the bedroom window. The flash rimmed her hair with fire and set him ablaze. Thunder cracked overhead and rumbled deep in his body.

His hands shook. "Sophie." God, he loved the sound of her name, the taste of it, a sweet whisper on his lips.

She flicked open the top button of her pajama shirt. Then the next. And the next. The folded edge fell back to skim the inner curves of her breasts.

When she dropped the thin shirt and bottoms to the floor, the dam broke on his control. He crushed her silken body to his and rubbed his chest against her firm breasts. He rocked his mouth over hers, and she molded her lips to his with a sexy moan. He rubbed the dusky nipples, puckered to hard points. She was sweet and tart and light and heat, and he craved her as a drowning man craved air.

Blood hammered in his head louder than thunder. "I need you, Sophie."

I need you. His words streaked joy inside Sophie. But did she want to be needed? She refused to examine it.

"I'm here." She stepped backward, pulling him down on the cool sheets with her.

He groaned his pleasure, his hard body pressing her into the soft mattress.

The skin-to-skin crush sent shock waves through her. Her heart went wild, and heat surged in her blood. Their tongues dodged and darted, coaxing and caressing. She rubbed her fingers over the coarse golden hair and smoothed her hands over the contours of his muscles. When she scraped her short nails down his lower spine, his growl of satisfaction reverberated inside her.

His hand slid across her abdomen and between her legs, to the slick folds that swelled for him. She shuddered with delight. He kissed her neck, licked at her needy nipples, then slid lower to find her with his tongue.

Pleasure speared her and tension coiled in her belly. "Now, Jack, now!"

In the next flash of lightning she saw a glint of foil. And then she took him into her body, and he stilled, his jaw clenched, straining for control. As the storm crashed and boomed outside, a raw jolt of power shot through her center that clenched and unclenched her muscles around him. Currents of sensation took her, tossed her, and she cried out his name.

A shudder rippled through him. "Sophie, Sophie, I've never felt like this. Come with me." And he began to thrust, plunging deep and pulling out, hot and wild and surging faster and faster.

She gripped his shoulders, writhing beneath him, breathing in gasps. Shivers pulsed inside her, sparks fired, shimmers lapped higher, higher. The storm slashed its fury at the windows. The cataclysm rolled through her and burst into white, pulsing shock waves as he spasmed with her, his big body shuddering uncontrollably.

They lay panting, wrapped together, joined as one, while they recovered from the storm.

"Damn, did I hurt you?" Jack said, rolling to the side and

smoothing back her hair. She couldn't see his eyes in the dark but felt the worry in the bunched muscles of his arms. He held her as though she were made of glass.

"I'm fine. More than fine." She turned on her side. Snuggling closer, she cupped his beard-roughened chin with her hand. "I think we were competing with the storm."

He chuckled, and the tension eased in the bicep beneath her head. "Nice bed. Beats the hard ground at a tomb." He drew one hand down the curve of her breast, to the indent of her waist and over the flare of her hip.

She sighed with delight at the feel of his rough hand. "I don't think that's the bed you're feeling."

"Better than a bed." He rolled on his side to face her and kissed her with a promise of more to come.

The lazy sweep of his tongue stirred a curl of need through her blood. She had thought she was thoroughly sated, but she wanted him again. And he wanted her, judging from the hard length pressing into her belly.

"Sophie, listen. The storm's past. It's just raining lightly. We can take it slow and easy, like the rain."

"Slow and easy," she agreed, but when he slid inside her, shock waves of need vibrated out to her fingertips.

"The clock is ticking, Sebastian."

"*Dak,* Ahmed. I know." Vadim gritted his teeth. The unconscious use of Cleatian could betray his anxiety. He had to be more careful, choose his words with caution. "My men have experienced difficulty. This American agent is slippery. I will have the package by Saturday. You can be certain."

"You have made such promises before. Was there not a play about a merchant of Venice who would extract a pound of flesh? I hope this situation will not come to that."

Vadim swallowed, schooled his voice to remain even. "I will bring the package to London myself." With the authorities looking for him, he didn't know how he might accomplish that, but it should calm his old friend.

"You have until Monday to turn over the package."

When he heard a loud click, Vadim also disconnected.

Monday.

Until then, he must maintain complete security. No one must find him. Not this task force. Not Ahmed Saqr.

Then, with or without the uranium, he must disappear.

By morning the rain had rolled northward, leaving the sky washed clean for clear blue skies and baking sun. Jack and Sophie made love again, with the sunlight streaming its blessing in the window.

They spent the day together. Jack invited Sophie to accompany him on his hill trek. He didn't resist when she coaxed him to talk about David.

She told him about her family, her stubborn sister and her mother, whose goal was to be CEO of the company where she worked. The corporate rat race wasn't for her, Sophie insisted, but what lay ahead for her remained murky.

Jack had a good idea about that, but she needed to find her path herself.

As darkness swallowed the watercolor-daubed sky, he tossed his duffel into the Opel's backseat.

He glanced at the closed front door and pictured Sophie in the dining room, at her saint search, fruitless so far. He was beginning to wonder if the antique-shop purchase was a fake. Another scheme set up by Vadim. A way to ingratiate himself into her bed.

Another nail in the dirtbag's coffin. Even if it hadn't worked.

The car key jabbed his palm, and he forced open his fist.

He'd told himself one more night with Sophie would be enough.

Wrong. The emptiness in his heart proved him a liar.

A thousand nights wouldn't be enough.

He dreaded saying goodbye, explaining why he had to leave her at the safe house alone.

But he couldn't stay. Especially after last night. More involvement with her would soften his resolve and be unfair to her. Maybe he could leave a note and just drive away.

Hell. He couldn't be that big a jerk. He owed her a face-to-face explanation. And reassurance.

When he turned back to the house, he found Sophie waiting in the doorway.

"I wondered if you were leaving without me." Her half smile and sad eyes said she suspected he was.

Two shiny clips caught back her hair, leaving curly wisps around her face and the rest on her bare shoulders in dark waves. Her crossed arms drew his gaze to the plumped mounds of her breasts in the V-neck sundress. She looked sexy as hell but determined, not the fey-looking fragile creature she usually appeared. Not Venus but an Italian Valkyrie.

Instead of chasing this bad guy, he'd rather carry her up to bed and take up where they'd left off this morning. But her little hum of impatience said she was waiting for his answer.

"I'm leaving, but not without telling you goodbye." His chest tightened at his glib words.

She sauntered closer, hips swaying, and challenged him with flashing eyes. "Sweet. That makes a mega difference."

Sophie's rare sarcasm speared him in the chest. Damn it, he was doing it this way to protect her. He felt his cheeks heat, jammed his hands in his pockets so he wouldn't reach for her. "I had word from Byrne last night. They've rolled up two of the Mafia thugs."

"Rolled up? You mean arrested?"

He nodded. "The motorcyclist and his buddy in the Fiesta. When they started asking around about two Americans, suspicious locals called the *polizia*. Byrne's cooperating Interpol agents stepped in."

"Now they'll find Sebastian Vadim?"

"Not that easy. Byrne said Tomasso—that's the man we called Slick—hired them as backup. They know squat about Vadim." He knew disappointment roughened his tone. Waiting for the next question, he held his breath.

"What about Slick—uh, Tomasso?"

"That's what I was coming in to tell you."

She arched one dark eyebrow and cocked her head, not giving him an inch. Where was the sweet, compliant Sophie? This Sophie was breathing fire that singed his skin and heated his blood at the same time.

He huffed out a sigh. "I talked to Byrne again just now. One of the hired thugs said they were supposed to meet Tomasso tomorrow morning in a hill town in this area. If I can grab him up, I might be able to get to Vadim."

"You, not Interpol." She rolled her eyes and gestured with both hands in expansive Italian fashion.

"They'll back me up if I need it. The other thugs were flashing a photo of you."

A thoughtful frown creased her brow. "Vadim had a camera when he took me sightseeing. I'm still fuzzy, but I remember that much."

"Makes sense. But they might not know what *I* look like. This Tomasso won't expect me to be alone." Finally, after some fast talking, Byrne had agreed to support Jack's plan. So with Sophie why did he feel like a kid conning his mom into buying him a pet boa constrictor?

"Tomasso might not even know where Vadim is." She heaved an impatient sigh. "Any more than I do."

"Vadim's rent-a-gorilla is a hell of a lot more likely to know where his boss is than you do. I realized it while I tramped those damned hills. Of all the houses Vadim owns or has access to, how could you know which one he's gone to ground in? And who's to say he hasn't moved ten times in the last two weeks?"

"Then why does he want me dead?"

"I think you know where the uranium is. There's some connection we're not making. Some clue we—*you're*—missing."

Tears sheened her eyes, but she jutted her chin up in defiance. "Don't you think I'm trying to remember?"

"Aw, Sophie, I'm sorry." He pulled her into his arms and did what he itched to do. He smoothed a hand over her back, threaded fingers through her silken hair and inhaled her unique scent, better than flowers. "I know you'd remember if you could."

"I go over and over in my mind what I do remember, but it doesn't help," she said, her breath warmly damp through his shirt. "Nothing connects. I see images of the two weeks at Vadim's villa. They're like clips from a weird, disjointed indie film."

"There's some clue I should bing on. I feel it in my gut. Something that bothers me, but I can't nail it down."

She gave her head a small shake, as if dismissing her distress. She stepped out of his arms. "This thug Tomasso is not Vadim. Can't you let Interpol or the *polizia* arrest him?"

"Don't you get it? I can't stand hearing long-distance about what's going on. All this damned marching in place has stretched my nerves until I feel like I'll snap like last night's lightning. I won't let Vadim get away." He punched the air in frustration.

Her gaze softened, and she slipped her arms around him. "You need to *do* something, to be in the action. I understand. But you're *not* going to leave me alone here."

He ought to just go, but she felt so good. He placed his hands on her shoulders. "You'll be safe. Nobody knows about this house."

She threw back her head and laughed. "Jack, *everyone* knows about this house. The whole town knows two Americans are staying in this farmhouse. What if Tomasso gets away and comes here? What if you don't return?"

The band around his chest tightened, but he wouldn't let

her dissuade him. "I won't take you along on an op. That's just plain nuts. The town where I'm headed is having a big market-and-antiques day. Hordes of shoppers. Too dangerous for you with that many people around."

"No way, Giovanni. I'm coming with you."

"What the hell do you think you're going to do?"

"For one, you don't speak Italian."

That hit too close to the mark, but he'd get around that problem. "Damn it, woman. I'm a trained operative."

"He's not looking for you. He's looking for me. I can be the bait. Let me help."

"Negative. I'll be back in a day or so. I'll leave you my other cell. Byrne is number one on the speed dial."

"*Magnifico.* A man thousands of miles across the Atlantic will save me if you miss Tomasso and he shows up here. Negative back at you, Jack. If you don't take me, I'll find a way to follow you. Arturo will let me borrow his *fruttivendolo* truck or Bianca at the trattoria will lend me her Renault."

Arguing would achieve nothing except sear his belly with acid. She didn't know where he was headed. He had to call her bluff.

Ducking his head so he wouldn't see the thunderbolts shooting from her eyes, he opened the car door. As he began to fold himself into the driver's seat, Sophie's voice stopped him faster than a stun gun.

"Fiorasole isn't far away. I'll see you there."

Chapter 14

Sophie nearly wept with relief that her words had stopped Jack. Now she had a better chance to convince him that he had no alternative but to let her help. If he found this Tomasso and learned Vadim's hideout, he would try to kill him.

But not with her glued to his side.

"How do you know the name of the market town?" He stalked around the car to confront her, fists on his lean hips.

Was it anger or resignation that deepened his voice and tightened the skin across his cheekbones? Her heart thudded, but she knew he'd never hurt her. She wouldn't back down.

She drew her lips into a satisfied-cat smile, although trepidation churned her stomach. "The Fiorasole Market Saturday is a big event in this area. Everyone goes. There are flyers all over Giordano advertising it."

Linking her arm with his, she began to stroll toward the back garden. When he didn't resist, she knew she'd won. She resisted a sigh of relief.

On the terrace she turned to him, flattening her palm over his scudding heart. The fragrance of oleander and spiky yellow broom wrapped around them in the encroaching dusk. "Stay here tonight and make a plan. We'll go to Fiorasole together tomorrow. It'll be all right. You'll see."

"You're not going to stop me from getting Vadim."

His perception shouldn't surprise her. He read people well. She might as well own up. "I intend to try. If you go after Vadim and kill him, supposing you live, you'll never find peace."

"Maybe not. But I will have kept my promise to my son and his mother. My pain will be eased."

His words tore at her heart. "I know about revenge, a poison deep in Italian roots. Revenge doesn't heal. Revenge only pollutes grief and infuses more pain."

He tilted his head and regarded her with too-sharp awareness. "You sound like the voice of experience. What revenge is in your past?"

No sidetracking allowed. She would save Great-Uncle Vinnie for another day. "*Hello,* we're talking about you, Jack. Not about me."

"*Hello,* but we *are* talking about you." He lifted her hand to his lips. Anxiety filled his eyes. "Don't ask me to dangle you on a hook. Byrne checked out this Tomasso. He's a soulless killer who works for a Mafia don."

Picturing the man, his dead eyes and his predatory demeanor, she shuddered, and not from the sensual touch of Jack's lips on her palm. The taste of fear was acrid on her tongue. Fear grabbed her by the throat. Fear could drag her down, but she wouldn't acquiesce.

"This situation's not the same, not like your family. I'm already in danger because of something I may know. Sebastian Vadim is responsible, not you."

"Damn it, I know that. But I care about you. A lot. Not to mention that you're a civilian under my protection, not a professional operative. What kind of protector throws his charge to the wolves?"

"A smart one who sees he has no choice?"

He emitted a growl from between clenched teeth and brushed a kiss on her lips. "A cornered one who has no choice. I must be—what did you say, *pazzo?* That means crazy, but what's the rest of it?"

"*Pazzo da legare.* It means tied up, ready for the loony bin. I didn't really mean it."

"Yeah, right. But this *pazzo* decision verifies it."

"So you'll agree? You'll let me help set the trap?"

The warmth of his smile wrapped around her. He cradled her head between his hands, curling warmth from her scalp down through her body. "I'm damned impressed at your courage. Yes, sweet Sophie, tomorrow we're partners."

"Partners," she agreed as he rocked his mouth over hers.

Courage? Sophia Constanza Elena Rinaldi, brave? She didn't feel brave. Fear chipped at her mind. Panic pounded with every beat of her heart. Perhaps Santa Elisabetta would give her the strength she would need tomorrow.

For tonight, the bliss of being in Jack's arms would block the fear.

On Saturday morning Jack and Sophie drove the fifteen kilometers to Fiorasole.

Beside him, outwardly calm and eager, Sophie gazed out at the vineyards and farmhouses. She wore sunshine-yellow—guaranteed to catch Tomasso's eye—a bright twisty thing on her French braid, a sleeveless top, loose-fitting capris and canvas shoes called espadrilles, the only footwear in her classy wardrobe she could run in.

He hoped like hell she wouldn't have to run.

Sophie was throwing herself into the Colosseum with a Mafia beast, with Jack as her sword-bearer. Byrne and his Interpol pals had thumbed-up the plan in true Roman fashion.

Jack had her back, but damn, Sophie wasn't an operative, and his gut said the danger in this arena was too great.

At first, the venerable market town looked benign and picturesque—wrought-iron gates, colorful doors and shutters, a couple of crumbled Etruscan tombs—and deserted. On the cobblestone through street Jack saw two small children kicking a soccer ball. Nobody else in sight.

When he braked the Opel at the piazza blocked off for the market, he nearly turned around and aborted the op.

Vendors' stalls and wagons, crammed with what appeared to be complete stores of wares, lined the piazza from entrance to the far end. On the left side, stragglers filled the steps of the redbrick *duomo*—a Romanesque gem, according to Sophie and her guidebook. A buzz of voices—vendors hawking their wares and shoppers haggling prices—assaulted his ears as soon as he doused the engine.

Abort the op? He couldn't.

He needed whatever scraps about Vadim that Tomasso knew. Compromising Sophie's safety for that purpose birthed a second clawed beast to rampage in his chest. Rubbing his sternum was an automatic reaction—as if that had a chance in hell of easing his dread.

"What's the matter?" Sophie's hesitant question betrayed her anxiety.

Anxious didn't begin to name the beasts in his chest. "This place is a circus and a beehive all rolled into one. Swarms of people. Stacks of crap as far as the eye can see. A maze of aisles."

Her eyes sparkled with anticipation, but her forehead crinkled with anxiety. "It reminds me of the Macy's after-Christmas sale. Only there's much more."

"This setup is worse than I expected. If Tomasso grabs you, some bozo with a side of pork or an antique lamp might block my way. Sophie—"

She squeezed his forearm where muscles jumped from white-knuckling the steering wheel. "Jack, you have everything set up. I'm wearing an earpiece transceiver and a button like yours—" she fingered her lapel pin "—and I have the mini flashlight hooked to my waistband. You won't lose me."

He jetted out a long breath, calming himself, cloaking himself with the job. If things turned sour, he could abort at any time. "Interpol's in place. I got the go-ahead." He touched the tiny transceiver hooked on his ear.

They'd worked out procedure and communications last night between calls to Byrne, whom he would owe major favors when he returned to the States. The Global Positioning System buttons and communication equipment had been delivered to him in the same envelope with the Opel's keys. The flashlight contained a panic button. From a command post nearby, Interpol was monitoring their locations on GPS. Jack could communicate with both via his lapel mic.

"Remember, stick to English so I can follow."

"Andiamo," Let's go, Sophie said with a teasing grin, but her hand shook as she slipped the straps of a cloth shopping bag over her arm.

He wanted to hold her tight, to tell her…to tell her…

Hell, he had no business making this personal. "Roger that."

After they left the Opel, Jack watched as Sophie ambled toward the crowded marketplace. She stopped at the first stall, where an entire roast pig stared glassy-eyed from a slab. The vendor—porky himself with little eyes in a fleshy face—sliced hunks of meat for another shopper to take home.

Moving on, Sophie turned and waved at Jack. He re-turned the farewell and turned away. Losing sight of her for even a nanosecond stung his nerves like bites from Florida fire ants.

He sauntered through the open door of the bar behind him. Shortly, an espresso in hand, he slipped out the back. Gulping down the brew as the Italians did slammed his system with caffeine. The potent stuff could power the Mars probe.

After leaving the shot-size cup on a barrel by the door, he jogged past the trash cans into the back street and circled around. Three shops down, Jack ducked through another shop and returned to the marketplace.

The shops on that side of the piazza occupied an ochre-brick building fronted with a colonnade. He lounged behind one of the columns and hoped he was inconspicuous. His height made that problematic, but remaining on the fringe was his only option. His position kept him out of the sun, but the day's heat and his stinging nerves dappled him with sweat.

He listened through his transceiver as Sophie bargained with vendors in a mix of English and phrase-book Italian. Her beauty and waifish vulnerability charmed the men. Her warmth won over the women. By the time she'd made her way down the aisle, she'd acquired more free samples than purchases.

And no Mafia hit men.

Thank God.

Jack rolled his shoulders. He wanted this possible lead to Vadim but not at the expense of Sophie's life or safety. If the rent-a-gorilla showed up—

Priorities, damn it. What the hell was wrong with him? He knew what had to be done. But a spiked pang had him rubbing his sternum again.

As Sophie made her way to the produce section, she began to relax. All around her thronged villagers and travelers, women and children, farmers and merchants—no Mafia hit men.

Yet. *Be alert, Sophia Constanza.*

Pretending to survey the scene around her, she swept the crowd with a searching glance. Jack had disappeared, as planned, but he was watching from cover, also as planned. She tried to prop up her courage with that thought.

Beside her a blond woman in a chic gray suit discussed a legal case with a man who'd just stepped out of *GQ*. The woman's demeanor conveyed cool confidence and expertise.

Yes, a professional who knew her role. A lawyer, a woman who'd found her calling and made a life for herself.

"*Mamma, Mamma,* come look!" A scabby-kneed little boy about five yanked at the blond woman's skirt.

She has a child? Sophie pretended to examine a head of lettuce while she observed the tableau with fascination.

Lawyer sophistication dissolved into maternal smiles. The woman knelt and hugged her son. "Yes, Emilio, what treasure have you found?"

GQ man frowned with what seemed mock ferocity. "We came here for fresh fruit and vegetables, not toys."

Little Emilio tugged on his hand. "No toys, *Babbo.* A man has puppies! Black-and-white ones."

The boy used the Tuscan term for *Daddy.* Sophie gaped as the laughing parents allowed their son to lead them away to temptation. No mistake—they were a family.

She replaced the lettuce and sorted through the pears. Well, lawyers had families, too. The woman must've established her career first.

Maybe. Probably.

Then again, it could happen the other way around.

Sophie wanted a family, too, just not yet. Still, if Jack let himself love her, could she give up her dreams?

Would she have to? Did independent have to mean alone?

"*Signora,* you want?" The vendor, a red-faced woman in an equally crimson apron, smiled and slanted glances at the pears Sophie was mangling.

"*Oh, sì, sì, mi dispiace.*" Fumbling in her purse, she managed to find the right euros to pay the woman. Uh-oh, she'd apologized automatically in Italian. With a shrug she decided that even the casual American tourist would know that much.

As she strolled down the next aisle with three bruised pears in her shopping bag, Sophie felt a chill in spite of the day's heat. Without turning around, she knew someone was following her.

Jack hustled behind another column and spotted Sophie in the throng. The yellow outfit gave her the visibility he'd hoped. She shone brighter than the Tuscan sun baking the piazza. From his vantage point he had a clear view as she strolled farther away from him. The side aisle's wagons and stalls appeared to hawk mostly T-shirts and linens.

When Sophie stopped before a stall, scarves and lengths of cloth that might be curtains or tablecloths floating from awnings blocked Jack's view. Damn, he could hear her but not see her. Not good enough.

He sidled around the piazza to the end of the colonnade. At the corner he caught glimpses of her through the waving fabrics—enough to satisfy him she was still safe.

Sophie thanked the vendor and was about to leave the booth when a raspy male voice murmured something in Italian. A display piled high with T-shirts hid the speaker from Jack, but the man's threatening tone hiked his pulse.

Before Jack could move for a better view, he heard Sophie. "What are you doing? Take your hands off me!"

The menacing voice again, in hesitant, heavily accented English, said, "You come. No trouble."

Jack's adrenaline spiked. The game was on.

But damn it, he couldn't see them for the crush of people and the angle.

The steady chorus around Sophie told him no one noticed that this man was kidnapping her. People seemed to be caught up in their own business. Italians were used to pushing and shoving.

But he slowed his pulse with one thought—witnesses would deter overt violence.

Into his mic Jack said in a low voice, "Tomasso has approached her. I'm moving in."

"Copy that," came the French-accented reply. "I 'ave 'er on the screen. Heading toward the *duomo*. Backup on the way."

Jack signed off, checked his weapon and started edging in the direction his contact had indicated.

Sophie's sharp intake of breath came next. "Is that a gun in my ribs?"

"No talk. You come."

The edge of fear around Sophie's bravado squeezed Jack's heart. No panic. She had the presence of mind to let him know Tomasso had a gun. Jack shoved emotion away, concentrated on control and experience.

Sophie and her captor came into sight. He saw them making their way toward the *duomo*'s open doorway.

Jack began to step from his shelter toward the market.

Cold steel pricked his neck.

He froze in place.

Jack, where are you? Sophie's mind screamed.

Terror constricted her throat. The oxygen in the crowded piazza seemed insufficient as she fought for air. Even if she could drag in enough breath to yell, she couldn't scream bloody murder. Tomasso would run away, and they'd lose him. She had to cooperate.

Maybe Jack hadn't heard her before. The mic wasn't working or his transceiver was turned too low.

Slowly she slid her left hand to her waistband, toward the panic button on the flashlight.

"What you do?" The man's words spat at her like bullets from his pistol. "Put hands down."

He hustled her up the *duomo* steps and inside.

"Why are we going into the church?" she managed to gasp out before the heavy wooden door slammed shut behind her.

Jack rammed back with one elbow as he went for his Glock with the other. A hard body shoved him against the column. His head cracked against the stone. Ignoring the clanging pain, he fought off waves of dizziness.

His attacker had been ready for a countermove, Jack realized as the man relieved him of his Glock. The knifepoint stung. This time it drew blood.

"Andiamo al duomo," the man said, his breath a rancid stench of garlic and dental neglect. *"Subito."*

To the church. Now. Jack knew enough Italian for that.

He got the picture. Tomasso had a new henchman, a man who'd been watching for Jack. Jack had been watching Sophie's back but not his own.

Fury drummed down his nerve endings. Fury at himself for allowing emotion to interfere with proper procedure. He'd conducted surveillance like an amateur.

Resisting Rot-Breath, even if he took him down, meant Tomasso would get away with Sophie. Sweat dripped down his forehead and stung his eyes. He had to keep cool and obey.

Rot-Breath would take him to Sophie.

Then he would come up with other options.

As he let the goon march him toward the *duomo,* Jack scanned the market. Only locals—women and children, robust farmers in rough country clothes.

Where the hell was his backup?

Inside the massive brick church Sophie shivered in the cool air. Candles' waxy scent and the musty odor of centuries-old mortar mingled in the *duomo*'s shadowed interior.

Her captor dragged her into a side chapel and shoved her against the wall. As she fell, her weight rocked a marble post. It wobbled on its base, then settled.

"Non ti muovere e stai zitta," he said as he gestured his meaning—stay put and be quiet.

The sight of his ugly black pistol was all Sophie needed to make her obey. She edged away from the marble post so as not to bring it down on her head. Apparently the pedestal for a statue, the heavy pillar stood empty.

Fear pounding in her veins, she huddled in the corner. This wasn't supposed to happen. He'd separated her from the crowd. Jack was supposed to stop him.

Would the GPS button work from inside a brick-and-stone

building? Where was Jack? Why didn't he reach her before this man dragged her away?

Sophie pressed her fists to her mouth to hold in the panicked sobs swamping her chest.

The shuffle of feet on the stone floor approached the chapel. Jack? He'd be killed. She had to warn him.

She swallowed her panic and yelled, "Jack! Look out!"

The thug Tomasso barked a laugh and ordered her to be silent.

She watched in mute shock as Jack stumbled into the chapel and fell to his knees. Blood trickled from beneath his ear. A man with a long ponytail and a wicked-bladed knife entered behind him.

"Sophie, are you okay?" Jack said, climbing to his feet.

She bobbed her head, but fear made her movements jerky as a broken puppet. "What did he do to you?"

"*Silenzio!*" Tomasso raised his pistol.

Flinching, Sophie subsided, but he stopped short of striking her.

With a nasty laugh he lowered the gun and stepped to one side, in front of the pedestal.

Jack shook his head slightly in warning. *Wait,* his eyes seemed to tell her.

Comforted that Jack would know what to do, Sophie crouched in her corner and reminded herself to breathe.

Backup, she remembered. Where were they?

"You called it, Tomasso," she heard the new man say in Italian. "This fool didn't know I was there until I had him."

Clearly buying Sophie's act that she knew no Italian, they talked freely of their triumph. She watched Jack for guidance while she listened.

Tomasso ordered the other man to make sure no one was in the nave or other side chapels. When the ponytailed man returned with the all-clear, Tomasso began to screw a long attachment onto his pistol.

Sophie knew little about guns but recognized a silencer

when she saw one. Her racing heart leaped up into her parched throat. The leader's next words confirmed her worst fears.

They were going to kill Jack right there and take her with them.

How could she warn Jack? What could she do?

When Jack saw the silencer on Tomasso's Beretta, he knew that he had little time to act or he would never get another chance.

Rot-Breath held only the knife. The Glock was jammed into his waistband. Tomasso was the immediate threat, but for the moment he ignored the two captives and blabbed away in rapid Italian with his henchman.

Jack stood legs apart, his weight balanced on the balls of his feet, his arms loose. Mental telepathy would've come in handy, but eye signals were all he could send Sophie.

Tomasso continued to stand where Jack wanted him—in front of their best chance. Their only weapon. A distraction at the least. He willed Sophie to interpret his glances….

He saw her frown, then look to her left and at Tomasso's back. Her eyes widened in comprehension. With snail-slow deliberation she placed her hands around the marble stand.

When she looked back up at Jack, he mouthed, *Now.*

She gave a mighty shove.

The pedestal toppled. It knocked Tomasso off his feet. Italian invectives echoed off the chapel's stone walls. The Beretta squirted from his hand and skated across the floor.

Jack had no time to go for it. He pivoted and aimed a kick at Rot-Breath's knife hand. The dagger clattered to the stones. He dived headfirst at the man's midsection.

The two men fell to the hard floor in a welter of tangled limbs. Jack's Glock slipped from Rot-Breath's waistband. It clanked onto the floor, and Jack grabbed it.

The henchman landed solid blows to Jack's belly and one to the jaw. He fought tough and street-dirty but was shorter than Jack and untrained. Jack managed to hold on to the gun.

Where the hell was Byrne's Interpol crew?

Crimson fury fueled Jack's strength, fury at all this bunch had done to Sophie, to him, to countless others. Fury at Vadim for hiring them. He delivered a solid chop to the throat, and the man collapsed like a tent. Just in case, Jack shoved the Glock's nose into the soft flesh beneath his chin.

"Well done," Matt Leoni's cheery voice said above him.

"You!" Behind Leoni stood *Commissario* De Carlo and two other guys Jack recognized. *Not Interpol but the task force.*

Had his good friend Byrne sunk him?

Would De Carlo take him into custody along with the Mafia rent-a-gorillas?

Leoni held Tomasso's Beretta in one hand.

Jack's heart sputtered before lurching into overdrive. *Sophie.* "Sophie, what about Sophie?"

"She's just fine." Humor glinted in Leoni's sleepy eyes.

Jack's shoulders relaxed, but white noise filled his ears and his head spun. He had to sit there, straddling his captive, while he got it together. The moment of terror followed by overwhelming relief drained him more than the fight.

"This creep's coming around. Better secure him."

Jack roused. He still had his gun, and Leoni was handing him cuffs. Things couldn't be all bad.

Pushing the coughing captive over onto his face, he snapped the plastic bands around his wrists. Then he stripped him of a second knife in an ankle sheath.

Jack pushed to his feet, under protest from various body parts. He touched his jaw, and his hand came away smeared with blood. Sore as hell but nothing broken. "What took you so long? I could have used some damned help a little earlier."

"We thought you might need to throw a few punches at somebody. Ms. Rinaldi had things well in hand." Leoni cut a meaningful glance toward his left.

Chapter 15

"Sophie, what—" Jack stared, struck dumb as a stone, at the scene in the corner.

Sophie sat on Tomasso. Correction—on top of the marble pedestal that held Tomasso down.

Leoni clapped Jack on the back. "A hell of a woman, but I guess you already know that."

Jack couldn't help grinning. He surmised what had happened. The pedestal apparently had done even more than distract Tomasso. It had fallen square on his lower torso and legs, knocking his Beretta away and pinning him prone to the floor. To make certain he stayed there, Sophie had straddled the pedestal and held the man's gun on him until the task force had arrived.

If only he had a camera.

In precise phrases, she translated between the hit man and the ATSA officer. Her cheeks were rosy with excitement, and

Jack fought an overwhelming urge to snatch her up and shelter her from the other men's admiring stares.

"When we showed up, she had the Beretta's silencer jabbed in his neck like a bayonet. I relieved her of the weapon. Don't want to lose our prime witness." The languid humor in Leoni's voice eased Jack's tension down another notch.

"They were going to kill us," Jack said. "Looks like she wasn't taking any chances."

An officer helped Sophie to her feet, and two others lifted the heavy weight from the hit man's lower body.

"He says he doesn't think anything's broken," she said.

As she crossed to Jack, he noted the worry etching deep lines in her brow. Her gaze skimmed him from head to toe. She touched a finger to the dried blood on his neck and, apparently satisfied the wound was superficial, smiled.

That sweet curve of her lips curled around the muscles of his chest and blotted out the other people in the room. When he opened his arms, she stepped into them.

Leoni's mouth twitched with a smile. Jack ignored him. He didn't care what the damn task force thought, the CO included.

If he'd followed regs, Sophie would be dead.

Only the feel of her against his body could completely dispel the lingering fear for her. "Everything's okay, Sophie. It's over," he murmured into her hair, its familiar fragrance the final reassurance he needed.

"Signora Rinaldi," said the silky voice of *Commissario* De Carlo, "you did a very brave thing. You are to be commended." With an avuncular crinkle to his eyes, he approached them as officers hauled the two Mafia hit men from the chapel.

Sophie lifted her head from Jack's chest and edged left, but he kept her tucked under his arm. "He was going to shoot Jack—er, Officer Thorne."

"Ah, of course." De Carlo passed a hand over his mouth. "I see you are recovered from your injuries."

"I'm still a little stiff, but yes."

"And this Mafia...*merdiaolo* didn't harm you? Pardon my language."

"*Grazie,* I'm fine."

Straightening to a military posture, he turned to Jack. "Officer Thorne, your independent actions have saved this young woman's life. My apologies to you for questioning her importance to Sebastian Vadim. And for doubting your integrity. There was a leak, as you suspected. You have your friend Byrne to thank for bypassing normal channels."

"He's not one to color within the lines." The exact reason Jack had called on Byrne in the first place. "The leak was somebody in Vadim's pocket, I assume."

"*Boh!*" the CO uttered in disgust. "The Venice *Questura* slipped up on background checks. Our leak was a filing clerk assigned to the task force. The man loses money in the casinos. Vadim paid him generously for information."

Sophie slipped from Jack's embrace and stepped forward. "So does that mean Officer Thorne is back on the task force?"

De Carlo made a small bow. "We shall see, *signora.* He and I will discuss that later."

Jack fought down the spike of uncertainty sparked by the CO's ominous undertone. "What will happen to Tomasso and the other man? I'd like to be in on the interrogation."

"*Assolutamente.* Your country house should serve. If you will show us the way."

"This is not a good development, Sebastian."

"I know, Ahmed. My men experienced...difficulty. I may need a bit more time. Perhaps Wednesday." Vadim dabbed his handkerchief across his forehead. Late June was hotter in Venice than he remembered.

Hotter still because his men in Tuscany had failed again. Worse, they had allowed themselves to be arrested.

"I can give you no more time. I want what I have already purchased. You have until Monday. No longer."

When he heard a loud click, Vadim also disconnected.

Monday. Only two days.

This problem was Jackson Thorne's fault. Vadim should've killed him the first time Thorne had interfered in his business. Fury and hatred blazed with the impact of a torch thrust into his bowels. He cursed in both Italian and Cleatian.

He was surrounded by incompetents. Sullying his hands with such messy chores was not his preference, but the unusual circumstances forced him to make an exception. He must go obtain the uranium himself.

Thorne would die, but first he would have to watch the lovely Sophie perish.

"So they won't talk? We have nothing?" Jack asked the CO as officers handed Tomasso and the other prisoner into a task-force van in the farmhouse's driveway.

Jack and Sophie in their rental car had led the entire party from Fiorasole for the prisoners' interrogation. Then six hours of questioning at the farmhouse dining room table had borne no fruit, only stony silence and evil looks.

"Niente. Questo m'aggrava!" De Carlo slapped his forehead to further express his frustration.

Jack understood, both the Italian and the aggravation. He was ticked as hell, too.

The dapper *commissario* smoothed his thinning hair and shrugged. *"Boh,* I should have known. There is no honor among thieves, only fear of reprisal."

Jack shifted his feet. He'd been waiting hours for De Carlo to follow up on his earlier promise that they would talk. Part of that talk ought to be returning Jack to the task-force investigation. He hoped. *"Commissario,* Sophie Rinaldi is safe here."

"Perhaps. Perhaps not. This Vadim is resourceful."

Jack's jaw muscle knotted. De Carlo was right, but Jack needed to make his move. "Someone else can guard her. Put me back on the task force. I know Vadim. I know more about him from what she's told me. Sir."

De Carlo looked down at the ground as if marshaling his thoughts. The light breeze feathering across their faces carried the verdant fragrance of freshly mowed grass.

When he raised his head, he said, "You joined this task force in order to take revenge on Vadim, the man responsible for your wife's and son's deaths, did you not?"

"That doesn't mean I won't do my job."

"*Di certo.* Certainly, I do not question your abilities. I simply do not want you doing *more* than your job."

When Jack frowned, De Carlo continued. "*Signore,* as a father three times over, I understand vendetta. If Sebastiano Vadim had killed my son, no barrier would stop me. No death would be too painful for him."

"Then you'll put me back on the team?"

"I cannot let personal desires come first. Vadim has committed too many crimes to escape justice. You must trust the task force. There is too much at stake here."

Jack's shoulders tightened with frustration. He'd been so focused on Vadim, he'd forgotten the other dangers. "Like the weapons-grade uranium that's still out there."

"*Sì,* the uranium." He glanced at the waiting car. The Alfa Romeo's taillights winked out as the driver gave up and doused the engine. A jet trail streaked across the fading pink-and-purple dome of the sky.

"I understand." But he didn't have to like it. He would detour around it if he had to.

De Carlo put out his hand. "You're a fine officer, Signore Thorne, as are the other ATSA personnel. I was skeptical at first about working with ATSA, but no more."

"Thank you." Even as he shook hands, the fury prowling inside Jack would give him no peace. He fought to control his words. "I need to talk with Vadim. To tell him he hasn't gotten away with those particular murders."

"Done. Once he is in custody." The *commissario* began to walk away toward the Alfa Romeo. The engine purred to life.

He turned. "*Signore,* revenge is a cruel master that brings no satisfaction. Losing your family need not be the end of your life. A man, especially a man who deals with the harsher side of life every day, needs balance to have a full life. The warmth and softness of a woman, the laughter of children."

Jack averted his eyes and shook his head. "I put my family in danger. They died because of the job. Once is more than enough."

"*Polizia* everywhere have families. *I* have a family. There are divorces and the normal difficulties of family life, but your loss was an unusual tragedy. Do not deny yourself a basic human need. *Buonasera.*"

On that instructional note of farewell De Carlo slid into the idling car, then rode away.

Jack watched the disappearing taillights until he stared into only dark shadows.

Sophie looked out the sitting room window. The last task-force vehicle rolled down the drive with the control officer, De Carlo. Its taillights glowed as night winked out the last mauve tint in the western sky.

Exhaustion enveloped her like a hot towel. She collapsed on the white leather sofa in the sitting room and closed her eyes. If only capturing Vadim's hired guns meant it was over.

But Matt Leoni had told her that neither man had revealed anything. "Vadim means nothing to them," he'd said. "You don't want to know what their don would do to them if they talked."

When Jack entered the house, she opened her eyes. She watched the fluid slide of his muscles as he paced the room. Golden bristle covered his clenched jaw, and he could've held a pencil between his rammed-together eyebrows.

"Disappointed?" she said, at a loss for consoling words.

"Disappointed doesn't come close." He rolled his shoulders and flopped down beside her, his long legs stretched in front of him. He lifted her hand and threaded his long fingers with hers. "But at least you're safe from those bums."

"Until Vadim hires more." Her heart gave a little hiccup at that thought, and she inhaled Jack's comforting scent.

"He won't have the chance."

Hope for an end to this mess sprouted in her chest. She scooted back on her cushion to sit up straight. "Does that mean De Carlo knows where he is? You're going with the task force to arrest him?"

Was this good or bad?

If Jack was part of an arrest unit, the company of others might deter him from going too far. Or did he want Vadim dead so much that he'd kill him without concern for himself? The rush of thoughts twisted through her, tangling in her tired brain and wrenching her heart.

He sighed. Or it might've been a growl. "Not exactly. We're no closer to him. Or the uranium. And I'm assigned to continue guarding you."

Unexpected, but a good thing if it kept him by her side. "I don't understand. De Carlo reinstated you to the task force, didn't he?"

"Officially. But he knows my connection to Vadim." Jack rested his head on the sofa and barked a humorless laugh. "He appreciates what I've done but considers me a loose cannon."

They sat quietly, hands linked, Sophie's head on his shoulder, as darkness filtered through the room.

As Jack saw matters, preventing the sale of the uranium to Ahmed Saqr didn't hinge on Vadim. The Yamari extremist was under surveillance, and officers would intercept the package.

Again the task force cut Jack out, but this time he wasn't going to sit idly by. He wouldn't let Vadim slip away for the sake of following De Carlo's damn orders.

The Mafia thugs were in custody. The leak was plugged. Nobody would blab Sophie's location. She was safe here.

Yeah, safe.

Definitely.

Some insurance wouldn't hurt. He would take care of it.

"Sophie, I'm leaving in the morning."

She went stiff and then twisted to peer at his face. "Didn't you just say De Carlo assigned you to keep guarding me? Or do those words have a nuance I'm missing?"

He hadn't meant to state it quite like that. But blunt was his style. Better to be straight with Sophie. "You're safe here. You can call the task force if there's a problem."

She placed a warm hand gently on his knee. "If you shoot Vadim, that's murder. Don't ruin your life for revenge."

He couldn't give in. As much as he loved the feel of her hand, of her nearness, he couldn't succumb to her softening influence.

Twisting away, he rose from the cushy sofa and stepped over the cocktail table as if it were a track hurdle.

From the other side he said, "You don't get it, do you? Ruin my life? *I have no life.* Not since I watched my three-year-old son bleed out and die before I could reach him. Revenge is the only thing I have to live for."

"That's no sort of life. You're letting what happened in the past steal your entire future."

"You're one to talk. You're trying to dig up the past as a guide to your future. Like the bones of your ancestors were tea leaves or something."

She blinked, taken aback by his retort. "Tea leaves? I'm just trying to get a clue so I'm not trapped in a life chosen by circumstances instead of by me. I want independence."

"You're looking in the wrong place."

Then her chin went up, her Valkyrie face, flames of determination alight in her brown eyes. "Then so are you. You're only—what?—thirty-two?

"Thirty-five."

"Only eight years older than me. Young. Look inside yourself. There's so much more than hatred and grief in you. You're honorable and protective, for starters."

"You still don't get it. I promised on David's grave. On his mother's grave."

"And afterward?"

"After doesn't matter."

"You'd spend the rest of your life in a small stone cell or in a prison of your own making. Pain and hatred, not promises, are stealing your future. Do you really think David and Tonia want you to sacrifice the rest of your life?"

Jack couldn't answer. If he said more, he'd lose it. Fists clenched at his side, he stalked to the window and stared out at the gathering purple over the distant hills.

Behind him he heard Sophie jet out a breath as if gathering herself for more battle. The woman was relentless.

She said, "Let me tell you about revenge."

"Italy is steeped in revenge. I know. Your story won't make any difference, but go ahead." The sound of her voice might get him through the night.

Until he could go after Vadim.

A bat swooped across the sky, hunting nocturnal insects. Tomorrow he'd go hunting for a killer—if he could find him. He turned around as Sophie began her narrative.

"My great-uncle Vinnie lost a great deal of money in a business deal. When he couldn't support his wife and daughter, Great-Aunt Rita left to live with her parents. Vinnie later learned the business deal had been a scam, some sort of confidence game. When he confronted the crook, he took a gun."

"He shot the guy?"

"Right. I don't know the details because this happened a long time ago in Florence. Somehow the case was declared self-defense and he went free. But only physically."

"What do you mean?"

"He got some of his money back from the dead man's estate and started over. But guilt ate at him, a nasty little monster nibbling at his soul from inside."

When Jack realized he was rubbing his chest, he jammed both hands in his jean pockets. The image was real, too real. But he didn't see himself in her scenario. Not the same.

"Vinnie began to drink and eventually lost everything. Rita divorced him. He never saw his child again. Not long afterward he died in a boating accident, but the family has always believed it was suicide. Guilt and grief—the added burdens of revenge—destroyed him. Great-Uncle Vinnie was my *nonna*'s brother."

Head tilted and espresso-brown eyes wary, she sat quietly on the sofa and waited for his reaction.

"I understand what you're trying to do, but the situation's not the same. Your relative lost his family because of revenge. I want revenge *for* my family. And for all those other poor bastards whose deaths he's responsible for."

"The children and political prisoners working in the diamond mines, you mean? Well, doesn't that just make you the avenging angel."

His head snapped up at her snarky tone. Real anger. An anomaly in Sophie, one he was seeing more often, for good or ill. But he'd made his decision. "Like I said, I'm leaving in the morning."

"And you think you can find Vadim when the entire task force and the Italian *polizia* haven't?"

He was about to say that he had to try, but she was right. He had no idea where Vadim was. "Is this lesson over, teacher?" he growled.

She folded her arms. "If you kill Vadim, what about the uranium? It's dangerous even if it's hidden. How will they find it?"

The possibilities hit him in the gut. Saqr wouldn't get the nuke, but somebody else might. What if other terrorists got hold of it? What if an innocent civilian found it and opened it? Or a child?

Jack sank into the nearest chair. "Sophie, when you're right, you're right. I need more information about Vadim and the uranium before I can go after him."

She leaned back, apparently satisfied she'd convinced him to stay.

He would. For now.

He saw her eyelashes flutter lower and lower. He should carry her up to bed, but questions lingered. "You were a pro in Fiorasole today. I'll never forget the sight of you sitting on ole Tomasso."

"You can believe I'll never forget it either."

"You listened to their conversation a long time. They might've let slip something useful before Tomasso prepared to shoot us." An involuntary shudder ripped through him at the thought of a bullet tearing into Sophie's tender flesh.

"Shoot you, not me." She sat up, yawning.

"What?" A hunch raised the hairs on his neck.

"That's why I tried to warn you. Or maybe you understood when he put the silencer on. Tomasso said they were going to shoot you and take me with them."

He leaped the hurdle to join her on the sofa. "Where? Where were they going to take you? To Vadim?"

She arched her back, stretching like a cat. A tired cat. "Vadim? No. Let me think."

"Go back over the conversation. Try to remember his exact words."

She closed her eyes as she seemed to replay the overheard dialogue on her mind's recorder.

Anticipation and worry congealed in his mind. Too many times he'd thought he had a break, only to reach a dead end.

Sophie's eyes flew open. "I remember something. Maybe it's important. He said, 'She'll take us to it.'"

"*It*. What—the *uranium?*" Jack leaped to his feet and

pulled her up to face him. He held on to her hands, letting her softness remind him not to push her too hard. "Then you do know where the uranium is."

"Or they think I do."

Dragging fingers through his hair, he considered. "It can't be just their idea. Vadim has to have told them you have it. But where? Your bags were checked. The Geiger counter and the other detectors found only traces of radiation around the house, enough to indicate the uranium had been there, but not enough to locate it inside a thick lead casing. Besides, it'd be very heavy."

But it wouldn't take up much room.

Suddenly he knew.

His heart hammered at his rib cage. He was a dumb fool. How could he have missed it?

"Oh, my God!" Alarm glazed Sophie's eyes to a deer-in-the-headlights stare. All color drained from her face as her fingers clamped his in a death grip.

He saw that she'd realized the same thing. "Sophie?"

"Heavy as a marble statuette?"

"Heavy as hell."

"It seemed heavier than it should be."

"You carried it in that tote all this time. His first errand boys might've intended to kill us with the gasoline. I bet it wasn't until later that Vadim learned you'd taken the statuette. That explains why the other attacks didn't escalate to explosives and incendiary devices. He gave orders not to damage the goods."

Apprehension pinched her mouth. "Maybe it *was* damaged. The cracked base where the bullet struck, do you think—"

He pulled her close, wrapped her in his arms. "No, it's all right. By this time, you—*we'd* be feeling sick if any radiation had leaked." He thought.

By God, he hoped that was true. He'd been so focused on getting Vadim that he hadn't paid close attention to the briefings on radiation dangers.

"You should call someone, shouldn't you?"

From the strain in her voice, he knew she wanted the danger removed as quickly as possible. So did he. "Yeah, De Carlo will send a Haz-Mat team—uh, a hazardous-materials disposal team—to check for radiation and carry it away. I'm afraid you'll have to give up Saint Elizabeth."

"*Boh,* as the Italians say. None of my computer searches found her. I don't think there is a Rinaldi saint. The figure's some other saint. The antique dealer cheated me."

"Or Vadim set you up. It looks like he was going to use you to transport the uranium out of the country."

Would he have instructed Saqr to steal it from her? What would he care if she were killed in the process?

A fire-breathing dragon roared up within Jack. De Carlo was right. No easy death for Vadim.

She nodded sad agreement. "What do we do now?"

Tiredness smudged violet around her beautiful eyes. Her shoulders sagged. The day's adventure and her fierce attack on his defenses had drained her.

Time to take charge and care for her.

He breathed deeply, banking his fury. Kissing her gently, he savored her sweet-as-honey taste and her delicate scent. "I'll call De Carlo. You go upstairs and move your stuff into another bedroom. Don't touch the statuette."

"I never want to see it again." Sophie headed for the hallway and the stairs.

He'd hidden the uranium in her saint.

The sheer gall and coldness of the man made Sophie's head ache. She'd been helpless and he'd tricked her. Conned her. Did she buy the figure or did he give her the one thing she couldn't resist to use her for his greedy and ruthless ends?

And then she'd hoped the little icon would help her in her search for family and ancestors.

What Jack had said popped into her brain. *Ancestral tea leaves?* Was that what she was doing?

Sophie trudged from the stairwell down the hall to the master bedroom. Her heart ached as if a big hand had reached inside and wrung it like a dish towel.

Had she wasted time looking for relatives in Florence and Rome? If she'd found any, what did that prove? *Look inside yourself.* Her advice to Jack applied to herself, as well. She had some thinking to do.

In the bedroom Sophie avoided glancing toward Santa Elisabetta and made a beeline to her luggage.

She kicked the twenty-four-incher. Not *her* luggage. The Versace suitcases were bought for her by Sebastian Vadim. Like the designer boutique clothing.

Like the marble saint stuffed with uranium.

She slammed the suitcase onto the bed and gathered garments from the armoire and tossed them in. At the first opportunity she'd give it all to Catholic Social Services.

Among her toiletries in the bureau she found the business card that had accompanied the statuette. Tears pricked her eyes. Her hand curled into a fist, crumpling the card. She spun on her heels and glared at the little saint.

Light from the table lamp reflected on the marble and seemed to make it glow. Radiation? No, just a reflection. But then she saw…she saw…

Everything.

She'd been existing deep beneath the sea, remembered sounds muted, images blurred. She burst to the surface. The clarity hit her in a glaring ray.

Images scrolled through her mind, not distant mirages but full scenes. Echoes like the flutter of bird wings dialed to full volume. Memories darted, hammered her from all sides.

Sophie's limbs drained of strength. She clutched at the edge of the bed.

She remembered.

In the office. The statuette. The phone call.

Running.

Terror.

Emotions battered her. Rage. Fear. Anguish.

The bottom dropped out of her stomach. Her brain spun so fast that her legs buckled and she fell to her knees sobbing.

Chapter 16

Jack disconnected and closed the sat phone.

De Carlo had said rounding up a Haz-Mat team would take time. He looked at his watch. They could arrive anytime between midnight and dawn. Hours to wait.

Was Sophie all right? After the uranium eureka moment, she'd left the room dragging like a kicked kitten.

He went to the foot of the stairs and listened. From the bedroom he heard slamming. Drawers. A door. The armoire. She was mad. Good. About time.

That emotion Jack could handle.

His stomach announced the late hour, so he wandered into the kitchen to see what he could rustle up for supper. Sophie'd been a cooking fool the past few days. There must be plenty of leftovers.

From the fridge he rooted out containers of ravioli, sautéed vegetables and thin slices of rolled-up prosciutto. A bottle of wine was all he needed to top off the meal. He peered in the plastic containers, shrugged and dumped everything into one saucepan. Why not? They'd all go into the mouth together.

He'd just turned the gas flame to low under the pan when a loud thump from upstairs jerked his head up.

Too solid for a suitcase, and she wouldn't touch the statuette. Would she? What the hell?

He dashed for the stairs and took them three at a time. "Sophie!"

He skidded to a halt in the doorway when he saw her crumpled on the throw rug beside the bed. Tears streamed down her flushed cheeks.

He knelt and curved an arm around her shaking shoulders. "Sophie, what is it?"

"Oh, Jack," she choked out on a sob, "I remember…that day…all of it."

Her memory had returned. He glanced at the marble saint, standing in bogus banality on its little table. The revelation must've triggered the memory recovery.

Murmuring soothing words, he gathered her up. She might have a steel core, but in his arms she felt as fragile as the ethereal sprite she appeared. He carried her down the hall to the smaller bedroom where he kept his stuff. He set her on the antique wrought-iron bed and handed her tissues. He stood by, not knowing what to do with his hands.

Not knowing what the hell to do, period.

What should he do but wait? He never knew what to do with a crying female. Tonia had used tears to manipulate him, but Sophie's were all too real.

She got to him down deep. Seeing her so distraught stabbed him like a hot needle. She was vulnerable and tough, impulsive yet steady. He loved her zest for life. Her loving heart challenged him like a nagging conscience. She forced him to confront conflicts he didn't know he had. She made him look inward and examine his damn emotions. His chest tightened with a tenderness that unnerved him.

He cared for her.

A lot.

More than he'd ever thought he could care for a woman.

But it had to stop at that. He had an obligation to fulfill, and she wanted no strings. Even if she did, she'd want more from him than he had to give.

In a few moments Sophie sniffled and gave him a shaky smile. "The memories rushed back like a tornado in my head. It overwhelmed me, I guess. I'm all right now."

"Sure you are." Chest burning with an ache to know everything she remembered, Jack sat beside her on the bed.

"I want to tell you about what happened, why Vadim tried to kill me." Her eyelids were puffy from crying, but her irises were clear and calm.

Talking about Vadim's hit-and-run might sweep away the last of her fears. And tell him his enemy's location.

Once the Haz-Mat team verified that the figure contained the uranium, there would be nothing to stop him from going after Vadim. "I'm listening."

Sophie leaned against him, her bare arm against his. She savored the clean scent of his sun-warmed skin, his hardness and warmth against her. His touch would strengthen her as she put the disjointed images together to tell him.

"I was to fly to Paris that day, June fifth, then take the Eurostar Chunnel train to London three days later and fly home from there. At breakfast Vadim had a present for me."

"The saint." On the side away from Sophie, Jack clenched his fist as though preparing to ram it into Vadim's face.

"Got it in one." She smiled. Now that the storm in her brain had ended, she regained a modicum of calm. "I was thrilled and touched that he'd gone to such trouble. I took the saint upstairs and set her beside the bed while I packed."

"Where we found her later."

"Exactly. The saint was too valuable a gift to accept, but I couldn't bring myself to refuse her."

"How could you refuse the family saint? He knew that."

She nodded. "I decided I would give him something special. I was going to order a case of his favorite local vintage from the village wine shop. Mom had wired me money for traveler's checks, the ones you found. There's no telephone in that bedroom, so I went downstairs to use the phone in the sitting room."

He turned, blue eyes laser-focused, trademark scowl in place, clearly anxious for what came next. "But you didn't."

She shook her head, tucked behind her ear loose tendrils of hair. "When I picked up the receiver, I heard Vadim's voice." Her shoulders raised in a hunched shudder. "He was plotting with…that terrorist. About *me*."

"The terrorist. Ahmed Saqr?"

"That's the name. You were right that I was the ignorant courier. I was to take the uranium as far as London. It was to go on to New York, but they didn't say how."

"Probably a container ship. Less chance of detection than by airplane." He rubbed his chin. "Vadim's scrambler allowed him the security to discuss the plan on the phone. He didn't count on you picking up the extension."

She pressed a hand to her stomach to calm it. "I had the impression Vadim helped devise the plan, even pushed it, but I didn't hear their target."

"Byrne told me. His snitch came through yesterday. The plan was to set off a dirty bomb in the diamond district."

"But that's horrible! Why?"

"Damn, I see Vadim's part in this," Jack said, fury contorting his mouth. "Saqr's radioactive explosion would strike at what he views as Western decadence and materialism. Hundreds, maybe thousands of people would die. Contamination would virtually entomb diamond trading records and diamonds for years. The economic chaos would affect thousands, maybe millions. It would devastate the legitimate diamond trade."

"I get it. Vadim could step in with his smuggled diamonds and take over the industry."

"Damn evil bastard!" Jack seemed to swallow further invectives. He sucked in a breath through his teeth and turned to her. Gentle concern in his eyes, he cupped her cheek. "And he caught you in the middle of his web."

She leaned into his rough palm. Reaching behind her with his other hand, he unclipped her hair and finger-combed it loose. When he began kneading her tight neck muscles, she nearly purred.

He might not express his feelings in words, but these small touches of comfort showed that he cared. She wondered if he realized.

"Did he hear you on the extension?" he said.

Her shoulders trembled in an involuntary shudder. "I must've made a noise. I was so shocked. When I knew he heard me, I hung up. I didn't know what to do. I had nowhere to hide." She recalled being too frightened to think clearly. "So I just…ran."

"The way Vadim went after you finally makes sense. He chased you down then because you could blow his plans out of the water."

"Later he had to make sure he could get the uranium-stuffed saint before he had his men, um, kill us." A niggling suspicion jarred her pulse, and she turned to face him. "Oh, Jack, do you think he knows why *you're* after him?"

He scowled, clearly thinking the notion over, but then shook his head. "I don't see how. But back to that day—do you remember him chasing you?"

She conjured up the events after her escape from the house. Tears flowed along with the memory, but the ending came up blank. "Yes, but not the actual impact."

"The doctor said you might not. Just as well."

"I remember charging down the driveway. The crunch of gravel behind me. And voices shouting in Italian and in English. That was you?"

"That was me." He pressed his lips to her forehead. "Is that everything?"

Sophie knew what he wanted to hear. She temporized by mopping her eyes with the tissue.

Jack was honorable and idealistic. He believed he had to seek vengeance, but in the end he wouldn't go through with murder. She wanted to trust him, *needed* to trust him.

After blowing her nose, she said, "I remember another outing to Venice. We spent the night at a palazzo in Santa Croce. Vadim said it belonged to a friend named Moretta, but he seemed very at home there."

"I doubt Vadim has friends. Moretta could be another alias. Interpol and the task force don't have the name. The Santa Croce district, huh? Where exactly is the palazzo?"

"On the Fondamenta Aldo." She paused but decided to tell him everything. "I don't know the address, but it's a faded rose-brick with wrought-iron balconies. What will you do?"

He kissed her again, gently on the lips this time. "I will bring your suitcases in here before I go check on dinner. I will ply you with food and Chianti and tuck you in bed. Then I'll wait up for the Haz-Mat guys."

Sophie watched Jack leave the room.

He hadn't said he would phone the task force about the Santa Croce palazzo. Would he throw away his life for revenge? Or did he listen to her arguments?

Feeling his pain had prompted her to stand up to him.

And *for him.*

Was that all she could do? Should she admit she'd fallen in love with him? Would that change anything? Probably not, since he didn't love her. He cared, but that was all. He wouldn't let himself feel more.

Telling him she loved him would make no difference except to load on more guilt.

She had no answers, only screaming nerves and a heart

wrenched by a wringer of doubt, fear and love—too many emotions to sort out.

Love hurt the most.

Love should be filled with joy and smiles, not pain and tears. Why did she have to fall in love with this man? She didn't want love if it made her heart ache like this.

A shower wouldn't help much, but perhaps it would cleanse the grimy feelings brought on by remembering Vadim's dirty manipulations. Gathering up her hair in the discarded comb clip, she scooted off the bed and headed to the bathroom.

More memories had emerged from the depths, not about Vadim but personal ones she hadn't told Jack. She needed time to mull them over and make decisions.

At twelve-thirty Jack closed the bedroom door on the sleeping Sophie and went downstairs to meet the Haz-Mat team. The official van had just pulled up outside.

He could still feel the warmth of her body and detect her scent on his skin. Leaving her would be the hardest thing he'd ever done. But he had no choice.

Sophie had proclaimed him chef supreme for his stew of leftovers. They'd laughed and eaten and drunk the wine on the terrace to a chorus of summer insects.

Then they'd made love in the antique bed.

He'd kissed her and she'd sighed. He skimmed his finger-tips up her spine and along the elegant arch of her neck, and she purred. He worshipped her taut breasts, laving and drawing her nipples into his mouth, and she moaned. She kissed him back with fierce passion, wrapping herself around him, greedy for him as he was for her.

His body had hardened to the point of pain. He ached to have her, to claim her. Even more, he needed to imprint Sophie on his spirit. So he ignored the other need.

He moved against her with infinite slowness, memorizing every inch of her fine-grained skin with every inch of his. He tasted her—her mouth, her ears, the delicate skin of her temples and her throat, down her womanly body to taste the feminine essence between her legs. When she arched off the bed and cried his name, he moved up and entered her. Just barely.

She gripped him with her legs, kissed his chest.

He gritted his teeth, and withdrew.

She arched up, urged him deeper.

He held himself above her, savored the tug of her body.

She moaned, clamped her hands on his butt and drew him down. "Jack, please!"

He contemplated her, so beautiful with her midnight hair spread over the pillow, her body dewy with perspiration, her rapid breaths perfumed with wine and kisses. And then he thrust all the way inside her, joining them body and spirit. Soul to soul.

"Sophie!" He was unable to wait any longer. His desperate need overwhelmed him, didn't allow slow or soft.

He filled her, thrust again, again, fast and furious. She'd stayed right with him, clutching at his back and murmuring her need, until she cried out, and the pressure of his climax sent him with her over the brink in a blinding release.

Afterward, he had held her close until she'd slept. He'd watched her, silently apologizing for leaving her, for hurting her. When he'd heard the van pull up in front of the house, he'd eased out of bed, lifted his Glock from the bedside stand and slipped on his jeans.

His hand on the door latch, he stowed the reverie for the future and opened the door.

A team of five covered in white protective suits trooped into the house and up to the room where the statuette was. Their leader ordered Jack in clipped Italian, *"Stai,"* which sounded an awful lot like a command to Fido. He remained at the foot of the stairs and listened to the click and beep of their equipment.

Ironic that he and Sophie had lived with the uranium for days and now he was being ordered to keep away for his safety.

Moments later the group descended with the uranium in a sealed kit. The Haz-Mat chief nodded and said, *"Radioattivo."* Radioactive. As he left, he handed Jack the hollowed-out statuette, apparently safe without its contents.

Jack set the little saint on a hall table. So they'd been right, only too slow to figure it out. Were they in danger for having been near it? But if the statuette was safe, maybe there'd been no leak. He didn't know enough Italian to ask.

After they left, Jack drove away down the hill road.

He found the winding route to the *Autostrade* and pointed the Opel north toward Florence on the A1. From Florence to Venice was two hundred and fifty-five kilometers, one hundred and fifty-eight miles. He should make it to Venice in three hours.

Still dark. Appropriate.

Or should he let the light of day shine on his revenge?

Revenge? Or would justice suffice?

Was his determination to kill Vadim screwed up? Or was it moral and just, as he'd always believed? He'd never questioned his goal before. He'd never had reason. No self-pity for him, but he felt like a clock wound too tight.

The hatred in his chest still clawed at him, but other emotions, other needs wedged in. The anguish and guilt that had held sway for five years no longer sustained him.

He'd changed. Sophie had changed him.

When he looked down the long barrel of the rest of his life, he no longer saw nothing.

He saw her.

Sophie was his life-giving connection. A shimmer of light in a cavern of darkness. He felt alive again, totally alive, when he was near her. She was his conscience, his lover, his friend, his—

Not his.

The thoughts tangled in his mind, like wires all knotted together. Sophie wouldn't be there for him. She wanted an independent life, a future she made for herself. He would never see her again.

His heart kicked hard against his rib cage, and he nearly went off the road. Horns blared as other cars careened past him. He gripped the wheel to wrench the car straight again.

Pain and grief had been his steady companions. They would remain with him. His lips compressed into a tight line. He shifted into fourth gear and flexed his fingers to ease the stiffness from his scars.

His watch read one-fifteen.

Was Sophie awake? Should he have left her a note? No, better to put her out of his mind. He'd made sure she was safe. De Carlo was sending an officer to patrol the grounds. Anything else Jack did would only hurt her more. His chest tightened until he thought his heart would tear apart.

Sophie.

Maybe he could give himself one chance.

He picked up the sat phone from the car seat and hit a number on the speed dial.

When Sophie heard the Opel roll away down the drive, she knew she'd failed. Jack was heading to Venice to kill Vadim.

Tears pricked her eyes, and she sat up in bed. *Stupida,* she had no time for weeping. Jack's life was at stake. She had to stop him. How, she didn't know.

She dragged herself from bed and slipped on his discarded dress shirt. After a trip to the bathroom, she searched the house for the cell phone. No sign of it or the sat phone. He'd taken both.

Eyeing the house phone, she smacked her forehead with the heel of her hand. She didn't know the numbers of either of Jack's phones.

If she phoned the task force, they might arrest him whether or not he'd done anything. She didn't trust *Commissario* De Carlo not to go in with guns blazing. If she didn't alert them, Vadim could kill Jack.

She had to try.

The automated response at the Venice *Questura* gave her De Carlo's voice mail, so she hung up and called again. After much button pushing, she reached a human being who would not give her the *commissario*'s mobile phone number. The stubborn officer agreed to inform him of her call.

Lord knew when he'd get the message. That left her only one option.

She had to go to Venice.

She sorted through the clothing in her suitcases. She settled on the pink cropped pants and blouse she'd worn the first day Jack had taken her to the villa—practical and not bought by Vadim. The yellow espadrilles didn't match, but they were better for walking than the prissy Gucci sandals.

She glanced at the banjo clock in the hall. One o'clock. Middle of the night. Nothing in Giordano was open.

Arturo lived above the *fruttivendolo*. Perhaps she could wake him and borrow his truck. Or she'd ask if he would drive her into Florence, where she could rent a car.

She made sure her traveler's checks were in her purse, then headed out the door.

"Good evening, Sophie. How convenient." Sebastian Vadim stepped from the shadows.

Sophie gasped and stumbled on the step. Two burly men grasped her by the arms.

"You will not run this time, my dear. Shall we go in?"

Sophie's heart raced. Her throat closed with fear, so she could utter only a faint squeak. How did he find her?

What if Jack came back when he found no one in Venice?

The two bodyguards half dragged, half walked her inside. White noise blared in her ears, making her head reel with dizziness. She saw no way to escape, no way to warn Jack.

The men threw her into a chair, and she clutched at its arms for something solid to hold on to.

"Ah, here is our little saint," Vadim said in barely accented English. A sly smile curved his lips. He removed black-rimmed glasses Sophie'd never seen before and dropped them in a pocket. "The very thing I came for."

For the first time Sophie noticed Santa Elisabetta standing on a nearby table. Her base was missing. She guessed the uranium was also missing.

Vadim would be furious.

"This visit may be briefer than I'd anticipated." From a small bag he carried he drew out a pair of heavy protective gloves and put them on.

She held her breath, biting her lower lip. He wore his usual silk suit and open-collared silk shirt, but his salt-and-pepper hair was bleached blond. A disguise, along with the glasses? How could she have ever liked this foul man? She'd once thought him kind and honorable, but now she sensed an aura of evil, of malevolence, that sent chills over her scalp.

He lifted the statuette. A frown furrowed his brow. He turned the marble piece over, exclaiming in Cleatian. He stalked over to her, shook it in front of her face. "Where is it? What have you done with it?"

Fury and righteous indignation swept fear aside. Sophie straightened her shoulders. "You mean the *stolen* uranium? The *polizia* confiscated it. They know about your plot. I remember *everything*."

She didn't see the blow coming that knocked her to the floor.

With a dejected slump to his shoulders, Jack slid his Glock into the belt holster. He surveyed the opulent parlor.

The rose-brick house was empty, shuttered and dark.

Did Vadim go to Cleatia? Could he get past the border?

Jack paced the Oriental carpet and thought. During his drive he'd notified De Carlo, but the task force was delayed. Now it didn't matter.

Without a clue to Vadim's whereabouts, Jack ought to return to Sophie. In case Vadim had more men looking for her.

And he ought to let her know nothing had happened to him.

Three-thirty. He hated to wake her, but she'd be worried if she found him gone. On his sat phone he punched in the number of the farmhouse.

"*Pronto,* hello. J-Jack?"

The tremble in her voice slugged him in the gut. "Sophie, it's me."

"Not alone. Don't—"

"She cannot speak with you now, Thorne. You will have to settle for me."

He had heard that voice only once, five years ago, but he recognized the smooth, accented tones. "*Vadim!*"

"Ah, I am flattered that you remember me."

Jack's pulse clattered. Ice-edged horror clawed down his spine. How in hell did Vadim find Sophie? "You bastard. If you hurt her—"

"An empty threat, Thorne. You will do nothing except what I say. You have been a thorn—so to speak—in my side for five years. Oh, yes, your search for me has not gone unnoticed. Now you have found me."

Jack slammed the palazzo's front door behind him and ran to the police launch. He'd contacted the task force earlier and set it up. He motioned to the startled driver to get going, then mouthed, "Police dock."

The open powerboat's inboard engine growled to life, and the wide-eyed young officer steered into the canal.

No time to waste. Vadim had Sophie. Jack had to save her. "What do you want?" he barked into the phone.

"A meeting. What else? I will pass the time with Signora Rinaldi until you arrive. She may not enjoy it as much as I, of course. You will want to hurry."

"Vadim, you freaking sick monster..." Jack's words blasted empty air.

Vadim had disconnected.

Chapter 17

Dressed in black ATSA jumpsuits—called "ninjas" in agency slang—Jack Thorne and Matt Leoni crouched beyond the Giordano farmhouse's terrace shrubbery.

The night was cool, but sweat trickled down Jack's spine. Dew soaked through the microfiber to his knee. Minor irritations he ignored as he focused night-vision binoculars on Vadim's two hulking henchmen. Each had a pistol in a shoulder holster. They were gabbing about who-knows-what on the terrace. Smoke wafted on the light breeze—*Nazionale* or some other European brand of cigarette.

Every nerve in Jack's body twanged on hyperalert. A heavy, slick ball of dread sat in his gut. He couldn't let someone else he loved die at Vadim's hand.

Sophie, be alive, be alive. Please, God, not Sophie.

For the moment, all he could do was watch and wait.

Thank God Leoni'd met him at the police dock. The deceptively lazy officer had taken it from there. From nowhere he'd commandeered a police helicopter to deliver the entire team and its commando arms and equipment to Giordano. They'd made the trip in record time.

At four-thirty, darkness still cloaked them from detection. High, thin clouds covered the waning moon. The officer sent earlier to check on Sophie's safety had been found dead, his neck broken. That implied Vadim hadn't come alone. A reconnoiter of his Mercedes and of the grounds determined that he had two hired guns for support.

Once the CO understood what Vadim wanted—Jack—he agreed that Jack could enter alone.

But first they had to neutralize the hired guns.

Leather scraped against stone as the two stepped on their cigarettes. They headed in opposite directions to circle the grounds, a patrol they apparently did once an hour.

Jack and Leoni exchanged hand signals as they followed, Leoni to the left, Jack to the right.

His target was squat and square, a cinder block of a man who might be strong but not agile. Speed and silence were key in taking him down.

Jack stayed low and behind the abundant cover until his man meandered well away from the house. At the first opening, he stepped out and delivered a solid punch downward to the collarbone, sinking the man to his knees with barely a sound. Jack slipped the weapon from his holster and used it to conk him on the temple. The thug dropped like the stone block he resembled.

One down.

Just in time. The first light of dawn was erasing the darkness, shading everything with gray tones. With quick and silent movements Jack secured the unconscious man's hands and feet with plastic cuffs and his mouth with tape. He slipped the man's Beretta into a ninja leg pocket.

In a moment, Leoni met him on the terrace. "Got mine," he whispered.

Standing to one side, Jack peered in. He could see through the dining room to the sitting room.

Vadim and Sophie sat in facing armchairs. Jack could see her only in profile, but she looked okay. Scared but unharmed. He exhaled slowly, releasing the fear she might already be dead. She stared at Vadim, but from so far back in her seat she could've been part of the upholstery.

Vadim leaned forward, talking to Sophie. More like pontificating, judging from his smirk. A smug expression Jack would erase soon.

Just behind them on a small table stood the saint figure.

So Vadim knew he'd lost the uranium. That was bound to make him even angrier. And maybe scared. Saqr wouldn't understand. Or forgive.

Good, Jack could play on his enemy's emotions.

I'm going in, he signaled to Leoni and adjusted his hidden mic.

Leoni tapped his transceiver and gave him a thumbs-up.

His Glock in his hand, Jack opened the terrace door and stepped inside.

The hall clock chimed the half hour, Sophie noted. Little more than an hour since Jack had telephoned. Two more hours until he could possibly arrive.

Her cheek throbbed where Vadim had struck her. He hadn't touched her again, although he'd implied to Jack he would. If she could keep him talking, perhaps he wouldn't hurt her more. At that feeble hope, her pulse threaded unevenly.

"You've used people all along," she said. To her, the statement was an accusation, but to him, it would be an opportunity to boast. She kept her hands clasped in her lap and tried to appear calm.

"Of course. People are so easily manipulated." He droned on about convincing the locals who lived near his Veneto villa that he was a respectable businessman.

When he wound down, she asked, "How did you find this house? How did you know I was here?"

A nasty smile curved his lips. "My men combed these hill towns. In the bars, people are friendly. They gossip. Some are in need of euros to buy more wine. Like your gardener."

"Silvio?" She'd smelled alcohol on his breath in the early mornings. And he'd known the night before the Fiorasole market day that she and Jack were going.

"He was most helpful, keeping my men informed. Tonight he demanded too much. He will not be troubled by his thirst— or his greed—again."

He'd killed poor old Silvio without a qualm. Or his body-guards had.

Sophie suppressed a shudder. Showing fear or shock might anger him again. And there was more she wanted to know. "You were planning to use me, but that was by chance, wasn't it?"

Vadim leaned back his head and laughed. "Naive child. You really believe that your luggage and credit-card disasters were coincidence?"

Her mouth dropped open. He couldn't possibly manipulate Alitalia or MasterCard. "How?"

His chest puffed out with pride at his machinations. "My dear cousin telephoned about your arrival. All I needed was to pass a few euros to a baggage handler and the hotel clerk."

A click came from across the hall. The French door from the terrace had opened and closed.

Frowning, Vadim rose from his chair. "Ugo, I ordered you to remain outside."

"Ugo won't be taking orders for a while." A man dressed in black stepped out of the darkened dining room and crossed the hall on silent feet. He held a pistol aimed at Vadim's heart. "He and his buddy are napping."

At the sound of the voice, Sophie's pulse leaped. "Jack!" Then her heart slammed up into her throat. What was going on?

"You!" Vadim yanked Sophie upward by her left arm.

The force shot shards of pain radiating from her sore shoulder. She gasped, then clamped her lips against her weakness.

He held her against his side with a firm grip. In his left hand Vadim, too, held a pistol.

He jammed the cold steel against her jaw.

Jack's eyes narrowed to slits of blue lasered at Vadim. Here was the hard-eyed, grim-faced man Sophie had first met. He flicked a glance toward her, then back. "You slime, you'll pay for hurting her."

Oh, don't let this escalate because of me.

Vadim's hand trapped her left arm, but her right was free. She started to touch her bruised cheek, but the pistol jabbed her neck again, and she let the hand fall. "He hit me only once. I'm okay. Jack—"

"She's a delicate creature," Vadim interrupted. "I waited so her brave protector could witness her pain." When Jack took a step forward, he edged away. Sophie's hip bumped against the side table.

"Let her go. This has nothing to do with Sophie. It's between you and me."

"Absolutely. And she *is* between you and me." No mistaking the deadly humor in his voice.

Bravado. Sweat streamed down Vadim's neck, soaking his shirt and stinking of fear. He was used to hired help doing the dirty work.

One wrong move and he would shoot Jack, then her. Her heart stuttered and her legs could barely hold her.

Jack shook his head, and one amber brow arched. "What are you getting at?"

"Your damned search for me caused me to keep on the move, to change names over and over. Too many times. You hurt my enterprises, as you did before. But no longer."

Surprise flashed in Jack's eyes that his pursuit had been more than a blip on his target's radar.

Sophie dug deep within her for courage. She had to do *something*. Create an opening for Jack.

Not daring to move her head, she cut a glance at the side table. Vadim had moved them even with the saint figure.

That was her chance.

If she could only reach it.

"If you let her go, you can walk away," Jack said. "She means nothing to you."

"Ah, but she means more to *you* than I realized. Alas, without my assistants to restrain you, I must forgo watching you suffer as she dies. I shall simply kill her. Then you."

Sophie bit her lower lip. If she reached for it, Vadim would feel her movement.

Did Jack notice? Did he see what she wanted to do?

His harsh expression didn't change except for a fine tightening of the skin across his cheekbones. "Not likely. Shoot her and you die. I may go down, but I'll take you with me. Let her go. Then it's just us."

"A duel? Or a cowboy gunfight? *Not likely.*" He sneered as he aped his opponent. "I prefer the odds the way they are."

Intent on taunting Jack, Vadim allowed his pistol to drop an inch. Then another.

Sophie prepared herself for the pain, but she had to make her move. She twisted against Vadim's iron grip. "You'll never get away. They'll hunt you down like the scum you are."

"Silence, bitch!" His fingers bit into her skin. He jerked her arm upward as though knowing the exact motion to trigger agony.

Jagged lances ripped into her shoulder. Sophie cried out in spite of herself.

"Sophie!" Jack took a step forward, his face twisted in a mirror of her pain.

Shoving her against the table, Vadim kept possession of her arm. He raised the pistol at Jack. "Do not move, Thorne. Or you will die first."

Burning spasms radiated from her shoulder, and she bit down hard on her lower lip. No, she wouldn't cry. Nothing to attract his attention. The taste of blood and terror bloomed coppery in her mouth.

Concentrate, Sophia Constanza, concentrate.

Bending over in pain, she curved her body over the statuette. Her fingers brushed cool marble.

Could she pick it up one-handed? She had to. There was no other choice.

"Vadim, you're finished." Jack's voice was low and icy, deadly in its calm. "You have no nuke, no hideaways and no assets. Ah, you do have one thing—a terrorist who wants your blood for reneging on a deal. You can't get away."

"I escaped before and I will again. You are a fool." Vadim's pistol angled down an inch. He was paying no attention to Sophie.

Her heart thumped wildly against her ribs. She closed her fingers around the saint's waist. *Forgive me, Saint Whoever.*

With all her strength she swung the statuette. Marble connected with metal and flesh in a resounding thunk.

The pistol flew away into a corner. The marble figure crashed to the floor and broke in two.

A shrieking Vadim clutched his hand.

Freed, Sophie sank to her knees.

Jack drove his shoulder into Vadim's gut. They fell to the carpet together.

Vadim aimed a punch, but Jack deflected it.

He slammed his pistol butt on the damaged left hand.

Vadim howled. He collapsed.

At last, Jack exulted in his triumph. He had the killer where he wanted him. Sophie was safe. The clawed beast inside him would be appeased. He nearly roared.

He propped his knee on Vadim's right arm and jabbed the pistol under his jaw, exactly as his enemy had done to Sophie. "Wrong, Vadim. There is no escape for you. Not even in death.

You killed my family. Your damned uranium would've killed thousands. The devil has a special place in hell for you."

Sweat rolled off the older man. His face blanched paler than his bleached hair. He cradled his mangled hand on his chest. The knuckles were torn and bloody. Two fingers bent at impossible angles. "Get it over with then."

Where was Leoni? Why didn't the task force come in? Did Vadim have men outside they didn't know about? Jack shoved aside the possibilities. He focused on the defeated man.

"Jack, no, this is wrong." In his peripheral vision he saw Sophie's wan face as she edged closer. Tears trickled down her purpling cheek.

He kept his eyes on Vadim. "Sophie, stay back. He's still dangerous. You know I have to kill him."

She crouched beside the abandoned wing chair, cradling her reinjured arm against her side. "You don't. Revenge will dishonor your son's memory. It won't bring him back. Would he have wanted you to throw away your life?"

He didn't know. Why had he never asked himself? He'd aimed for his son's murderer for five years. How could he abandon his goal? The urge to weep and scream filled his chest. "There's nothing else. I've lived only to find Vadim and kill him."

He heard her draw a deep breath. "You have more than you know to live for. Live for *me*. I love you."

She loved him. A giddy sense of euphoria welled up in his chest. But he couldn't let emotion dull the deadly ray of hatred. "He has to die. He killed my family. He would've killed you."

"I want a life with you, not painful memories scarring my heart. If you kill Vadim, you're only perpetuating the pain by passing it on to me. Let the task force have Vadim. You came for me. That tells me you care for me."

He couldn't deny his feelings. Until he had his gun at his enemy's head, he'd focused on saving Sophie. Only on Sophie. Revenge for his family had flown from his thoughts.

"Choose life, Jack. Choose life."

Life. *Life with Sophie.* This amazing woman he loved. And he did love her. She was his passion, his friend, his better nature. She loved him.

Was it possible? Could he?

The task force would see that Vadim was tried and convicted. He wouldn't go free. Ever. "How do you feel about a life sentence in an Italian prison, Vadim? Stone walls and bars. A kind of hell for a man like you."

Vadim glared back in silence.

Jack saw that his search for revenge rose from his own grief and guilt, not from what his family would've wanted. Perhaps saving Sophie and stopping Vadim from selling death meant more than revenge.

Jack turned his gaze toward her. The pleading in her eyes made his heart knock like a clogged engine.

Vadim erupted from his grip. A slender blade flashed in his damaged hand.

Pain like a flaming torch ripped into Jack, and he fell backward. He looked down for the source of the pain.

A knife hilt stuck out of his chest. *"No!"*

Sophie screamed.

On his feet now, Vadim held Jack's Glock. He backed against the wall. Three feet to the right was a door to a small patio. "Still think I can't escape?"

Jack's hand hovered over the hilt. Vadim must've had the knife inside his jacket. Blood seeped from around the wound. That could wait. He had to stop Vadim.

He bent on his side as if to protect himself. He flipped open the jumpsuit leg pocket and curled his hand around the confiscated Beretta.

Where the hell were Leoni and the cavalry?

"Jack, oh, Jack!" Sophie began crawling toward him.

"No. Stay…there. Safer." His voice was a frog imitation. He could barely breathe for the invisible SUV on his chest.

Clicking off the safety, he slid out the Beretta.

Vadim edged along the wall until Sophie came into his view where she huddled by the chair. "Thorne, you're dying, but you'll live long enough to see I keep my promises."

He raised the automatic, pointed it at Sophie.

Jack fired.

Gun bursts echoed like a hundred weapons exploding in unison.

Vadim jerked like a mad puppet. He slid to the floor. The Glock clattered from his lifeless fingers. A trail of blood smeared the wall behind him.

Doors slammed. Shoes scraped on the tile floor. Voices barked orders.

Jack had no strength to hold the Beretta. He let it fall.

Sophie, where was Sophie?

He wanted to tell her…he had to tell her… But blackness overtook him.

Chapter 18

"So that's it," Leoni said. "Uranium's secured. Vadim's dead. Everything's wrapped up. Unlike you. I figured you'd be packaged and bound up like an old pharaoh." He dipped a mock bow at Jack's small chest bandage.

"No mummy. I'm supposed to breathe deep and cough. Hurts like hell." Like a stone slab from an Etruscan tomb weighted his chest, but not enough pain for more morphine.

Damn tubes and monitors wrapped the bed in spider strands. Oxygen tubes up his nose. More tubes in his arm. Even one in his chest. Freaking blinking lights all around.

Apparently they'd rushed him unconscious and barely breathing to Careggi Hospital in Florence. He'd spent yesterday in surgery or drifting in a morphine haze.

Never mind that De Carlo had pulled strings, paid—what was it?—*bustarelle* to arrange all the comforts. The private room reeked of disinfectant and felt like a prison.

He itched to get out. Now.

Where was Sophie? Why didn't she come to see him? Had she gone back to the States already?

What she'd said, was it only an expedient lie?

His breath hitched with a sharp pain—an Etruscan ghost stomping on the stone slab.

Blood loss from the stabbing had been minimized because he'd left the knife in, but the blade had punctured one lung.

When his breathing evened and the pain ebbed, he said, "The two Mafia bodyguards, what about them?"

"Ugo's the weak link. Not the smoothest tenor in the opera, but he's singing. De Carlo's strutting like a rooster about getting the goods on one of the big dons."

Jack smiled. "Maybe the Italian government's anti-Mafia agency will give him a medal."

"I'm glad I'm outta here. If that happens, there'll be no living with the guy. ATSA's sending me to London to advise the Scotland Yard Anti-Terror Squad on rolling up Ahmed Saqr. I don't get why they want *me,* but orders are orders."

"Sounds good." Jack extended his hand, but he couldn't reach far with all the damn tubes. "Thanks for giving me a chance back there."

Leoni had told him that he'd delayed bringing in the others until he could be sure Sophie was out of the line of fire and until Jack had time to confront his enemy.

As backup, a sniper had kept his rifle aimed at Vadim's heart from the moment Jack had entered the house. When Jack had fired at Vadim, so had the sniper and three other officers.

"No prob, big guy. I was counting on Sophie's powers of persuasion. But you, I wasn't so sure of." He clasped Jack's hand. "So when can you go home?"

The big question. "Today, if I had any say. But Doc says my lung has to heal some before I can fly." He'd said a lot more than that but agreed that Jack would be good to go in a week, barring complications.

"Okay, then. I have a flight to catch. Do what those pretty nurses tell you." With a mock salute, Leoni left him.

Barring complications. Major irony there. He pondered the biggest complication of all.

Sophie.

Yeah, she'd taught him that justice could be served without vengeance. Vadim had created his own undoing. He'd died in a hail of bullets, only one of them Jack's.

She'd taught him other things, too. In this bed, trussed up like Gulliver, he had lots of time to think about them.

And about her.

She'd slipped into his heart and soul like sunshine burning away the clouds. He needed her in his life if he was to have any kind of a life at all.

Where the hell was Sophie?

Heart fluttering like a flag in a windstorm, Sophie hesitated at the door to Jack's room. She smoothed her knit top and straightened her skirt, her favorite flowered one. Thank goodness she had her clothes back.

Was she ready for this?

You can do it, Sophia Constanza Elena Rinaldi.

On that self-cheer, she pushed open the door. She managed to pull her lips into a smile.

"The nurse said it was okay to come in." She stepped inside and let the door swish shut behind her.

A machine beside the bed bubbled as fluid from Jack's chest drained into it.

The nurse had warned her, but seeing Jack was something else again. At the sight of his bare bandaged chest and the blinking monitors, she nearly burst into tears.

Jack pushed himself more upright on his stack of pillows. The exertion must've cost him, because he immediately grimaced as though he'd been stabbed again. "Sophie, you came."

"Of course I came. I just had to wait until the task force

finished interviewing me. They had more questions than Alex Trebek asks on a year of *Jeopardy!*"

She kept her tone light but let her gaze drink him in. Oh, God, he'd been hurt so badly. His wide shoulders and long legs were too big for the bed, and he looked too pale beneath the amber stubble on his chin. All those tubes and monitors, much more than she'd needed.

She felt her forehead crinkle and deliberately smoothed her features.

Her gaze tangled in his. The contradictory anxiety and relief that she glimpsed in his usually shuttered gaze fueled her resolve. "Are you in a lot of pain?"

"Only when I breathe."

"Jackson Thorne making a joke? You must be delirious."

"Delirious to see you. Or maybe it's the morphine," he said. "De Carlo wasn't too hard on you?"

She shook her head, and her hair skimmed her shoulders. To her satisfaction, his eyes followed the movement and swept down to her breasts.

He'll be all right. "Matt kept him from using thumbscrews."

"Matt?"

"Leoni. He's been very sweet."

Jack frowned. His gaze sharpened, then slammed into a formidable glare.

Was he jealous? The notion lapped anticipation higher within her. There was hope yet that he loved her.

But he wasn't ready to admit anything. She could see him blanking his expression already. He didn't want her to see his feelings, so he would change the subject.

He cleared his throat. "The uranium was secure. The seals were soft but leaking minimal. No more than an X-ray, the technician said."

She hoped that her smile wasn't too cat-in-cream smug. "Matt told me. They found my luggage in Vadim's house in Venice, too. Everything was there, including my camera and addresses of my cousins here in Florence. I don't have to wear *his* clothes anymore. I have my own."

"You look great."

He didn't. Sweat beaded his forehead. Pain or nerves? "Thanks. Kind of ironic. The first time we met, *you* came to see *me* in the hospital."

She approached the bed and placed her hand in his.

He linked their fingers together. His avid gaze beamed his hunger for her as he browsed from her hair—a mess from the wind—to her mouth and lower. To her arm. "The sling. Vadim hurt you?"

She smoothed a hand over her bound shoulder. "I wrenched it a little when I whacked him with the marble statuette. Guess it wasn't totally healed."

"You slugged him a good one. A little practice and the Nationals'll recruit you. But I'm sorry about the saint."

"It doesn't matter. She wasn't real, and I don't need her anymore."

"You saved our lives. I saw you try for the figure, but I didn't expect it to work. My hat's off to you. Mind-blowing courage, Sophie."

She grinned. "I was so scared I thought I'd faint. Where the nerve came from to swing that saint, I have no idea." A blush heated her cheeks as she remembered mining for courage. "When he stabbed you, it was horrible. With a dagger in your chest, you shot him. You were the brave one."

"I couldn't let him shoot you. Forget him. We're a hell of a pair, all bound up like this." Did his voice sound too desperate?

Jack wanted them to be a pair, but she was keeping it light. To avoid talking about her saying that she loved him? His stomach clenched.

"Yes, but your wound is a lot deeper than mine." Her voice turned serious and her eyes darkened with emotion. "And you'll always have scars."

They weren't talking about their physical wounds anymore.

He hoped.

Please, God, let me read her right. Don't let me lose her.

"I've already healed some," he said, taking a practice run up to the big hurdle. "I might need some TLC for the rest. You could nurse me until I can take you back to Saint Mark's like I promised. Unless you have other plans."

In his condition he couldn't hold his breath, but his heartbeat was on hold waiting for her answer.

She lifted her chin. "De Carlo said that your ATSA assistant director authorized new plane tickets for me."

His free hand gripped the bedsheet. "Oh."

"But the date's open on them."

He sighed. "You're a wicked tease. You know that?"

"Only with you. But I'm going to be direct so we understand each other. You prodded me these past few weeks to assert myself. So here goes. What I said at the farmhouse, I meant. I am in love with you. And I think you love me."

His heart started again, then leaped over track hurdles his body couldn't. He lifted their joined hands to his lips and searched for the words. He had to get this right.

She peered at him, apprehension in her eyes. "Well?"

"Yes, Sophie. I love your breathless charm, your kindness. You're so beautiful and you seem so fragile that I want to protect you, but you have Amazon strength inside."

He paused to catch his breath, inhaled oxygen. He made himself breathe deeply, past the stone-slab pressure.

"Are you okay? Should I get the nurse?" Fear flashed in her eyes, and she started to turn away.

Shoving away the pain, he tugged her back. "I'm fine. Let me finish. You blow me away. I love that you made me search my soul and find myself. I love your name. I love saying it. Sophie, Sophie, Sophie, *I love you.*"

Tears welled in her eyes, and her lip trembled. "Oh, my. I don't know what to say."

"That's a first." He handed her the tissue box sitting beside his bed. "I don't want to screw this up, so I'll warn you. My ex-wife said I was too distant. Too reserved."

"Yeah, right. You think?"

He grinned. She knew him too well already. He patted the bed beside him. "I never told her I loved her. I let the distance grow. What love used to be between us died. There's more to communication than those three words, and the break wasn't all my fault, but you get the idea. I don't want to make the same mistakes with you."

"I won't let you." Smiling, Sophie eased down to sit on the bed. She clasped his hand again. "So I have to make you tell me at least twice a day that you love me. Maybe three times. You could say it again now."

"Sophie, I love you." He tugged her closer, nudging the oxygen tube aside so he could rock his mouth over hers. Her tongue caressed his as she kissed him back.

He let the taste and the scent and the feel of her flow through him, a healing balm better than any medicine.

When the kiss ended, she gazed at him with serious intent, no more teasing. "I want you in my life, but I know what you said about danger to family. More than most, I appreciate the hazards of your job."

"I was seeing through a prism of grief and hatred. Cops of all kinds have families. What happened with Vadim was one in a million. De Carlo, of all people, reminded me of that."

After he'd inhaled more oxygen, he said, "What about your search for independence?"

"Independence doesn't mean I have to be alone. I've done some thinking, too, learned some things about myself. You know those cousins in Florence?"

He nodded. "Their addresses were in your suitcase."

"When my memory returned, I remembered meeting them. I think that was the reason I blocked out the entire vacation, not just Vadim. My cousin Enrico is a professor at the University of Florence, and his sister is a nurse."

His grin nearly blinded her. "I'd laugh if it didn't hurt like hell. Teaching and nursing—professions you were trying to deny."

"Exactly. You said I was fighting my true nature. You were right. I loved teaching the Donati kids and helping them develop and grow."

"No wonder you couldn't figure out your direction. You were in a tunnel and ignoring the light at the end."

She smiled. "After I nurse you back to health, I want to finish my degree—in education."

"Sounds like a plan. But an incomplete one." He kissed her nose. "Marry me, Sophie. I want to wake up beside you every morning. I want to cook pasta and Tuscan chicken with you. Make babies with me, Sophie. I love you."

There, he'd said it again. Easier the second time. Or was it the third?

Her eyes widened. She pressed a hand to her heart. "Oh, my, once again I'm speechless."

"All you need is one word. Sophie, say yes and let me breathe again. I have only one healthy lung here."

A slow smile curved her lips. More tears sparkled on her lashes. "Yes, Jack, I'll marry you and make babies with you."

Waves of joy and relief nearly lifted him off the bed.

Propping herself so she wouldn't hurt him or her shoulder, she kissed him gently.

He couldn't hold her as tightly as he wanted, but he could sate himself on her taste. Her mouth was sweet and insistent, and when lack of breath made him pull back, he ached for more.

She squeezed his hand. "David will always be your son. Will you take me to the cemetery in Miami? I want to put flowers on his grave and say a prayer. For Tonia, too."

"We had our differences, but she was a good mother." Then his throat clogged for some reason, so he merely nodded and kissed her again.

Happiness burst inside him like Fourth of July sparklers,

disintegrating the remnants of the clawed monster that had tormented him for what seemed like eons.

Her mind had blotted out her painful and deadly memories, and he had obsessed on his until they'd poisoned him.

No longer.

He couldn't change the past any more than he could forget it, but he could choose to move on.

Together Jack and Sophie would make a new future.

*Experience the anticipation, the thrill of the chase
and the sheer rush of falling in love!*

*Turn the page for a sneak preview
of a new book from Harlequin Romance
THE REBEL PRINCE
by Raye Morgan*

*On sale August 29th
wherever books are sold*

"OH, NO!"

The reaction slipped out before Emma Valentine could stop it, for there stood the very man she most wanted to avoid seeing again.

He didn't look any happier to see her.

"Well, come on, get on board," he said gruffly. "I won't bite." One eyebrow rose. "Though I might nibble a little," he added, mostly to amuse himself.

But she wasn't paying any attention to what he was saying. She was staring at him, taking in the royal blue uniform he was wearing, with gold braid and glistening badges decorating the sleeves, epaulettes and an upright collar. Ribbons and medals covered the breast of the short, fitted jacket. A gold-encrusted sabre hung at his side. And suddenly it was clear to her who this man really was.

She gulped wordlessly. Reaching out, he took her elbow

and pulled her aboard. The doors slid closed. And finally she found her tongue.

"You…you're the prince."

He nodded, barely glancing at her. "Yes. Of course."

She raised a hand and covered her mouth for a moment. "I should have known."

"Of course you should have. I don't know why you didn't." He punched the ground-floor button to get the elevator moving again, then turned to look down at her. "A relatively bright five-year-old child would have tumbled to the truth right away."

Her shock faded as her indignation at his tone asserted itself. He might be the prince, but he was still just as annoying as he had been earlier that day.

"A relatively bright five-year-old child without a bump on the head from a badly thrown water polo ball, maybe," she said defensively. She wasn't feeling woozy any longer and she wasn't about to let him bully her, no matter how royal he was. "I was unconscious half the time."

"And just clueless the other half, I guess," he said, looking bemused.

The arrogance of the man was really galling.

"I suppose you think your 'royalness' is so obvious it sort of shimmers around you for all to see?" she challenged. "Or better yet, oozes from your pores like…like sweat on a hot day?"

"Something like that," he acknowledged calmly. "Most people tumble to it pretty quickly. In fact, it's hard to hide even when I want to avoid dealing with it."

"Poor baby," she said, still resenting his manner. "I guess that works better with injured people who are half asleep." Looking at him, she felt a strange emotion she couldn't identify. It was as though she wanted to prove something to him, but she wasn't sure what. "And anyway, you know you did your best to fool me," she added.

His brows knit together as though he really didn't know what she was talking about. "I didn't do a thing."

"You told me your name was Monty."

"It is." He shrugged. "I have a lot of names. Some of them are too rude to be spoken to my face, I'm sure." He glanced at her sideways, his hand on the hilt of his sabre. "Perhaps you're contemplating one of those right now."

You bet I am.

That was what she would like to say. But it suddenly occurred to her that she was supposed to be working for this man. If she wanted to keep the job of coronation chef, maybe she'd better keep her opinions to herself. So she clamped her mouth shut, took a deep breath and looked away, trying hard to calm down.

The elevator ground to a halt and the doors slid open laboriously. She moved to step forward, hoping to make her escape, but his hand shot out again and caught her elbow.

"Wait a minute. *You're* a woman," he said, as though that thought had just presented itself to him.

"That's a rare ability for insight you have there, Your Highness," she snapped before she could stop herself. And then she winced. She was going to have to do better than that if she was going to keep this relationship on an even keel.

But he was ignoring her dig. Nodding, he stared at her with a speculative gleam in his golden eyes. "I've been looking for a woman, but you'll do."

She blanched, stiffening. "I'll do for what?"

He made a head gesture in a direction she knew was opposite of where she was going and his grip tightened on her elbow.

"Come with me," he said abruptly, making it an order.

She dug in her heels, thinking fast. She didn't much like orders. "Wait! I can't. I have to get to the kitchen."

"Not yet. I need you."

"You what?" Her breathless gasp of surprise was soft, but she knew he'd heard it.

"I need you," he said firmly. "Oh, don't look so shocked. I'm not planning to throw you into the hay and have my way with you. I need you for something a bit more mundane than that."

She felt color rushing into her cheeks and she silently begged it to stop. Here she was, formless and stodgy in her chef's whites. No makeup, no stiletto heels. Hardly the picture of the femmes fatales he was undoubtedly used to. The likelihood that he would have any carnal interest in her was remote at best. To have him think she was hysterically defending her virtue was humiliating.

"Well, what if I don't want to go with you?" she said in hopes of deflecting his attention from her blush.

"Too bad."

"What?"

Amusement sparkled in his eyes. He was certainly enjoying this. And that only made her more determined to resist him.

"I'm the prince, remember? And we're in the castle. My orders take precedence. It's that old pesky divine rights thing."

Her jaw jutted out. Despite her embarrassment, she couldn't let that pass.

"Over my free will? Never!"

Exasperation filled his face.

"Hey, call out the historians. Someone will write a book about you and your courageous principles." His eyes glittered sardonically. "But in the meantime, Emma Valentine, you're coming with me."

**Introducing an exciting appearance
by legendary
New York Times bestselling author**

DIANA PALMER
HEARTBREAKER

He's the ultimate bachelor…
but he may have just met
the one woman to change his ways!

Join the drama in the story of a confirmed
bachelor, an amnesiac beauty and their
unexpected passionate romance.

**"Diana Palmer is a mesmerizing storyteller
who captures the essence of what
a romance should be."—*Affaire de Coeur***

**Heartbreaker *is available from Silhouette Desire
in September 2006.***

If you enjoyed what you just read,
then we've got an offer you can't resist!

Take 2 bestselling love stories FREE!

Plus get a FREE surprise gift!

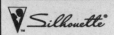

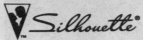

COMING NEXT MONTH

SIMCNM0806